As soon as I awoke on the morning of my fourteenth birthday I knew it was going to be a Keeping Day. I can always tell about things like that, because I'm sensitive.

There are moments when everything's so sharp and bright it almost seems I cannot bear the pain and beauty of the world. But whenever I find myself thinking that way, I cross my fingers quick and take the wish back. Because if I wasn't sensitive, I would never have stumbled onto being a writer, which is my secret dream, and I never would have found the Keeping Days.

I found the first Keeping Days four years ago, the summer I was ten. It was an August evening. From far, far down the street came the sound of Mama's bell. All at once I could feel it all inside of me. I knew I had found a Keeping Day.

# The KEEPING DAYS

## NORMA JOHNSTON

**tempo books**

GROSSET & DUNLAP
A Filmways Company
Publishers • New York

*This book is in memory*
*Of my grandmother,*
*Margaret Messler Pierce,*
*From whose family came much of this story.*
* * * * * *

*This book is for*
*My students and friends—*
*Allison, Anne, Karen, Leslie,*
*Mary, Peggy, Wendy—*
*Who gave me Keeping Days.*

THE KEEPING DAYS

Copyright © 1973 by Norma Johnston
All Rights Reserved
ISBN: 0-448-17307-7
Ace Tempo Books Edition: September 1981
By Arrangement with Atheneum Publishers
Tempo Books is registered in the U.S. Patent Office
Printed in the United States of America
Published simultaneously in Canada

# CONTENTS

|  I | June | 1 |
| II | July | 21 |
| III | August | 49 |
| IV | August | 69 |
| V | September | 85 |
| VI | September | 105 |
| VII | October | 119 |
| VIII | October | 147 |
| IX | November | 161 |
| X | December | 191 |
| XI | December | 213 |

God made man,
Male,
And female.
He set them in families.
And the meaning of family
Is mutual love and responsibility.
And the meaning of responsibility
Is the discipline of love.

*—Darius Leander Swann,*
THE CIRCLE BEYOND FEAR

# CHAPTER I

## *June*

As soon as I awoke on the morning of my fourteenth birthday I knew it was going to be a Keeping Day. I can always tell about things like that, because I'm sensitive. I might as well tell you that straight off, because Mama always does. She seems to think it explains a lot.

"Tish is the sensitive one," Mama says when introducing me to folks, rather like a mother hen presenting the gosling in her flock. "Bronwyn's the beauty, Benjamin the brilliant one, Marnie my most difficult"— Mama always sighs at that point—"Peter the nature lover, and Melissa the baby." Missy at four is hardly a baby any more, but she laps it up, the little monster, while the rest of us manage glassy grins and cuss in private.

The way Mama ticks us off is for all the world like Peter labeling his insect collection, and leaves us feeling as if we too were impaled on pins. I tried explaining this to Mama once, but she just snorted. "Too sensitive," she said briskly. "Got to get over it. Time you did." Mama always talks like that, dropping half her sentences as though she's going somewhere in a hurry and hasn't time. Mama always reminds me of a little brown wren, small and compact and efficient, her brown hair

1

skewered up every which way and not a spark of sensitivity in her soul.

There are times I almost envy Mama that, times when I ache for some poor outsider who's being snubbed by Mary Lou Hodge's crowd, or even moments when everything's so sharp and bright it almost seems I cannot bear the pain and beauty of the world. But whenever I find myself thinking that way, I cross my fingers quick and take the wish back. Because if I wasn't sensitive, I would never have stumbled onto being a writer, which is my secret dream, and I never would have found the Keeping Days.

I found the first Keeping Day four years ago, the summer I was ten, right after my sister Missy was born. It was an August evening, and the dishes were done, and all the kids were playing Kick the Can in the street. When it started getting dark, we drifted down to Lathams' side lawn, the way everybody did that summer. Kenny Latham had found a nest of baby rabbits, and my sister Bronwyn, who was thirteen then and older than the rest, had the rabbits in her lap and was trying to feed them milk from a medicine dropper. When I looked up, the sky behind the maple tree was purple. Lights were going on in windows, and from houses all along Vyse Avenue our mothers started calling. "Celinda . . . ." "Herbert . . . ." "Mary Lou . . . ." From far, far down the street came the sound of Mama's bell. All at once I could feel it all inside of me, the purple and silver, the shimmer of fireflies and flowers, the tender look in my sister's eyes, and the familiar silver tinkle of the bell. And I knew I had found a Keeping Day.

From that night on I've cherished them, two or three a year, the way my sister Bronwyn lays aside the pearls she's given on special occasions to make a necklace of some day. One day, when I am grown and have really lived, I hope to make a book about the Keeping Days.

And on nights now after awful days, when I'm lying awake in the dark, I take my Keeping Days out and tell them over to myself, the way Mrs. Breidenbach next door tells her beads. And I become glad once again that I have this cradle gift.

I was so particularly glad on my fourteenth birthday morning, that I even woke up smiling. My toes were curling, and I had queer feelings inside, as if a whole cage of butterflies was trying to burst free. Bronwyn was already up so I had our room to myself for a change. The warm June breeze was billowing the muslin curtains with their pleated frills, and outside in our old apple tree a regular gossip session was going on. "Today's Tish's birthday," the oriole sang and, "Birthday!" the catbird echoed from the roof. The air was so fraught with promise that I rolled out of bed and peered hopefully in the bedroom mirror.

Mama's fond of saying that when a girl's in her teens she changes overnight, but I've just about given up hope. The face that looked back at me was revoltingly familiar, thin and golden-olive-skinned, like all us Sterling kids—a heritage, Pa claims, from some illegitimate Indian ancestor in colonial days. My hair's dirty blonde or faded brown, depending on your point of view, and straight as a poker to boot. And even in my nightie you could see I have hardly any bosom, which I think is perfectly revolting at my age. But even this crude reality failed to spoil my expectations for the day.

I cantered downstairs like our old mare Nellie setting out for a picnic, and you could fairly smell the festivity in the air, even though everyone was behaving like it was a perfectly normal day. Missy was playing with her dolls on the landing. Peter's praying mantis had escaped again, and he was trying to coax it down off the curtains before Mama found out. Ben was stringing lanterns for my party; Marnie was trying to stand on her head; and

Bron was practicing a new song her beau had brought her.

Every time I look at Bronwyn I'm thankful I'm sensitive, because Bron certainly got all the rest of the cradle gifts. She looks like an autumn leaf, all brown and coral and gold, she sings like an angel, and she's just plain nice besides. "Sweethearts can live on love alone," sang Bronwyn. "Happy birthday, hon."

Mama called in from the kitchen. "You, Tish? Time you're up. Work to do." I waltzed out into the kitchen and hugged Mama from behind.

"Isn't it a *lovely* day!"

"Going to be a scorcher." Mama pushed her hair back from her forehead and rubbed the back of her neck. The heat always bothers her, and it seems to be doing so earlier than usual this year; she looked rather grey and pale. "Should have known better than have my children this time of year," she grumbled. "Tell Ben get the berries picked early."

"Ben's fixing my lanterns."

Mama sniffed. She wasn't happy about the party. She wanted me to have the same old ice-cream-and-cake in the afternoon as I'd had all my life. What I'd had in mind was an evening affair, with dancing, but we had compromised on a strawberry-social sort of thing, in the yard, from seven to nine. And I hadn't gotten that till we'd had a Family Council meeting at which I burst into tears and fled the council table. Behind me I heard Pa slam his hand on the table in exasperation.

"For goodness sake, Evie, tell the child she can have it before she drowns us all!"

"Very well, Mr. Sterling," Mama had answered stiffly. "Spoiling the child, I'm sure. Too sensitive now."

"Touchy, you mean," Pa grunted. But he winked at me when Mama wasn't looking.

The atmosphere between me and Mama had been

fraught with electricity ever since. Mama flares up easy, and she has an annoying habit of remembering and stewing over small errors weeks after they've occurred, but it isn't like her to hang onto an irritation as ceaselessly as on this particular occasion. I still can't quite figure out why she was so sore—it wasn't, after all, as if I'd gotten my own way completely. It is probably partly because this year for some reason she still hasn't gotten around to summer housecleaning yet, and to Mama even a kids' party means the house should look like Queen Victoria was coming to tea. Partly, too, it could be because Pa wasn't much help. He loves kids, and usually is great at dreaming up party plans, but this month he's been spending longer and longer hours down at the courthouse where he is a court reporter, taking down and then transcribing every word the lawyers and witnesses say when they come up to trial before old Judge Simms.

Pa was gone again, even though it was Saturday, I noticed, as I took advantage of Mama's preoccupation to fix a birthday breakfast of bread, butter and sugar, a delicacy I adore and Mama does not approve. But Mama herself had been percolating like an overheated coffeepot. Already, at ten a.m., she had made two cakes and a big bowl of chicken salad, and was starting to mix her homemade ice cream. I hoped Pa or Ben would be around when it came time to turn the freezer crank.

Time seemed suspended all day, the way time does when some mysterious promise seems to be hovering around a corner out of reach. The June heat built, ruffled by a tremulous breeze as midafternoon wore on its dawdling way. Everything seemed on tiptoe waiting. By four o'clock everything was ready, and there was nothing left to be done but keep Missy and Cicero, our almost-sheepdog, from disturbing the unnatural neatness of house and yard. I solved that problem by tying the latter to a tree way out back, and tossing the former over to her best friend's house where she could concoct mudpies in harmless bliss.

Three hours till the party. Three hours till I'd find my Keeping Day. The minutes crawled. I kept hoping my own best friend would manage to get over, but Celinda is rarely able to escape her mother's clutches on a Saturday. Mrs. Dodds, among her other idiosyncrasies, considers idleness a sin, and guards Celinda from it like a dragon. Who did come over, to my chagrin, was my Aunt Kate, Pa's older sister and our cater-corner backyard neighbor. I can give you an idea of our Aunt Kate by telling you that Sourpuss Sadie, the bane of all local Latin students, is our auntie's dearest friend. Aunt Kate is dish-faced and medium-sized, but she contrives to look gaunt and angular and ten feet tall. Today she surveyed the backyard with eyes as sharp as her own spyglass and sniffed disapprovingly.

"Evening party this year, Evie? Don't you think Letitia's rather young? You know what went on at the Hodges' party." Since Mrs. Hodge, who is given to weeping and wailing, is a member of the local Ladies' Aid, Mary Lou's precocious attempts on the opposite sex are as common knowledge among the grown-ups as they are among our crowd at school. Aunt K picked up a punch cup and raised an eyebrow. "Your good cut glass for a children's party? You *are* an optimist, Evie."

"Oh, I don't know, Kate," Mama said sweetly. "Letitia's 'most grown up now. Fourteen. Like her to have things nice. Started walking out with Mr. Sterling when I wasn't much older." That was a whopper. Mama was sixteen when she first met Pa, and if I'd even suggested I was old enough for a steady beau, she'd have tanned my hide. But this was turning into another minor skirmish in the twenty-years' war of Mama vs. Kate, which altered everything. Aunt K's visit was proving a blessing in disguise, for Mama'd completely forgotten she was opposed to the party and mad at me. I kept my mouth shut and prepared to enjoy the battle.

Aunt K's sharp eyes skipped around. "Edward home? Hope you're not tackling anything like this when he's not around. Can't trust children today. Poor Alice Hodge . . . ."

"Trust *my* children!" Mama's chin came up in that way she has, and her eyes were snapping. "Mr. Sterling home this evening. Wouldn't want to miss the celebration. Highly in favor. Have some lemonade, Kate. Look like you need it."

Mama's loathing of Aunt Kate is a family legend, but she seemed to be winning this round and enjoying herself immensely, so I took off as the ladies transferred the field of battle to the front porch. By the time Mama got finished with Aunt K, she might even have talked herself into letting me have dancing, especially if I wasn't around to hear.

The party was going to be divine. I always could sense such things, and the knowledge made me feel so good that even our quite unexciting backyard took on an air of magic. The clotheslines had been taken down, and Peter forced to remove his caterpillar jars from the back railing. A faint clank and muffled cussing told me that Ben was up in the apple tree trying to figure out how to string the lanterns. I sat down on the back steps in the afternoon sun, tried to spread the skirt of my sailor suit the way Bron does her coral party dress, and closed my eyes.

. . . *I'd be sitting on the bench in the far corner of the garden. The scent of Mama's crimson rambler would fill the twilight,* . . . *no, gloaming. The scent would fill the purple gloaming. In my white mull dress, my waist would look tiny and fragile beneath the soft curve of my bosom.* (I planned to rip the ruffles off an old petticoat and pin them to the front of my Ferris waist.) *He would look at me as if he'd never seen me before. "Why, Tish, you've— grown up," he would say.* (I didn't have the faintest idea who he would be, but that was unimportant.) *"Do you think so?" I'd whisper, a catch in my throat. He would lean toward me so close I would almost faint. "Tish," he'd say huskily, "you're—lovely . . . ."*

"Hello, LeTEEsha!" I opened my eyes and crashed down to earth with a thud. Mary Lou Hodge was smirking at me from across the side fence. I felt exactly as if she'd walked into the room while I was taking a bath, and I was glad she didn't have enough imagination to read my mind.

"What do you want?" I asked ungraciously.

"Just wanted to wish you happy birthday, LeTEEsha." I should explain that in our family Mama names the boys and Pa the girls, and on account of his wide-ranging reading, Pa does make the weirdest choices. Everyone knows how I feel about the name Letitia, so I was aware that Mary Lou was only calling me that for pure orneriness. I was also aware that the real reason she'd come over was her terrific crush on Ben. It is a good thing she does not know what he really thinks of her, on account of he usually refers to her as That Female Idiot. Ben is fifteen and an intellectual giant, but he has not yet discovered Sex.

"Couldn't you wait till tonight?" I asked, referring both to wishing me a happy birthday and ogling Ben.

"I don't know whether I'm coming tonight." Mary Lou flounced her skirts and simpered in the direction of the apple tree.

"He'll be here, so you might as well come," I said, not adding that she'd been invited only because our mothers are in Ladies' Aid together.

Mary Lou had the grace to blush. "That's not what I meant," she said hastily. "It's just that now I'm in high school, daylight parties seem so juvenile." Mary Lou adores rubbing in the fact that she's a high school freshman while I'm stuck in eighth grade for another two weeks.

Before I could think of a suitable retort, my sister Marnie came ambling out of the house, licking frosting off a spoon. Marnie at twelve is still under the impression she should have been a boy, and she can be devastatingly blunt.

"What she means," Marnie said now, clearly, "is that you can't get away with playing kissing games till after dark."

There was a choking sound from the direction of the apple tree.

"That's why Tish is having an early party," Marnie continued with appalling candor. "Our Aunt Kate told Mama how you had all the boys behind the barn playing Post Office at your party, and Mama says she won't have such goings-on around her."

Mary Lou turned the color of a beet. "I guess she won't have to worry, Miss Marianna Busybody Sterling! Nobody'd want to play Post Office with your skinny sister!" She flounced off down the street, and I went upstairs to start getting dressed for the party.

Only instead of getting dressed I flopped down on the bed and depression settled like a sudden fog. I thought about how much I hate Mary Lou, and how I am going to have revenge on her in the book I shall write someday. It is going to be a very profound book, and very sad, because it is going to make everybody realize what it's like to be sensitive and misunderstood, and how one suffers on account of people being unwittingly cruel. Only they will realize too late, for I shan't allow it to be published till I've passed on. They'll put my picture on the cover, looking so pale and lovely that it hurts. That little bitch Mary Lou Hodge will come to the funeral

with eyes so swollen with remorse that for once no one
will think she's pretty. And Mama will say brokenly,
"We had a genius among us, and we did not appreciate.
Had we but known!"

I lay there wallowing in the vision till it seemed so real
I got goosebumps on my arms. I had to jump up and
look in the mirror to be sure I was still alive. But it was
my own face that looked back at me, so everyday dull,
like some mask behind which my real self was imprisoned. And suddenly I had this terrible urge to find
that other person who lived inside. I snatched the ribbon
off my braid and ran my fingers through my hair till it
hung like a silken veil about my face. I pulled off my
middy and flung it on the bed, and jerked myself into
Bronwyn's coral party dress, and pulled the straps of the
despised Ferris waist down off my shoulders.

I turned to the mirror very slowly with half-closed
eyes. For a breathless minute I felt queer inside.

Then the door opened. My brother Ben's head poked
in.

"Hey, Tish, the Mouse is downstairs with your
present." Then, slowly, "Holy Jehosophat! If Bron
catches you, she'll skin you alive!"

I wanted to sink through the floor.

"Besides," Ben added kindly, "you haven't got the
shape."

He departed, pulling the door shut behind him, and
leaving me turned as hot a color as the coral dress, clear
down to its drooping neckline. Ben's eyes had shown me
how I really looked, a child parading in a borrowed
image, like Missy dressing up in Mama's clothes. Only I
wasn't a child any more. I wanted to die, but instead I
crammed Bron's dress back into the wardrobe, and
pulled on that loathsome middy. I bundled my hair
back, avoiding encounters with the mirror, and, feeling

like some fairy-tale character imprisoned by a spell, went down to see Celinda.

Celinda Dodds is my most intimate friend, and dearer to me than a sister, but I have to admit Ben is right. Despite her heart-shaped face, navy-blue eyes and pale wavy hair, she is mousy. Nobody but me has ever seen her the way she can be sometimes, those blue eyes sparkling with mischief. I would cheerfully kick her occasionally if it would do any good. It's not really Celinda's fault; her mother comes from Massachusetts and thinks everything that's fun is a sin.

It was like Celinda to manage bringing her gift over early, for we know each other so well that our presents are usually very personal. "Happy birthday," Celinda said, and held out her package. Her eyes were black with excitement, and she looked almost pretty. The present was a notebook with a real leather cover and marbleized liners, filled with positively reams of paper. Mrs. Dodds believes too much pocket money is an instrument of the Devil, so I knew Celinda must have saved for weeks and weeks.

"It's to write the—you know," Celinda said, meaning the Keeping Days, only being too tactful to mention them in front of the family. The Sterling clan is addicted to teasing, and my writing dream has so far been too fragile a plant to risk in public exposure.

"It's just about the most perfect present I've ever had," I said, and hugged her, and Ben made disgusted noises in his throat, and Celinda blushed. And Mama said, "Now, Benjamin," and I dragged Celinda upstairs to sit on the edge of my bed while I dressed for the party.

Mama won't let me wear my hair up yet, or a real corset, just that old baby Ferris waist, which doesn't encourage any shape at all, but I pinned the ruffles across it and tied a Roman sash around my waist instead of

where it belongs around my hips. Now you could at
least see my tiny waistline, and Celinda and I decided
that all things considered I didn't look too bad.

When we went downstairs Mama was setting an extra
place at the table for Celinda and saying, "might as well
stay, no sense running back and forth." Then she looked
at me and untied my sash and tied it again real firm
down where it belonged.

Pa came home, looking hot and rumpled in his tan
summer suit, and Ben appeared, having done honor to
the party by scrubbing till his skin shone and putting on
his best red-and-white striped shirt. In their presence,
Celinda's glow went out and she shut up like a clam.
Celinda's more than a little intimidated by Pa's gruff-
ness and his quite impressive beard, which amazes me
on account of her own father looks like one of the
gloomier of the Old Testament prophets. She slipped
into the seat beside mine, and Pa asked how come just a
cold supper, and Mama reminded him about the party,
and Pa said, "Tarnation too much socializing, be glad
when they're all married off." He looked at Bron
hopefully, and Bron blushed, and Mama sniffed. And
before we knew it, it was time for the party.

Land, but it was pretty! Ben had run the lanterns all
through the apple tree and around the trellises clear over
to my Aunt Kate's yard—Aunt K'd probably have her
spyglass working overtime anyway, so he thought he
might as well make it easier for her to see. Mama's
peonies and roses glowed against the fence, and all our
relations' garden furniture was scattered on the grass.
The table was set with Mama's cutwork cloth and her
porcelain berry dishes, and there was another table
beside it for the presents—in our neighborhood, even at
my age, folks bring presents.

"Brought the family's out, too," Mama said, coming
out and taking off her apron. She'd put on a crisp white

pique waist, and done her hair up with her tortoise comb. Through the open window came snatches of music as Bron played the piano in the parlor. It was almost like a scene in a story in the *Ladies' Home Journal*.

I scrunched up my eyes and concentrated hard. *My fourteenth birthday*, I thought, *on the twenty-second of June, Nineteen-hundred*. I was making a memory. I felt all tiptoe and trembly in my stomach, the way I had all day, as though something wonderful was about to happen.

I opened my eyes, and what happened was Mary Lou Hodge, mincing into the yard on real French heels, and after her came the rest of the crowd; the boys first, naturally. Celinda once said if the Pied Piper'd been a woman, he'd have looked exactly like Mary Lou Hodge. At first everyone just stood around and looked uncomfortable, and the girls fluffed their skirts and the boys poked each other in the ribs and suggested things like mumblety-peg. Then Doug Latham got a few of the boys off behind the apple tree and from the howls of laughter I deduced he was telling racy stories, of which he has quite a few on account of hanging around with the traveling salesmen at his father's grain and hardware store.

Marnie, who finds it hard to remember she's not a boy herself in spite of being all tricked out in her best white dress, was over there too, and Mama looked anxious and kept casting worried glances at the next yard— my Aunt Kate not only has good eyesight, but good ears as well. Only pretty soon Ben kicked Marnie out, and then Mary Lou sort of sauntered over, tossing her strawberry-blonde curls and flipping her skirts so her petticoats showed, and after a while everybody was mixing just fine. With the exceptions, of course, of Junius Albright and Celinda, but we were used to them. Celinda's a pill at parties, and Junius is a pill, period.

Ben, who's more charitable than the rest of the boys, says what else could we expect from a kid who's been raised by Sourpuss Sadie. His mother, the wife of Pa's best friend, died ten years ago, and since then he's lived with his Aunt Sadie, who is peculiar to say the least. He has a thatch of brown hair, ears like the handles on a loving-cup, and a face that turns red if you so much as look at him, which hardly anyone ever does.

Bronwyn's beau Herbie Willis dropped by, and her girl friend Selma and Selma's beau Fred, and Bron brought them all out in the back with us. Herbie, who fancies himself as God's gift to the senior class girls, had on a fancy striped shirt and a flower in his buttonhole. He and Fred treated us like we were real young ladies, so the rest of the fellows spruced up, too, and pretty soon it was almost as good as if I'd had a real evening dance. The sky behind the apple tree turned purple, and the lanterns glowed like jewels. Herbie had brought his guitar, and he sat on the back steps strumming love songs and gazing soulfully at Bron. And you should have seen the way Doug Latham was looking at Mary Lou! Pretty soon they sort of disappeared into the back of the garden, and Mama looked nervous again, only just then Bronwyn came out of the house carrying the birthday cake and everyone started to sing.

In twenty minutes the cake was gone, clear down to the last glob of frosting on the doily, and Mama was looking at Pa and beginning to indicate it was time for folks to leave. Mary Lou gave a coy little squeal.

"Ooh, Letitia, you haven't opened your presents!"

I'd been hoping nobody would notice, on account of I feel like a fool having to gush over things, especially in front of the boys. But Mama was wearing her brisk, no-nonsense expression that meant I had to be gracious or else.

Just to get even I opened Mary Lou's first, which

proved to be an Elsie Dinsmore book for which I'd been too old for simply ages, and goodness knows Mary Lou is too, since she's always telling everybody about the dirty French novels she reads. One of the boys snickered, and the girls, particularly Celinda, cast me sympathizing glances, which sustained me through opening the rest of the gifts. They were so nice that if I hadn't been feeling conspicuous I would have been quite thrilled. There were two sets of collar pins, a locket on a chain, an autograph book, and all sorts of lovely stuff. There was a butterfly mounted in a pin tray from my brother Peter, a bottle of real cologne from Bron, and even a big stone painted up fancy for a paperweight from Missy. From Pa came a gorgeous leather-bound volume of *Idylls of the King,* which he knows I absolutely adore. I started to open a big flat box that I knew was from Mama, since she always wraps things the same, in white tissue with big pink bows. I lifted the top off, and felt my cheeks getting hot, and slammed the lid down quickly.

"Aren't you going to show us, Letitia?" That was Mary Lou Hodge, naturally.

"Not this one," I said shortly. But Ben happened to be standing next to Mary Lou, so she was acting coy. "Ooh, just an itsy peek," she squealed, and grabbed for it, and the box tipped over, spilling the awful, beautiful, handmade undergarments out onto the ground.

For a minute I prayed I'd die.

It was Doug Latham, of course, who picked up the bloomers. One of the boys snickered, and then I heard somebody say, "I don't think it's so funny."

It was Kenny Latham, Doug's younger brother. He's always been the quiet type, but if I ever liked boys at all I could almost love him for what he did just then. He took the awful thing away from his brother and turned to Mama. "Did you do this embroidery, Mrs. Sterling? My mother's fond of embroidering, too." His voice was squeaky, but he looked sober and respectful. Mama's face had this queer kind of shattered look.

Suddenly a great sob burst from me. As it did, I was able to move again, and I went running up the back steps into the house, up the stairs, and into my room. I threw myself across the bed, unmindful of my dress or of the ruffles, and I sobbed and sobbed. Always before when I'd cried, it struck me how romantic it was, and then I'd stop crying and couldn't seem to start. This time I didn't care that nobody was there to see me. I didn't *want* anybody to see me, I could never face anyone again. I cried till my face was raw and blotchy, and it dawned on me that the thing Mama'd spoken of had happened. I had changed, inside.

Somebody came in and sat down beside me, and a cool hand stroked the hair back from my brow. "Tish, honey." Bron's hands were cool and smelled of that sweet cologne she wears.

I rolled over and looked at her. "Bron, how could Mama? How *could* she?"

"Honey, Mama's old. Nearly forty! She's forgotten how awful it can be. You do forget, as you get older." Bron sounded almost sad. "You won't believe it, but when you're my age, tonight will seem funny."

"No, it won't. Bron, I'm so humiliated. I just can't face them."

"Yes, you can. Don't worry about Mary Lou." Bron giggled softly. "Doug Latham bet Ben she didn't wear any, and when she got huffy they told her to prove it, and now she don't dare say a word." Bron went to the washstand and poured water into a bowl and wrung out a cloth. "Here, wipe your face. Mama says you can dance for half an hour."

Mama's right, girls do change. A year ago, or a week, I couldn't have done it, but I went downstairs and out onto the back porch and smiled at everybody just like nothing had happened. "Inside, everybody!" I called gaily. "We're going to dance. It's my birthday, so I get to choose. Kenny, will you help me start off?"

So the party wasn't spoiled. Everyone laughed and kidded and acted as if they'd forgotten the whole thing. Mary Lou even had the grace to look ashamed. And I kept on smiling until the last kid had gone, until I was up in bed beside Bron and the light was out. Then the tears came again, but differently, the slow quiet ones like soft rain falling.

"Tish, honey?" Bron's arm was around me. "Don't cry, honey, it wasn't so bad."

"It's not that," I wept. "It's over. My birthday's over."

In the darkness I heard Bron laugh softly. "I told you it wouldn't seem so bad after a while." Her voice sounded tender and long years older. "An hour ago you couldn't live through another minute, and now you're crying because it didn't last longer."

But it wasn't that. My birthday was over, and it hadn't been a Keeping Day. The miracle had never quite happened. I felt cheated of something very precious, and it was all tied up with Mama and that blasted underwear.

"How could Mama do it?" I thought. But I knew the answer. Mama hadn't meant to humiliate me. She just didn't understand. She would never understand. It was time I got used to it.

I lay awake in the moonlight, unable to sleep as the hours crept by. Beside me Bron had kicked off the covers and lay curled like a kitten, hugging her pillow and half of mine as well. It is strange, I reflected, how hard it is to sleep after a special day. It's as if your mind has wrapped arms around the day, the way Bron has the pillows, and won't let go.

I felt myself getting sensitive and perceptive again,

only suddenly and quite strangely I didn't want to. I didn't want to be sensitive any more if it meant feeling like this. I swallowed hard and decided perhaps some more ice cream would be a good idea.

When I went down to the ice box I saw the back door standing open, and a figure in white was moving through the garden. I went out on the porch. Mama, in her wrapper with her hair down her back, was walking past the rose bushes snipping off hocks. She looked younger like this, and softer; not brisk at all.

"Hello, honey." Mama smiled. "Come on out. Too nice a night for sleep."

I went out and sat down on the bench.

"A nice birthday?" Mama asked.

"Scrumptious. Thanks for letting us dance." I felt suddenly shy. With Mama! I touched the ruffle of my new nightgown. "It's beautiful, Mama," I said softly.

"Got another present for you, too." Mama finished the roses and sat down beside me. "Occurred to me when I saw what Celinda'd brought, you might rather have this than anything else." She took it from her pocket and handed it to me, a small blue book with "Girlhood Fancies" in gold upon the cover.

"Go ahead, open it," Mama said.

It wasn't a book at all, but a Journal, like Celinda'd given me. Only this one was already filled with writing. The moonlight was bright enough for me to make out the words.

"*. . . what is there about me that makes me so different that nobody understands? When I was little I used to think I'd been left on the doorstep in a basket. Now I'm older and know better, but it still seems queer. How can I be my parents' child when we don't even speak each other's language?*"

I glanced at Mama but Mama, her hands locked behind her head in the way she has, was looking at the moon. I turned more pages.

"*. . . today I feel alive, alive! This beautiful day is calling me, all blue sky and sunlight, and I can feel it inside of me, through and through. When I ran down to breakfast, I felt like singing, 'Isn't it a lovely day!' Ma just grunted, 'Dreadful hot for bakin'.' Is that what happens to you when you get old? Does the part of you that feels crumple up and die, like losing sight or hearing? I'm never going to get too old to feel!*"

"Mama," I said softly, "who wrote this?"

"I did," said Mama, "the year I was fourteen."

Side by side in the rose-spangled garden, Mama and I sat in silence looking at the moon.

# CHAPTER II

## *July*

July always brings the dog days in our neighborhood. Pa says they're called that because the heavy-blanket heat makes everyone foam at the mouth and snap at each other's heels like a pack of mad dogs. It was certainly true of our family this year.

June wound out its firefly-spangled way. Bronwyn graduated from high school wearing white silk mull embroidered all over with butterflies, carrying an armload of white roses from Herbie Willis and looking as radiant as Titania herself. A few days later came my graduation from grammar school. I had a white organdie trimmed with rows of tucks and I looked, unfortunately, exactly like myself. At least my hair was improved, thanks to Mama's curling-iron; poor Celinda had to wear her usual braid and her mother wouldn't even let her loop it up.

Then school was over, and we all made deep dives into our lovely indolent summertime pursuits. I was indulging in an orgy of Shakespeare, with Pa's highest approbation, and Celinda was deep in *Jane Eyre*—*not* with her mother's approval, which explains why she was reading it in our treehouse on the sly. Mrs. Dodds' disapproval didn't always stop Celinda from doing some-

thing, it just stopped her from enjoying it. Peter went
through every vacant lot in a two-mile radius, seeking
additions to his insect collection; Ben went fishing with
Doug Latham and the other fellows; and Marnie spent
her time falling out of trees, bruising her shins, and making a pest of herself tagging after the boys. Missy, who
wasn't in school yet and therefore didn't understand
about vacations, did pretty much what she always did.
Mama went into her seasonal frenzy of sewing-washing-
ironing-till-all-hours, which she must get a queer kind of
pleasure out of since she does it every year, and Aunt
Kate had a field day, in the long summer twilights,
watching the whole neighborhood with her spyglass.

That was June. Then along came July, and the sereni-
ty exploded like a firecracker on the Fourth.

The first thing that happened was that Bron and
Herbie had a spat. Bron never fights, and so she didn't
exactly really fight, but she put on her regal, distant
manner and her eyes were shooting sparks. The spat
started on the Fourth of July. Herbie took Bron out riding after the usual family picnic, but she came home un-
usually early. I was sitting up in bed, reading *Romeo and
Juliet,* when I heard the screen door slam and Herbie's
footsteps retreat rapidly down the street. Bron hadn't
asked him in, which was unusual. She came into the
bedroom, her hair tumbling down around her flushed
face, and banged her hat and parasol down upon the
bureau. "Men!" she said eloquently.

"What happened?" This was even more interesting
than Shakespeare.

"Herbie tried to get fresh, and was mad when I
wouldn't let him." Bron came over for me to unbutton
her dress. "He's tried it before, but usually I can handle
it. Only ever since he invested all that money in those
graduation flowers, he thinks he's got a—a vested interest in me!" She banged things around some more.

Bron's not mushy, but she's not a touch-me-not, either, and she'd certainly given Herbie enough reason to think she did like him specially. She blew out the light and slid into bed, and presently her voice came to me through the darkness.

"Tish? The funny thing was, it *was* sweet of him to give me that bouquet. And I liked it that he wanted to—touch me. I was going to let him kiss me when it dawned on me that that's all it was—*letting* him. I really didn't care whether he did or not. And that's not a good enough reason to kiss a boy, is it?"

Herbie must have been really mad, because he didn't stop by as usual that Sunday morning to walk to church with our family. Bron kept dawdling, putting off our leavetaking. Finally Pa, who's a vestryman, said, "Tarnation thunder, I'll be getting there too late to take up the offering. Evie, can't you ever manage to teach these children some sense of time?"

Mama pressed her lips tight together, then hollered up the stairs, "Bronwyn Isolde, get down here directly!"

Bron, recognizing the danger signals, hustled. Only by then Ben discovered that Missy'd been investigating a mud puddle in her white pique coat, which didn't improve Mama's disposition. Neither did the fact that when we passed Aunt K's yard she came sailing out to stake a proprietary claim on Pa's arm. Mama snorted and tucked her hand through Pa's other arm, which she rarely does, and all in all we made quite an entrance into church.

We filed into the family pew, which you might know is way down front, just as everybody stood for the *Gloria Patri*. The service rattled along through the *Te Deum*, the Lesson and the usual prayers. Then, as we got up from the kneeling benches, I heard Bron gasp. "Oh, the rat. The absolute, unmitigated rat."

"Who? What? Where?" Marnie demanded, so loudly

that Mama jabbed her in the ribs. Bron jerked her head toward the right side of the church, and there was Herbie, seated in state alongside Viney Hodge. Viney is Mary Lou's sister, who graduated with Bron, and she's exactly what Mary Lou's going to turn into in another few years if she's not careful. There's a word for Viney which I discovered in my exploration of Pa's books, but if I ever tried using it, I'd get my mouth washed out with soap.

Bron has the disposition of an angel most of the time, but she's not a Sterling for nothing, and by the time the Recessional reverberated through the nave, the family temper was fast emerging. She sailed down the aisle in a crackle of organdie, and as she passed Herbie and Viney she snapped her parasol open with an ominous click. Herbie looked uncomfortable and Viney triumphant, and Aunt K said "Humph!" significantly, and Mama pressed her lips together. Fortunately, at this juncture, Mr. Albright came up to speak to Pa and walked along with us toward home. Since Mama and Aunt Kate were already hitched onto Pa's either side, he bowed to Bron, murmured, "Miss Sterling?" and offered his arm. Bron took it with a flourish. Mr. Albright is very dashing, with beautiful sideburns, even if he is as old as Pa, so Bron's exit from the fray was in my estimation not bad at all. I sneaked a look back and had the satisfaction of seeing Herbie's jaw drop three notches.

When we reached Albright's, Pa announced he had to stop off to talk business with Mr. Albright. That was mean of Pa, for it left Mama and Aunt K to walk together, and it's an open family secret they can't abide each other. They marched on side by side through the shiny Sunday morning, as stiffly polite to each other as a pair of skirmishing generals. If I ever tried it, I'd get my face smacked for sure, but that's the kind of cattiness grown-ups get away with in the name of good manners.

Ben and Peter, recognizing the signs, prudently took themselves off as soon as Pa departed, but we girls were stuck.

By the time we reached Aunt K's yard the skirmishing had reached the cloying sweetness stage. Mama was getting the worst of it, and I was having trouble making Marnie keep her mouth shut. Marnie, whatever her faults, is fiercely loyal. We all stopped at Aunt K's gate, and I could sense Mama fishing around for a parting shot, when Missy decided to be appealing. "Pretty!" she announced, beaming like a cherub, and pointed at Aunt K's roses.

"Oh, nothing much," Aunt K allowed, in the typical Sterling way of turning off a compliment, but her grim face softened.

"Oh, I don't know, Kate," Mama said sweetly. "I thought your roses were doing particularly well this year." That was a dastardly shot, for Mama has a green thumb and Aunt Kate decidedly hasn't. I felt like applauding. Aunt Kate bridled.

"Of course being a woman alone I don't have the advantage of help with the heavy work. But of course not having children tramping around does make a yard look better. I have a batch of new rosebushes being delivered next Saturday if I can just find a boy to dig the trenches. I thought of asking Benjamin, but I suppose he's too busy hanging around with that wild Latham boy. Does Edward approve of your letting Ben run around with him so much, Evie? If they're not picked up by the police one of these days, I'll be very much surprised. Anyway," Aunt K reverted back to her garden problem, "I'll pay Ben, of course, if he'll do the job properly. When we were young, Edward was always glad to do things for the family and wouldn't think of accepting pay, but children aren't brought up like that any more."

Mama's eyes shot sparks. "Why, Ben would be glad

to help you Saturday morning, Kate. And I know he
wouldn't dream of accepting money." She was so angry
she was actually speaking in complete sentences for a
change.

"Mama, don't let it get to you," Bron soothed, when
Aunt K had mercifully gone inside. "She's just a sour
old maid. She isn't worth it!"

"Not going to lower myself to be uncivil." Mama
tossed her head. "Your father's sister; his place to handle her." She fairly bristled righteousness, but when we
reached home she banged the pots and pans around so
it's a wonder dinner ever reached the table, and the fact
that she had to keep it hot a whole hour waiting for Pa
did not help things at all.

When Ben found out what had happened, he was
furious. "Christopher Columbus, Ma, couldn't you
have asked me first? I promised Doug Latham I'd go to
the ball game with him Saturday."

Perhaps because she knew Ben had a point, Mama
retreated into parental prerogatives. "Didn't think I had
to ask my children whether I could rely on them! Kate
put me on the spot. Besides, you see too much of that
Latham boy. Away from home too much. Neglecting
your chores. Bad influence."

I groaned. Mama knows perfectly well she's not going
to win anybody's support by attacking his friends. Ben
flushed. "Doug's all right. And I guess he's right that
you're trying to turn me into a Mama's boy. Anyway, I
promised Doug I'd go with him Saturday, and I'm not
going back on my word."

On Monday Pa telephoned from the courthouse to
say he would be quite late and not to wait dinner; Ben
was out somewhere with Doug Latham and forgot to
come home; Bron, who had had an afternoon of sympathetic solicitude and gossip from Selma, had a sick head-

ache; and Missy played dress-up in Bron's coral dress and fell in another puddle. It was a charming day.

For a girl who didn't care whether she kissed Herbie Willis or not, Bron was taking his defection pretty hard. She grew rather pale and languid, drooped around the side porch rereading poetry that even I think is pretty goopy, and whenever Mama wanted her to help with the housework claimed she had a sick headache, which meant that I got stuck with the job instead.

Mama was having splitting headaches, too, only she reacts to them in a different way. She regards any physical disability in us as a sign of weakness, and in herself as a personal insult. Consequently she chose this week to launch into a full-scale siege of cleaning attic and cellar, plus taking up, airing and beating all the carpets in the house.

On Wednesday afternoon Bron entertained the girls from the Dorcas League who were planning their basket party for Saturday night. Mama wasn't overjoyed about this on account of the housecleaning and her headache, and Bron wasn't exactly enchanted either because Viney Hodge is a member of the League too and Bron wasn't feeling any too Christian toward Viney. The basket party was a girl-ask-man fund-raising affair at which the basket suppers were to be auctioned off, and Viney made much of the fact that she already had Herbie lined up to be her escort.

"Who are you asking, Bronwyn?" she demanded archly. Viney, like Mary Lou, goes in for kittenishness and giggles. "That cute Mr. Albright who walked you home from church?"

Ben, who was home for a change and raiding the refreshments, hooted. "He's as old as Pa, and a widower to boot, and so dignified he gives you icicles in July."

Bron tossed her head. "He's a very nice man, and a staunch supporter of the church, Pa says so. I just bet he would come if I asked him."

"Ooh, why don't you?" Viney squealed. "I dare you to!"

Bron smiled enigmatically. "Maybe I will."

That night Mr. Albright walked Bron home from choir practice, and she got in later than usual. "Well, I did it," she said flatly. "He's going to escort me to the basket party." She sounded a bit forlorn and sad.

On Thursday Missy tattled to Mama that Ben and Doug were smoking roll-your-owns out behind the barn —an excellent spot to be unobserved by Mama, but in a direct line from Aunt Kate's window. Mama was so mad she made the mistake of telling Ben she didn't care if she never saw hide nor hair of either one of them again. Ben said that was fine with him, too, and took off. Mama was all primed to dump the whole situation in Pa's lap, but Pa didn't make it home for dinner again.

Friday was a scorcher. It was also the day Mama had designated for taking up the downstairs carpets, and Ben, having taken Mama at her word, was nowhere to be found. That meant it was Bron, Marnie and I who dragged the heavy rolls outside, hindered by Peter's attempts to rescue every larva or beetle that turned up in the newspapers underneath. Marnie got interested in the old funny papers that had been put down last year for padding, and spread-eagled on the floor to read. After a few hours my arms felt as if they'd been wrenched from their sockets, and Bron's hair curled damply around her flushed face.

Mama's hair was falling down, too, but she looked rather greyish-white despite the heat. She appeared to have been losing weight lately, too. Ben had really been a skunk to skip out, despite the provocation. But I could hardly blame him, for Mama was being such an Early Christian Martyr she was just unbearable.

We finally got the carpets rolled away and the summer matting down. Mama sat down on the porch swing abruptly and closed her eyes.

Bron looked at her. "Mama, you stay here in the shade. I'll make some lemonade. And Tish and I will fix supper."

Into this house of shining floors and exhausted females came Papa, fresh as a daisy in his white linen suit, to announce he was going upstate to visit another courthouse over the weekend, and wanted Mama to be ready to leave with him in half an hour.

Mama stared at him. "You crazy with the heat? In the middle of housecleaning. And what about the children?"

"They're old enough to be left. Bron and Ben can look after the younger ones."

Mama sniffed. "Ben can't even look after himself. Almost burnt the house down yesterday. Land knows where he is today. Needs a father's guidance, but you're too busy staying downtown late and traipsing off to more courthouses just for the fun of it. Anyway, I'm too busy to go off on a moment's notice like that."

"All right, all right!" Pa said irritably. "I just thought the trip would do you good and give us a chance to talk to each other for a change. When I was getting started as a court reporter, before we were married, I used to visit other courtrooms and take the dictation down just for practice. Kate used to come with me. It was kind of fun."

"Kate doesn't have family responsibilities tying her down," Mama retorted. "And you could talk to me more if you came home from work on time."

But by that time Pa had gone into the house to pack his bag. He departed, announcing he'd be home in time for supper Sunday night. Mama didn't deign to answer. She retired early in a little cloud of righteous indignation, which prevented her from discovering that Ben didn't come home all night. Bron was worried.

"Oh, let him be," Marnie advised sensibly. "He can't freeze, and he's too fond of his own skin to starve. He'll come home when he gets hungry enough, and by that time maybe Mama will have calmed down."

The head of steam Mama'd worked up sustained her, despite the circles under her eyes, through taking up the bedroom carpets the next morning. We were just launching into a full-scale beating of the first one when Aunt Kate hollered over the fence.

"Tarnation," Mama muttered under her breath, and then louder, sweetly, "What is it, Kate?"

"Just wondered when that boy of yours was going to show up to dig those trenches. The rosebushes are here now, and they'll die fast in this heat."

"Good grief!" Mama turned to us, looking pale. "Forgot all about it. Where *is* Ben?"

Bron and I looked at each other. Then Marnie, who obviously was having a struggle with herself, blurted out, "He hitched a freight to the ball game with Doug Latham."

Bron grabbed her by the shoulders. "And you let him go?"

"I'm no tattler," Marnie announced righteously. But she quailed under the look in Bron's eyes. "Oh, all right," she said in a low voice, and turned toward the fence. "Aunt Kate! Ben had to do something with someone else, so I'm going to do the digging for you. I'm plenty strong." Marnie can really be a lamb when she puts her mind to it.

"I'll come too." Peter heroically broke off communications with a friendly caterpillar.

"And don't take any money, either!" Bron hissed after their departing backs.

It was a weekend I wish were more forgettable. Bron, Mama and I coped with the carpets. Bron went to the basket social with Mr. Albright. She came home late, and she didn't tell me anything about it. Herbie sat with Viney in church again. Ben still hadn't come home, and by midafternoon on Sunday Mama was not only mad, she was also worried sick.

"Could break his leg, hopping freights," she muttered, pacing the floor. "Could lose a limb. Could be lying in a hospital somewhere right now." Or, alternatively, "Where *is* your father? Fool men are never around when you really need them!"

"Mama, sit down," Bron kept saying. "Have some coffee." "Have something to eat." But Mama just kept batting her away.

The late evening twilight was just greying the sky when we beheld Pa and Ben strolling up from the corner together, arm in arm.

"Well, of all the . . . !" Mama's energy came back in a blaze. By the time they came up the path she was waiting for them on the porch, like a figure of Fate.

"Evening, Evie," Pa was starting mildly, when Mama interrupted.

"Hope your son's been telling you what he's been up to! Haven't seen hide nor hair of him for three days. Off hopping freights with his hooligan friend when I expressly told him not to. Makes a fool of me to your sister just when she's letting me know what she thinks of how I bring up your children."

"Mama, you make a fool of me in front of my friends, too." Ben's voice was quiet, but I could see the telltale muscle twitching in his cheek. "You should ask me first before you take my time for granted."

"Ben Sterling, who do you . . . ."

"All right, all right, Evie!" Pa interrupted. "Can't this wait? I've had a long trip."

"Trip!" Mama turned on him. "Better you'd been home to handle your son. I can't, I'm sure. *And* your sister."

"Now, Evie." Pa sounded tired. "Kate means well. She's a lonely woman . . . ."

"That's right. Stand up for her. Not your wife. I knock myself out making a nice home for you, and you're not home enough to notice, let alone help. Don't know what good it is having men around the house if they're never there when you need them!"

Pa looked at Mama. "Ben's right," he said. "You do take too much for granted."

Mama didn't even answer; she just marched upstairs and into their room and slammed the door. For the first time in our lives, we heard the key rasp in the lock.

Pa snatched off his glasses. "Tarnation, woman, that's enough!" he hollered up the stairs. "When you're ready to speak civil, you can send for me. Meanwhile I'll be staying where a man does get appreciated!" He stomped down the steps, around the yard, and through the gate to Aunt Kate's.

It was strange how, in the hottest spell of summer when clothes cling clammily to your skin, you can have goose-bumps and your bones feel winter-cold. I could never, in my life, remember such a week as the next one.

Ben was seldom home; he took to his old habit of entering and exiting the house via the window, the kitchen roof and the apple tree to avoid encounters with Mama. I didn't blame him. Mama was as sour as a pickled lime, and she whirled around the house like one of Missy's perpetual motion tops. She couldn't seem to stop, and she went at everything she attacked, from carpet sweeping to ironing, as if she were attacking Pa himself. I could tell from the strain in her eyes that her head was splitting, and there were little white lines around her mouth, but being Ma she wouldn't give in. And the way she snapped our heads off every time we opened our mouths, she shut off any sympathy like a leaky faucet.

Missy alternately made a babyish pest of herself or was touchingly, angelically subdued. "She knows something's wrong, poor monkey," Bron said somberly the afternoon we found her sound asleep under the table with Cicero as a pillow.

I wished I could go to Celinda and bawl the whole mess out on her sympathetic shoulder, but Sterlings don't wash their dirty laundry in public, even before such a close and dear friend as Cee. I did spend as much time as possible with her, grateful for her unspoken concern. Like Ben, I was home no more than I absolutely had to be, because it was a cross between a morgue and a crazy house. Sometimes I felt like a dirty dog deserting Mama, not even helping, but when I was around her I came so close to exploding I knew I had to get out of there before I did something really drastic.

I would have talked to Ben, if he'd been around, but Ben was on one of those rare, unreachable rampages that were a combination of Sterling temper, pride, bravado, and a stubbornly shut mind and mouth. Pa must have been much like Ben once, I thought, only he'd learned to control the family temperament. Up till now.

*Pa.* He was the one I really wanted to talk to, the one I wanted to run to like a child to have my world put right. Only I couldn't do that. He wasn't very far away. All I had to do was push open the gate between Aunt Kate's yard and ours. But I couldn't do it. Don't ask me why; I just couldn't, that's all.

I might have talked to Bron, but she was not around very often either, and when she was she had retreated into a kind of adult unreachability. Besides she had additional problems of her own.

"Herbie's been seeing Viney every day," Celinda told me. "Papa was telling Mama about it at dinner last night. The police chief caught them together out under the footbridge." The footbridge is our favored local spot

for illicit amours, which our parents think Cee and I
don't know about, but we do on account of our un-
avoidable association with Mary Lou Hodge and her
dirty mind.

"What were they doing?" I asked with interest.

Celinda turned red and looked away.

"Do you suppose Bron knows?" Even as I spoke I
knew it was a silly question. We both knew the length
and breadth of our local grapevine.

Evidently a lot of other people must have heard as
well. That night while we were eating supper in awkward
silence, our telephone rang. Bron answered. I heard her
say, "Yes, this is Miss Sterling," and for the rest of the
brief conversation she was being very la-di-dah grown-
up. When she came back to the table she announced,
avoiding everyone's eyes, "That was Mr. Albright. He
wants to take me to a concert at the Opera House on
Saturday night."

"Suit yourself, I'm sure," Mama sniffed. "Sure it
doesn't matter to anyone here what I think about anything anyway." She pushed back her chair and stomped
upstairs again to her room.

Bron sat down heavily. "Oh, dear."

"Let her alone," Ben said bluntly. *"Women!"*

"If *we* were acting that way . . ." Marnie began self-
righteously.

"Oh, shut *up!*" Bron snapped with irritation. And she
too swirled out.

You can get an idea how we felt when I say that even
Ben didn't want any homemade dessert.

It was nice for Bron to have something to look forward to, even if it was with somebody as old as Mr.
Albright. I wondered whether he knew about our family
mess. Mr. Albright was just about Pa's best friend. But
Pa, too, lived by the Sterling family code.

I didn't imagine things could get any worse, but I

should have known better. When I finally showed up home Friday afternoon I was greeted by a queer smell drifting down from the attic stairs. Bron and I converged on the attic at the same time. Bron, with the prudence of long experience, shut the hall door behind us as we bolted up.

"Oh dear God, what on earth . . . ."

"It's all right." Peter lifted a dirty face, looking out of breath and more than a little scared. A faint curl of smoke still eddied out from under the blankets heaped in a corner of the floor.

Bron grabbed Peter's shoulders and shook him till his teeth rattled. *"What happened?* This is no time for misplaced loyalty. If Ben's smoking had set fire to this house . . . ."

"He didn't mean to, Bron!" Two tears trickled in grimy little rivulets down Peter's cheeks. "Doug Latham whistled up from the street, and at the same time Mama started yelling for him. He had to skin out fast. But he thought the cigarette was out before he went!"

Bron and I looked at each other. Ben knows perfectly well how our parents feel about his smoking on the sly, and this was the first time he'd ever tried it right in the house. Thank goodness, I thought fervently, that Mama had barricaded herself and her sick headache behind a tightly shut door. And thank heaven for Peter's celebrated powers of scientific observation!

Bron handed Peter a clean handkerchief and looked away tactfully while he wiped his eyes. "It's a good thing we had one man around the house to cope," she said briskly. "You can go now, Peter. We'll clean up the mess."

Peter escaped with the celerity of a greased pig, and Bron and I opened the windows and swept up the evidence in silence. I was proud of the way my brother and sister handled things, but deep inside me I was scared.

Scared sick. I saw the same feeling reflected in Bron's eyes. What we all needed, unequivocally, was Pa and Mama giving order to the universe again. Things like Ben's rebellion were too big for us to cope with.

I was thinking about this in the dim dark and middle of the night, wishing I could light the lamp without waking Bron, when I heard Marnie prowling in the hall. And it suddenly occurred to me that there had been an unconscionable lot of butts in the attic for Ben alone. I opened the bedroom door.

Marnie was rummaging in the linen closet. "Missy wet the bed again," she grumbled. "I thought she'd outgrown that."

"I'll help." I followed Marnie into their room, plopped Missy on the window seat and changed her, still drugged with sleep, into a clean nightie while Marnie remade the bed.

"All right, punkin. Come on." Marnie came over to lift the weary bundle from my arms. Her face was tender in the moonlight, and softer.

"Marnie? Were you smoking with Ben in the attic?"

"Who said that?"

"Nobody. Bron doesn't know, but I counted the butts and I guessed." I let the silence settle. "They started a fire in the pile of dress-up clothes. If Peter hadn't noticed, the house might have burned down."

"Gloryoski." Marnie's face went white and she sat down suddenly, Missy and all. "Oh, Tish."

"It's all right. I won't say anything. But for heaven's sake, you idiot, stay out of trouble at least till all this blows over! I don't think we could take much more."

Marnie dumped Missy into bed and rose abruptly. "I'm going to go down and put the sheets to soak."

Some time later she floated back up on a pleasant cloud of conscious rectitude to announce she'd put *all* the laundry in to soak, and think how pleased and surprised Mama would be.

One of the results of lying awake nights worrying is that you sleep late mornings. I awoke the next day to the sounds of a flaming row downstairs. Mama's voice was raised, shrill as an old witch. "Look what you've done! Colors all run in with the whites, and fine things mixed up with the heavy sheets. Think you could at least not *make* extra trouble for me when I feel like this."

"Oh, hell and damn!" Marnie shouted rudely. I ran downstairs. The tears were gushing down Marnie's flushed face—Marnie, who never cried!—and her eyes were enormous. "No wonder nobody ever gives you any help. We can't do anything right! I wish this blasted house had burned down around your ears!" She stormed out, banging the door so hard the windows rattled.

Mama just stood there, staring. Missy hid beneath the table. Bron quietly started cleaning up the kitchen, and coward that I was, I fled. I didn't even wait for breakfast, just got dressed as fast as I could and exited via Ben's route of roof and apple tree. But the memory of my mother's face followed me all day like the Hound of Heaven.

By afternoon, after wandering aimlessly all morning, I took refuge in the Public Library. The strain of being around Celinda and not spilling to her had gotten on my nerves, and anyway I knew she was hurt that I wouldn't confide. I had a raging headache composed of worry, guilty conscience, lack of sleep and not having eaten anything all day. The Public Library threw me out on the streets at six, and I wandered around town for another couple of hours, feeling I knew exactly how the Ancient Mariner must have felt with that damned albatross tied round his neck.

At last my wanderings led me unconsciously to Vyse
Avenue. The lamp was lit in Aunt K's dining room, and
I could see her and Pa sitting at opposite ends of the
table. It seemed queer to see Pa at a table with only one
other person, not right somehow. I stood for a long
minute with my hand on Aunt K's gate, and then went
on.

The front of our house was in darkness, but a light
burned in the kitchen. Cicero was whining on the back
stoop, looking forlorn. I scratched his ears and let him
in. In the kitchen Ben, looking harried, was dishing fried
eggs out to Missy and Peter. "About time you showed
up," he grumbled. "Look, is this stuff fit for the punkin
to eat?"

"Where is everybody?"

"Ma's lying down, says she feels rotten, which means
mad and for tarnation sake to let her alone. Bron's out
with her aged beau, and land knows where Marnie is. I
haven't seen her all day."

Ben looked so beat and worried that I took the frying
pan out of his hands. "You sit down and I'll serve." I
got out bread and bacon, milk for the children, and
started a pot of coffee for Ben and me. Mama doesn't
approve of our drinking coffee, but what she didn't
know couldn't hurt us. I was beginning to wonder darkly whether Mama was ever going to get over this. It
wasn't like her to go locking herself off this way. I remembered some of Aunt K's grim tales of women who'd
taken to their beds and never gotten out of them, "for
sheer spite, too," and shivered.

Sunday is usually the climax and keynote of our week,
at once chaotic and reassuring, filled with the fragrance
of cooking and the bustle of getting ready for church.
When I woke up this Sunday, there was no friendly bitter smell of perking coffee, not even the sound of
Mama's snapping around and Missy's whining while her

hair got curled. I looked at the clock and poked Bron's sleeping back violently. "Wake up! We're going to be late for church."

"Wha . . . ?" Bron rolled over, flushed with sleep. Then she too looked at the clock and jumped up. "Glory, Pa will kill us!" She tackled the chore of getting Missy and Marnie Sunday-decent while I roused the boys and went down to start the stove. Presently Bron came down, her forehead puckered. "Mama's not coming. She says her head aches, and to see what we can find in the icebox for our dinner." We looked at each other. Ordinarily Mama's as strict as Pa about not missing church.

I burned the oatmeal, and we were late for service. I felt queer inside, walking down that aisle before everyone's eyes without Pa and Mama at our head. When we reached our pew, I knelt down on the bench and buried my face in my arm, and the stately familiar service rolled over and around me while I was lost in the lonely world of my own prayers.

Pa didn't even get to sit with us. He was serving as vestryman that week. When the service was over, I ducked out quickly. I couldn't speak to Pa, for the first time in a week, before this mob of acquaintances and strangers.

There wasn't much in the icebox to make dinner out of, on account of apparently Mama hadn't thought of replenishing it during the week. Ben looked in distaste at the collation Bron and I finally managed to produce. "Too bad it didn't occur to Aunt K to exhibit Christian charity and invite us over there to dinner."

"Aunt K's a rotten cook, and you know it," Marnie said bluntly.

"Then why does Papa eat there all the time?" Missy asked. There was a dead silence, and then everybody talked at once.

The afternoon dragged along. Ben and Marnie vanished as usual. Peter was preoccupied with his lepidop-
terae, and Missy squirreled away in some corner of her
own. Bron was out on the hammock with a handkerchief and a book of poetry. Herbie, Marnie had told
me, had escorted Viney to church again. I tried to write
in my Journal but the words wouldn't come; I lay on my
stomach on the treehouse floor reading all the poems
and stories I'd ever written, and ended by tearing them
all up. I thought when I wrote them that I'd known what
suffering was, but I'd been wrong.

Toward twilight, without being called, everyone came
straggling home to the side porch where we always have
Sunday night supper in the summer. Bron made cin-
namon toast and lemonade, and I tried to read aloud in
Pa's place, but the pretense was no good. Bron had gone
upstairs to knock on Mama's door, but she got no answer, and the door remained closed.

Late, late that night I lay in bed so wide awake that
my eyes fairly burned. The night was so still that not a
breath stirred the lank curtains at the windows, and my
thin nightgown clung damply to my back. I stared out
through the green arms of the apple tree at the faint
glow emanating from Aunt K's spare room. Pa always
sat up reading when he couldn't sleep.

I thought Bron was asleep because she lay so quiet,
but when I shifted position she sat up abruptly, hugging
her knees. "This can't go on." She got up and rapped on
the wall of our brothers' room. "Ben? You boys come in
here, and bring Marnie. We're having a Family Council."

I stared at her. "On our own?"

"Well, if parents refuse to act like adults, *somebody*
has to take the initiative," Bron snapped, sounding exactly like Aunt Kate.

The others came in, Ben with a sleeping Missy slung

over his shoulder like a sack of potatoes. "If it's a family conference I thought the punkin ought to be here, too," he said, dumping her on the window seat.

"It's still not the *whole* family," Peter pointed out devastatingly. We looked at each other.

"Ben's right." Bron flung back her hair. "There's no point in our talking. It's Pa and Mama who have to have it out."

"They won't," Ben said bluntly. "Any more than any of us would ever be first to give in if Pa didn't make us take a good look at ourselves and squirm."

"Mama's awake," Marnie contributed. "I heard her snuffling when we came by her door."

For some reason, that shook us as nothing else. Mama, as much as Marnie, considered tears a sign of weakness. Bron stood up. "I'll get her out of there if I have to climb in through the window. Marnie, make coffee."

I swallowed hard. "I'll get Pa." Silent as Indian scouts we scattered to our tasks.

In Aunt Kate's yard I paused to reconnoiter. All was dark and silent except where one light burned. I climbed precariously up the trellis and succeeded in throwing a handful of pebbles through the open window. After the second handful, Pa's startled face appeared beside me.

"Tish! What are you . . . ."

"Hush, Pa! Pa, come outside, please! I've got to talk to you."

Pa looked at me. "I'll be out directly. Now get off that trellis before you break your neck."

I waited under the rose arbor, hands clenched tightly, until Pa stepped cautiously out on the back stoop. Like me, he had pulled clothes hastily over his nightgown. "Tish, is anyone sick?"

"No. I just had to talk."

Pa tucked my hand through his arm and we walked

out into Vyse Avenue, spectral in the moonlight.

"How are things going?" Pa asked presently.

"Not good." Unaccountably my teeth started chattering, and then the dam burst. "Oh, Pa, we've tried to fill your place, but all of us put together can't do it. The—center's gone out of things. I never appreciated before how much you give us."

Pa gave a short laugh. "I'm afraid your mother doesn't think so."

"She will. Maybe she does already. If you'll just come home with me now and talk to her."

"It's not that simple, Tish." Pa sounded infinitely old. "A man needs to feel he's respected as a human being, that his wife sees *him,* all of him, not just the weaknesses he knows about already."

"Since when did you ever teach us anything had to be simple or easy!" The words burst out before I knew they were coming, and they hit Pa, I could see they did. I might as well be hung for a sheep as a lamb, I thought. "You always told us it took the really big person to make the first move. Can't you do that now, even if it does mean eating the Sterling pride?"

Pa looked at me, and I was afraid I'd gone too far. Then his shoulders sagged. "Out of the mouths of babes," he said. "All right, Tish. You win. Let's go home."

I didn't like the price of victory if it made Pa look like that. But I didn't dare think about that now. There were bigger obstacles ahead. My heart pounded harder than ever as we went up the kitchen steps.

Mama was in the kitchen, obviously in the middle of a row with Bron. When she saw Pa, she flushed and jerked her head away, pulling her wrapper tight together at the throat. Pa closed the door and leaned against it, waiting. Bron and Ben and I looked at each other and wondered where to start. It wasn't as exciting as we once had thought, having the leadership depend on us.

Finally Ben cleared his throat. "Let's—go into the dining room," he said. That was where we always sat for formal conferences. Pa led the way, but instead of going to the head he drew a side chair out, looked pointedly at Mama, and waited. Mama sniffed and flounced into it with poor grace. Pa, deliberately, sat down across from her. Ben looked at Bron and me, then stepped to Pa's usual place at the table's head.

"All right," Mama said ominously. "We're waiting."

"That's what we're doing," Ben said quietly. "Waiting for you two to act like grown-ups instead of what you're always calling us—spoiled kids."

I would have applauded if I hadn't been so scared.

"We're not a family any more," Bron said. "We need you back."

"Glad you recognize that," Mama retorted. But the wind had been taken out of her sails, as all could see.

"We're to blame, too." I looked at my mother's rigid face, then down at my hands. "We've taken for granted that you'd always be around for us. We've never thought of you as having needs."

There was silence, and I knew Mama was caught in the crossfire of her two favorite speeches, the one about Families Should Always Be There for Each Other, and the one on Children Should Consider Parents' Feelings. Part of me enjoyed the paradox, but the rest of me had a very empty feeling.

Pa coughed. "I appreciate your perception, Tish. But it's natural for *children* to take parents for granted. They need the security of being able to."

"Maybe that's true at Missy's age, or Peter's," Bron said earnestly. Peter looked aggrieved at being lumped with Missy, but Marnie nodded.

"Where do parents get the idea we've got to see them as gods? We ought to—to be able to respect each other as human beings. Definitely," she added darkly, "what we need around here is more respect. For all of us."

"Even when we're being pains. Like not doing things that embarrass each other—or not picking on things we're ashamed about already. And trust in each other's good intentions, even when they don't work out." I remembered my orgy of self-pity the night of my birthday party. "More concern for others, and less over whether they hurt us."

"Glad you're finally realizing it," Mama spoke in a raspy echo of her usual tartness.

"We're talking to *you,* too, Mama," Bron retorted.

Before Mama could answer, Ben's voice sliced in, clean and sharp. "I guess what we're saying is we don't need little tin gods. Or caretakers. But is it too much to ask for human beings who practice what they preach about understanding and respect, instead of getting wrapped up in their own stubborn pride? Because how in tarnation can you two expect us to act like adults when you don't yourselves?"

His words fell like a weighted rock, and in the little hush of shock that followed, he thrust his legs out and his chin forward in a replica of Pa's own gesture. Mama's breath came back to her in a rush, and for the first time she looked straight at Pa. "See what happens when a father lets his children run wild. Outrageous for them to talk that way to their parents."

"Shut up, Evie," Pa ordered, not taking his eyes from Ben.

Mama gasped. "How dare you—tarnation, *look* at me!"

"Why?" Pa asked. "How long has it been since you've looked at us, Evie, or listened to us either? If you had, you might have noticed it's your own highhandedness pushed me out of taking a hand with the children."

"If you'd been here more, instead of traipsing around from court to court . . . ."

"That traipsing around, Evie," Pa said evenly, "was in the interest of keeping a roof over your head. Or haven't you noticed that the city administration's changed? I guess you've forgotten my job's a political appointment. And maybe it hasn't occurred to you that it's hard for a man in his mid-forties to find another job. Tish is right, you are insensitive."

I wanted to sink through the floor. But Mama was too shocked and angry to notice me. "How's a woman to know a man has worries if he shuts her out like she's just a hired housekeeper? And makes her feel she's not a very good one at that? How can she feel like standing behind him when he doesn't stand behind *her*? If every time she needs a word of tenderness what she hears instead is, 'Tarnation, woman, why can't you iron my shirts as well as Kate?' I'm *tired* of ironing!" Mama's eyes were very black. "I'm tired of trying to keep my house as neat as a single woman's who's got no children muddying it up as soon as she's got something done. I'm tired of trying to keep your son from burning the house down around our ears, and one of your daughters from running wild. I'm just plain tired! And as for my dragging around the house like a sick cat, Mr. Sterling—" She took a deep breath and her chin jerked a mile high. "I wouldn't be that way if I wasn't, at my age, carrying another child of yours when I don't know how to cope with the ones I have already!"

In the hush Pa's voice went on like a low scratched gramophone record. "And another thing. After twenty years a man gets tired of hearing his wife call him, 'Mr. Sterling' as if they'd only just been introduced."

"Oh, Edward," Mama whispered, staring at him, and started to cry. I saw Pa move toward her. Bron rose quickly.

"We'll make coffee." She steered us firmly toward the kitchen, all but Missy who had fallen asleep with her head on the table. The door swung shut behind us. I felt queer and shaky, as if I were starting to get better from a long siege of the grippe. Mama was going to have a baby, and Pa might lose his job, but the important thing was that we were back to being a family again.

Only it wasn't in quite the same way it had been before. I could feel this in my marrow much later, when we had finally taken the coffee tray, with the brew long since boiled thick and bitter, into the dining room and were sitting, a whole family once again, in our accustomed places. We had never felt so awkward with each other, and yet so close.

We talked for a long while, quite quietly and calmly— about Pa's job, and money, and the new baby, and being a family. For the first time, I realized, Pa and Mama were really talking to us as if we were grown-up. I'd wanted that for a long while, and it was queer that I should find myself almost envying Missy, who huddled sleepily in Mama's lap and didn't understand a word of what was going on.

I didn't write that day down in my Journal right away. I didn't have to. It was already imprisoned in my memory, whole and complete, including the parts I wanted passionately to forget.

I didn't write it down. But deep within me—not in my heart of hearts, the way the novelists say, but in my blood and bones, I knew that it had been a Keeping Day. And that was what hurt.

We'd come to a place in the path of our lives where we'd had to leap across a chasm. We'd made it, and we had the heady knowledge we'd been able to make the jump, and the sense of being a few giant steps further along our way. But never again could we walk in the sublime confidence of those who didn't know the chasms could be there.

I had never known that a Keeping Day could be a descent into hell.

# CHAPTER III

## *August*

Mama was having another baby. I wondered where we were going to put it on account of we're pretty crowded in the house already.

So much had been said that night in so few words that it was kind of like we'd gulped a full meal down whole and now were having trouble getting it digested. We hadn't quite had time for the tasting and chewing, so it was pretty hard to keep all the pieces straight, let alone the implications.

For about a week we went around the house practically on tiptoe, being so considerate of each other you'd have thought we were strangers instead of being related. Marnie helped with the dishes for three days straight without being reminded. Ben actually went over and volunteered Aunt K a day of free yard work. Doug Latham was conspicuous by his absence, but I heard by the grapevine that he was sporting a black eye, the result of having made an apron-string type of comment to Ben about his aforesaid voluntary labor. And Missy got spoiled rotten because all of us were trying to make up to her for the neglect of the week before.

Pa came home on time for dinner every night, and

Mama, in spite of the fact that the smell of food made her turn peagreen, was cooking all his favorite dishes like corned beef and cabbage and lemon meringue pie. Being Mama, she refused all offers of assistance on the grounds she could do things better by herself, and then was cross as two sticks as a result of feeling thoroughly limp.

Pa was treating Mama like she was a piece of Great-Grandma Stryker's crystal, which embarrassed Mama. She went around muttering, "Stuff and nonsense, feel conspicuous, my seventh child after all, perfectly healthy woman," which was a contradiction in terms because in alternate breaths she was griping about how rotten she felt and how nobody cared. I could have kicked Mama, because here was Pa trying to show her how he did care, and she was tramping on it the way the hayers do the buttercups in Grandpa Stryker's fields. Considering how Mama loathes Aunt Kate, they've got a lot of the same bad habits.

I guess I realized from the first that Mama was as taken aback at the notion of a baby as the rest of us were. Like I said, where were we going to put it? I mean, babies are wonderful, but we really didn't need another. Missy was still pretty much a baby herself; she still wet the bed and she was at that showoffy, wanting-attention stage. I remembered how long it had taken Mama to get back on her feet after Missy was born, and how tired she'd looked till the two a.m. feedings had been outgrown. Missy had been a squaller, tuning up around suppertime and in full voice till after midnight, and Pa didn't have much patience with crying. I felt kind of sad to think of the poor little thing arriving and finding nobody particularly glad to see it.

Over and above the fact of the baby, stood the thing that made it a problem, the possibility of Pa's losing his job. That had been insufficiently discussed at the family conference that night, and we all sensed it was better not to broach the subject with either parent thereafter. We did, however, discuss it on our own. The attic, usual site of younger-generation conferences, being hotter than Hades at this time of year, we shifted to the treehouse. Even Bron climbed up, a thing she hadn't done in years. She sat on the floor, her feet tucked under her flowered dimity skirt, looking solemn and determined.

"I shall get a job, of course. I planned to, anyway, now that I'm out of school. Mama'll balk, naturally, but I'll have to make her see it's both sensible and proper."

"What can you do?" Ben demanded skeptically.

"I don't know. Be a governess, maybe; I don't think you need a Normal School diploma for that. Or get Pa to teach me shorthand so I can be a stenographer." Bron's face had the exalted look of a young Florence Nightingale.

"I still don't see why Pa should lose his job, anyway," I said plaintively. "He's good at it."

Ben shrugged cynically. "That's beside the point. Old Judge Simms, who gave Pa the job, is retiring this month. The new man's from a different political party, and besides he'll probably want to give the job to one of his own party cronies." He was silent for a moment. "To think of Pa waiting all these weeks for the axe to fall, and never letting on!"

"He probably thought we knew," Bron said bluntly. "He told us Judge Simms was going to retire. And we talk about parents being blind!"

We sat and stared at each other for a while as all the implications came thudding around our ears.

"What will we do," I asked finally in a small voice, "if it does happen?"

"Move someplace cheaper, probably. Maybe out to Pennsylvania with Grandpa Stryker. I'll be graduating in two years, and then I can work. Or maybe even quit

sooner." I knew exactly how much that sentence cost
Ben. For years he's been looking forward to going to
Harvard, like the Sterling men have done for gener-
ations.

"The last thing we need at this point," Marnie said
profoundly, "is another mouth to feed." You can
always count on Marnie to put into words what everyone else is being too delicate to say.

Ben doubled his fists. "Listen, stupid, if you even
breathe a word like that to Ma or Pa, I'll knock your
head off, even if you are a girl." He looked at me. "And
don't you go spilling the whole story to the Mouse,
either."

I bridled. "As if I would, Ben Sterling!"

I did, however, tell Cee about the baby when I for-
tuitously bumped into her at the Public Library the next
afternoon. Celinda took one look at me and dragged me
into our private corner, a bay window in the history section, which is out of the librarian's earshot. "Tish Sterling, what's happened to you?" she demanded.

"What do you mean?"

"For the past four weeks you've looked like death
warmed over. Now you look as if something very good
and very bad had happened at once." Celinda stopped.
"Look, Tish, if it's none of my business, I'll understand,
really I will. But you look the way I feel when I've got to
talk and have no one to run to."

I looked at her and my good intentions went out the
nearest window. "Mama's in the family way."

"Oh." Celinda turned pink.

I thanked my stars that in my family, what with six
kids, a brother who's animal-mad and a grandfather
who's a farmer, reproduction is taken pretty much for
granted.

"When's it coming?" Celinda asked presently.

"I don't know. End of winter sometime."

"Then that's why your mother's been so cranky lately."

I nodded, glad I wouldn't be tempted into revealing there were other factors involved in that particular situation.

"Tish, think what fun it will be to have a baby in the house again. Remember how we used to play with Missy? Maybe you'll get to be godmother. Bron was godmother for Missy, wasn't she?" Celinda's eyes were glowing. "I always wished I had a baby brother or sister."

"You can have my share of this one when it comes to walking the floor nights," I said, and meant it.

The library clock struck five at this juncture and I said goodbye hastily and let out for home, on account of it's a good half hour's walk uphill from the library and we were all still at the walk-on-eggs, be-helpful-to-Mama stage. The heat slowed down my usual speed. I was panting as I started up the last rise, and I could feel the cool dampness of perspiration trickling around my ears. I heard horse's hooves clippety-clopping up the hill behind me, and I moved over to avoid the inevitable cloud of dust. Then a shadow loomed beside me and stopped. It was Mr. Albright, coming home from his law office in the surrey.

"Hop in," he invited genially. "Too hot for hill climbing on a day like this." I obeyed, wishing for both Bron's and Pa's sakes that I didn't look so messy. Mr. Albright was immaculate in a white linen suit like Pa's and a red-and-white striped band on his flat straw hat. Fortunately he didn't try to make conversation. I wondered what he and Bron found to talk about when they were out together. If he'd been hoping Bron would be on the porch when he reached our house, he was disappointed, but he reined up in fine style anyway, and actually got out to help me down just as if I were as old as Bron.

"Tell your father I'd like to have a talk with him, one of these evenings when he's free," he said, departing.

I went into the house to be greeted by a blast of heat from the kitchen and to find that Mama, true to form, had worn herself out cooking a fancy meal on top of trying to start her preserving. In addition to which, it was already long past the time for Pa to be getting home.

"Roast getting all dried out," Mama said darkly. "Knew it was too good to last. Don't know why I kill myself when nobody really cares."

Marnie groaned under her breath, and Ben and I rolled our eyes at each other.

Missy came ambling in from the kitchen, chewing on an unscrubbed carrot. "Cicero just stole the roast beef off the table," she contributed. Cicero himself followed her in, looking idiotically pleased with himself and slobbering beef juice all over the hall floor. We held our breaths. Mama stared at Cicero and turned white and red and suddenly, shockingly, burst out, "Oh, hell and damn!" exactly like Marnie, and started to laugh. She laughed until she cried, rocking back and forth, hugging her stomach, the tears streaming down her face.

"Mama, you've been in the heat for too long. Come right outside and sit down!" Bron looked alarmed. Mama shook her head and kept on laughing, and at that moment, blessedly, in walked Pa. He took one look at Cicero, whose tail was going like a Fourth of July flag, and his lips twitched, but with great discretion he did not laugh.

"Peter, drag that beast out and tie him in the yard. And we're all going to sit out on the side porch for a spell. You, too, Evie." We're always relieved when Pa takes charge. I think this time even Mama was glad as we followed him gratefully out to the old wicker furniture in the shade. The air was growing cooler now, and the fragrance of Mama's flowers drifted up to us.

"First of all, we're going to sit here till we get cooled off, no need to rush for supper. Second, we're going to get cleaned up and go down to the Park Cafe to eat. They've put in some outdoor tables that look like fun."

"Can't afford to waste the money," Mama murmured.

Pa chose to ignore that. "Third, we're going to have a Family Council meeting. I've come to some decisions." His eyes traveled around the rapt circle. "Your Ma's right," he said, "we are too much bother for her to cope with just now. I know you've all done your best lately, but that doesn't help because the problem's in your Ma herself. She's just fundamentally incapable of taking things easy. It's not good for her. That's why you've been so hard to live with lately, Evie."

Mama opened her mouth indignantly, thought better of it, and shut it again.

"So I decided since I can't change your Ma's nature, I'm simply going to have to change the situation," Pa went on smoothly. "I'm going to send you all away for the summer."

"Away!"

"To your Grandpa Stryker's farm. I wrote him three days ago and I got his letter back today, saying he'll meet the Saturday train." Pa looked at Mama. "Be a good rest for you, Evie; you can get away from everything here and be with your father, and the children can run loose on the farm without your having to worry."

"You coming, too?" Mama asked.

Pa shook his head. "I'll get down for a week, perhaps, at the end of summer. Meanwhile I'll keep the house open and eat with Kate."

Mama was shaking her head. "Children can go. That dratted dog, too, he belongs on a farm. I'll stay here. Be a treat just having the house to myself in peace and quiet. Besides, won't have Kate thinking I don't look after my own husband." Pa started to speak, and Mama put her hand up and turned pink. "I'd *like* to be here with you."

Coming from Mama, that was the equivalent of a whole chapter of mush in a romantic novel.

It would be nice if I could say that we continued living on this plane, all sensitive and considerate of each other. Unfortunately real life isn't like that, at least not in our family, and the delicate plant of conscious love soon wilted under the hot blast of our independent natures. What we pictured that afternoon, I'm sure, was a water-color portrait of filial devotion, with all of us tiptoeing around Mama who lay on a chaise lounge, being pale and lovely and above all appreciative. We should have known that Mama couldn't fit that role.

What we got instead was Mama trying to finish up the housecleaning fast while we were home to help; Mama mending-scrubbing-ironing every stitch we owned so we'd look presentable to go to Gramps; Mama hollering at Ben to come carry hot water buckets for her just when he was on top of a ladder painting the trellis like she'd been after him to do for months, and then being mad as hops when she had to wait for him to climb down. We got Pa coming home evenings with a worried look on his face, finding Mama grey and worn-out and crosser than ever; Pa taking us into his study wearing his "I am grave-ly disappointed" face and telling us that after the Fami-ly Council he had hoped we would find it in our hearts to be of some assistance to our poor mother, and that even if we weren't going to help he didn't think it was too much to ask us at least not to make extra work.

It was one of those situations in which anything you do is wrong, and doing nothing only makes things worse. Marnie solved the problem characteristically by just staying away from home, which in view of her sus-ceptibility to foot-in-mouth disease was probably the best thing she could have done. Lord knows what she was up to, or where, but I told myself that the scare she'd gotten from the attic fire would probably keep her out of really drastic scrapes. I almost envied her ability to shuck off responsibility like that. Bron was out most of the day; she was looking for a job, which no one was supposed to know, on account of she didn't want to fight it out with Pa and Mama till she had a definite offer somewhere. This meant Ben and I had to cover for her whenever Mama wondered at her absence. It also meant that the major responsibility for trying to cope devolved on the two of us because Peter, for all that he has the amiability of an angel, is too little and too preoccupied with his own affairs to be depended on for much.

There were times during Pa's nightly reproach sessions when Ben and I fairly itched to tattle on both Marnie and Mama, but we gritted our teeth, stared at the floor and tried to control our Sterling tempers. Unfortunately this made us look sullen, which only made our parents madder. I cussed to Ben in private and prayed for patience.

Ben has the brains to look at things logically. "Hang on," he advised me when I came exploding into the privacy of the treehouse Friday afternoon; "we'll be leaving in the morning."

"If I should live so long," I muttered darkly, still smarting. I hadn't minded making a martyr of myself doing three baskets of ironing on the hottest day of the year; I hadn't wanted Mama on her feet by the hot stove, and I'd actually been happy thinking here was something concrete I could do to help. I *had* minded Mama descending on me, calling me a tarnation fool because I wasn't doing it exactly the way she'd have done it, didn't I *know* after all these years that she always starched Missy's pinafore ruffles by dipping them in sugar water before ironing, and what was I trying to do, anyway, make her extra work, on account of she was going to have to do at least three things over.

"The trouble with us," Ben said, "is that we've been looking at the problem hind-side-to. We've been trying to take the work off Mama's hands."

"She *wants* it off her hands—"

"Wrong, she wants us to fall down in appreciation because she's knocking herself out." Ben took a cigarette paper and some tobacco from his pocket and started fashioning a roll-your-own.

I stared at him. "Ben Sterling—"

"Shut up. I'm thinking," Ben said absently, lighting up. "What we have to do is find some way to get Ma to stop working without feeling superfluous, and a way for us to help without impinging on her prerogatives, as keeper of the house." When Ben uses words like that I may not understand him, but I know he's usually making sense.

"Mama's always bustled around like mad, but she's worse than ever now. I thought after Pa came home things would get better, but they haven't."

"I guess she's worried about Whatsitsname." That was how we had taken to referring to the baby. "Ma's pretty old. It's not too good for a woman her age to be having another kid."

We looked at each other. I started feeling shaky. "Ben, you don't think—if Mama's too old, why is she having one?"

"Because she's *not* too old, if you know what I mean."

One of the things that irritates me about my brother Ben is that he's always trying to be smart when we need him serious.

"Benjamin!" Mama's voice came hollering from the kitchen doorway. "Have to give Cicero a shampoo. Can't take him to your grandfather's looking like a dirty mop."

"Oh, drat." Ben stubbed out his cigarette and tucked the butt carefully away for future use. "Look, Tish, run down to Lathams' for me and tell Doug I won't be able to pitch for him today, after all. Tell him I guess I won't see him again till we get back in the fall." Ben looked tired. He had, I remembered, been dragging trunks and boxes up and downstairs for Mama all that morning.

"You go play ball. Peter and I'll do Cicero," I said.

This seemed a safe offer. It definitely was not impinging on Mama's preserves, on account she loathes bathing Cicero as much as he loathes being laundered, and the combination of outdoors and animals was right up Pete's alley. As for me, on a day like this being splashed by Cicero was almost as good as being Missy's age and young enough to go wading in a washtub in the shade. I collared Peter, and he collared Cicero who was hiding in the cool dust beneath the front porch, and together we persuaded him to sit in the washtub underneath the backyard pump.

I had just gotten one side of him nicely soaped and was proceeding under his chin when Aunt Kate's grey cat came ambling through the juniper bushes, and Cicero decided he'd been amiable long enough. He leaped out of the tub in one great splash, the cat jumped spitting to the fence, and the two of them took off down Bryant Avenue with Peter and me in perspiring pursuit.

We must have been quite a sight. Peter and I were both soaked; my hair had come undone, and I'd taken off my stockings and shoes. As for Cicero, one side of him was snow white foam that shook off evanescent bubbles as he ran; the other side was sodden and down-plastered. He looked like a refugee from a circus side-show. With Tom in the lead, his tail bristled to three times its normal size, we careened in and out of people's lawns and gardens.

Mary Lou Hodge, all gussied up in a frilly new dress,

was sitting on her front steps with Doug Latham and a couple of other boys. She took one look and began jumping up and down, screeching "Mad dog! Mad dog!" Immediately about five or six adults materialized out of nowhere. Tom and Cicero, seeing them coming, reversed their field and hightailed it toward home, and I tore after them, leaving Peter to explain that Cicero was suffering from soapsuds, not rabies.

We converged on our corner just as Mama made the fatal mistake of opening our front screen door. Tom, seeing refuge, skinned in past her. Cicero, galumphing after him, knocked Mama clear over. I heard her cuss, and then I heard her scream. I bolted inside into a scene of horror.

Spread out across the sofa like a snowy glacier were the pride of Mama's heart, her summer organdie curtains, ironed at last. At least, they had been snowy. Now a trail of muddy footprints led up to the pinnacle of the sofa where Tom perched, spitting. Cicero sprang at him, and cat and curtains came down together in a welter of dirt and suds.

For a minute, I couldn't choke back a laugh.

Mama's voice came in a harsh quivering whisper. "Get those beasts out of here and then just—get—out! Might have known you couldn't be trusted with a simple thing like washing a dog. Head in the clouds so much you're good for nothing! Why your sister can't be home doing something constructive for a change 'stead of mooning over that dratted boy. Tarnation selfish, worthless lot, every one of you. Don't know how glad I am to be getting rid of you tomorrow!"

I thought of Bron, trudging wearily around in search of a job she wasn't trained to fill, wondering how she was going to be able to preserve both Mama's sense of decorum and Pa's pride. I thought of Ben, being willing to give up his plans for college. I thought of all the acres of window-panes I'd polished that morning before I'd done all that ironing, and something snapped. "Not half so glad as we'll be to be gone! No wonder Pa almost couldn't stand it here. We never can please you, no matter how we try. I've been so sorry for poor little Whatsitsname, with nobody wanting it, but I guess you don't really want the rest of us, either. You wouldn't care if we never came home."

"Think we'd all be happier if you lived somewhere else," Mama said levelly. We stared at each other across the electric silence.

Mama gathered up her ruined curtains and went to the kitchen without another word. Peter came home and finished washing the dog. I went out of the house and walked and walked.

It may sound funny coming from me, but I do hate family fights. Even if you win, which neither of us had that day, you still feel as if you've lost half your life-blood afterwards. I felt so sick I didn't even go over to Celinda's to say goodbye, the way I'd planned. I walked till my legs ached and twilight was falling, trying to beat out my angry self-reproach, but it wasn't any good.

Fortunately, Pa didn't come home to supper, so we didn't have to explain to him. Mama'd locked herself in her room, and we kids fed ourselves leftovers. We were right back where we'd been a few weeks before. I almost hated poor little Whatsitsname for precipitating this mess.

Later, lying wakeful in the hot bedroom beside Bron, who was sleeping soundly, worn out from her unsuccessful job hunt, I heard Mama banging trunk lids around downstairs, but I didn't go down.

Pa was taking us to the railroad station early the next morning. Mama didn't come down to breakfast or to see us off. She had a sick headache and wanted to sleep, Pa said. I told myself that this was just as well. The sick feeling in my stomach persisted, despite the rising tide of elation as preparations for our migration accelerated.

Traveling by railroad train to Grandpa Stryker's was quite an event. We had only done so once, before Missy was born, and that had decidedly been *with* our parents and *without* a dog. Pa borrowed Mr. Albright's rig, which was bigger than ours, to take us to the station, and even so Cicero's crate took up so much space that he had to let Ben and Peter go down to the station alone on the trolley cars. We got there before they did, and by the time they'd arrived we'd mislaid two suitcases, Missy had spilt ice cream down her front, and Cicero had broken out of the crate and been chased all over the station. We were assisted in this endeavor by a policeman, a ticket agent, and two passing college boys who were hoping to make an impression on Bron. Cicero was finally reincarcerated after knocking down only one old lady and two children. He lay on the floor of his crate, trying to look put-upon, and licking the ice cream off Missy's dress.

"Good thing your Ma's not here," Pa said, grinning.

The trip itself was long, hot, dusty and unexciting. Bron, who was feeling her responsibility as eldest, overdid the authority, in Ben's and my opinion. Marnie found a bunch of young boys to talk to. Peter persuaded the conductor to let him spend most of the trip in the baggage car with Cicero, where he read penny-dreadful novels and munched peanuts in dirt and contentment. Missy wandered up and down the aisle, confiding our entire family history to anyone who'd listen and being invited into innumerable laps. I devoted myself to writing a detailed inventory of the train's appurtenances, from the frayed red plush upholstery to the tasseled fringe above the fly-specked windows, in case I should ever want to use it in a book, and above all to trying to forget the situation between me and Mama.

Just as dusk was falling, the conductor poked his head into our car. "You all the young'uns bound for Albion Junction? We're just pulling in there now."

Bron sat up and tried to wake Missy, who only burrowed more sleepily against her side. Ben went to disengage Marnie and Peter. I straightened my hat and peered out the dirty window. The train had pulled into a clearing by a crossing where red lanterns winked. Farm fields gleamed like darkling emeralds in the gloaming until they met the green-black of the encircling trees. And there in the clearing beside a big farm wagon, with a sprig of marguerites tucked rakishly behind his ear, stood my Grandpa Stryker.

How can I describe my grandfather? He's just *Gramps*. He is tall and thin and very straight, despite his droopy shoulders. His eyes are piercing blue. He has scraggly grey whiskers. He exudes an enormous peace. Just to walk around with him for fifteen minutes makes your heart grow quiet. I tumbled off the train steps into his outstretched arms, and felt for the first time in weeks as if I had come home.

The rest of the trip was a blurred kaleidoscope of darkness and swinging lanterns, of the sweet fragrant hay in the wagon bed and the steady clip-clop of Old Mag's hooves, and finally of Gramps' kitchen table set with mountainous platters of fried potatoes, ham, and eggs. Then the velvet blackness of the front bedroom, punctuated with the bass rumbling of bullfrogs in the river, and the tingling rough-dryness of old linen sheets.

I opened my eyes the next morning into a world of sunlight and peace. Somewhere out in the barnyard an old rooster bragged to his harem, and I could hear the joyous baa-ing of this year's lambs capering around their corral. Even the white ducks out on the river were feeling conversational, and the early morning bird chorus soared high above them all. I stretched luxuriously, wiggled my toes, and felt like peace on earth.

I'd forgotten that Gramps' world had this feeling. Or perhaps I'd been too young to notice it before—or need it, rather. The memory of the last encounter with Mama, with her grey face, angrily narrowed eyes and set chin came back to haunt me. No matter how wrong or stubborn Mama was, I shouldn't have come away without breaking the no-speakingness between us. But I didn't want to think about that now. I slid out of bed cautiously without waking Bron, pulled on a cotton dress, and wandered down the rag-carpeted front stairs.

Gramps' house is a mixture of his ideas of masculine practicality and of nostalgic reminders of Gran, who died when I was small. I have vague, contradictory memories of a plump grandmotherly lap and of a tidy Puritan precision. Gran was a Massachusetts schoolma'am, which accounts no doubt for Mama's brisk ways and lack of imagination. Gran's rocker stood by the kitchen fireplace, with a fat cat dozing in it, but Gramps used its back as a rack to dry his dish towels on, and he'd long since dispensed with tablecloths or curtains. Gramps was nowhere in sight nor sound, but a pot of his lethally strong coffee was boiling on the stove. I went out the back door and encountered him coming in from milking, carrying two foaming pails.

"Hey there. Figgered my second breakfast time might be just about right for your first."

"The others are still asleep."

"Well, let 'em be. Guess they need sleep more than anything else." It was Sunday morning, but Gramps was refreshingly liberal on the subject of church attendance. "By the way, Melissa's round and about. Dressed only in her drawers, but it's hot enough that won't hurt her, and there aren't any neighbors close enough to see. Gave her some milk fresh from the cow, and a couple of apples to tide her over, so she'll be all right."

Gramps placed a loaf of bread against his shirtfront and sawed off slices with a butcher knife while I watched, fascinated. He handed me a slice, waggling his heady brows. "Your Pa writes your ma's feeling poorly, hey?"

Gramps has no delicate reservations about plain speech, so apparently Pa hadn't written him about the baby. And I was decidedly not ready to have the morning's brightness shattered by another go-round on that subject. "She's tired and cranky," I said shortly.

"So she's bein' an Early Christian Martyr by stayin' in town 'stead of comin' out here. That's Evie all over." I didn't answer. Gramps glanced at me shrewdly, but he only said mildly, "I'm goin' out to the fields. You young'uns can suit yourselves what you want to do." He drained his coffee cup and ambled out.

It hadn't been very nice of me to let that Christian Martyr comment pass, even though it was an all too apt description. After all, Mama had stayed home mainly to be with Pa. That meant a lot to Pa, especially right now. As far as playing martyr was concerned, there wasn't one of us who was in any position to throw stones, was there? And face it, I was tickled to death to be here without Mama—just as glad as she was to get rid of me, probably.

Oh, drat and blast, I thought, the morning was spoiled now, anyhow.

I decided to go for a walk, alone, before anyone else got up and before Missy discovered me and demanded to come along. I took my big Leghorn hat to keep the sun off my face, deliberated over shoes and decided against them, and went out the front door.

Gramps' house, of Pennsylvania stone, was built two centuries ago when travel was more convenient by water than by land, so it sits quite literally on the river bank. The stream's too narrow at this point to be a respectable river, but it widens considerably a couple of miles further down. Willows arch over it, making a pale green canopy through which the sun sends yellow ribbons, and moss and violets grow along its banks. I set off through the pale airy tunnel and tried diligently not to think.

The air grew warmer; birdsong was replaced by the hum of bees, and the sun rose higher. Occasionally I passed a boy fishing, or a stiffly starched family setting off for church. Sometimes they waved, and I waved back, but kept on walking. I walked till the backs of my legs ached from the unaccustomed exercise, and the depression rolled off my shoulders like a discarded cloak, and I heard the full-throated church bell pealing out across the fields.

It seemed funny, when for once no one was pushing me off to church, I actually felt like going. I retied my ribbon, adjusted my hat, and started inland, hoping nobody would notice my bare feet.

The church stood on a rise of ground above the fields, dingy red brick and very small. Service had already started, but the doors were open. I slipped inside, unnoticed. "Congregational Chapel," the sign outside had said, and it was vastly different from our church at home. There were no kneeling-benches, no stained-glass windows, no candles nor altar nor organ; only a piano that was missing a couple of keys, and a speaker's stand on a platform up front, dead center before a clear glass window through which the sun was streaming. There were scarcely two dozen people in the congregation, most of them old. The minister was young, though, with the most gorgeous dark blue eyes. Bron should have come with me, I thought.

He sounded young, too, which meant he tried too hard, the way I do when I have to make a speech in school. I have to give him credit, though, for digging up a part of the Bible I'd never heard of before. It was about slavery in ancient Israel, which in one form seemed similar to the indentured servitude of colonial days, which we studied about in history class last year. Apparently an old Israelite who'd been sold into slavery to pay his debts could go free after seven years. There was one problem. If he'd married another slave and had children, the wife and children still remained the property of the master, the man alone could go free. If he wanted to stay with his family, he had to legally consent to bondage for life. It was a pretty horrible thought.

Evidently, the young minister said, a good many men on the threshold of freedom must have deliberately accepted the fetters forged by love. "But is not this an experience common to us all?" he asked. "The ties of love grow gradually, at first frail and then tenacious. Deep elemental forces are in conflict within us all. Instinctively we seek freedom; exemption from subjugation to the will of others; ability to follow our own impulses without restraint. But when we really love and are loved, we voluntarily renounce that independence. We are no longer free to act as we please, because we can't shake off the knowledge that whatever we do affects those we love and who love us. Love at its best always means the acceptance of bonds. This is what *family* means—the family of God, and the human family—mutual love and responsibility, and the discipline of love."

Like two naughty imps sliding in on a sunbeam, two thoughts popped into my head. "That's what's missing in our family," was the first. And the second was, "Why —if that's what family is—then I don't want it!" I didn't want to live all my life with the knowledge that my parents, that anyone I loved, could be hurt by anything I did that was true to myself. I didn't want the knowledge that sometimes the only way I could make others happy was by giving up things that were really me. That over and over again, like a wheel endlessly turning, I was

going to have to choose who would be hurt. I wasn't
ready for voluntary bonds, yet, because I'd never known
what it was to be really free.

Maybe I'd never really known what love was, either.
Maybe I never would.

# CHAPTER IV

## *August*

I didn't like myself very much that Sunday morning.
I didn't like what I was thinking, either, or the empty
loneliness that seemed to cast a shadow on the sun. But
the thoughts and feelings were there, whether I wanted
them or not, and would not be denied.

I was grateful, when I reached the house again, that
no one bothered to ask where I'd been. Everyone
seemed to be caught in summer's spell. Gramps had set
Sunday dinner on a table by the river in his usual style,
which meant lots of emphasis on what went into one's
stomach, and very little on the way it was served. There
weren't three matching plates on the table, and Gran's
solid silver rubbed elbows with a couple of kitchen
forks, but there was home-cured ham and fresh corn and
melt-in-your-mouth peach pie—Gramps is a real good
baker.

The young ones, savages that they are, piled in. Missy
was still blissfully running around in her underdrawers,
clutching an ear of corn in one hand and a piece of ham
in the other.

"What difference does it make?" Bron said, watching.
"She's happy, and who's to see?" Bron still sounded

tired. The boys had gone swimming in the river in
rolled-up old trousers, and Marnie in a faded old dress;
she looked a mess, and it was fortunate that Mama
couldn't see. Neither Bron nor I ate much, and nobody
felt like talking except Missy who rambled on and on,
intoxicated by the lack of competition. Ben lit a roll-
your-own right in front of Gramps who, after a minute,
took out his familiar, evil-smelling pipe. He sat puffing
away, keeping up his end of the conversation with Missy, his shrewd old eyes taking in everything the rest of us
weren't saying.

Late in the afternoon Gramps buttonholed me down
on the dock. "Going upriver to see if I can catch a mess
of fish for supper. Come along." I had no intention
whatsoever of going, but it is fundamentally impossible
to say no to Gramps, so presently there I was, sailing
along in the rowboat that Gramps' strong arms sent ef-
fortlessly upstream. We sat in silence till we reached the
widest part of the river and he locked oars.

"Now what in tarnation thunder," he inquired, "is
the matter with you all? You know your Pa's letters, a
lot of gorgeous words that don't boil down to nothin'.
What's wrong?" He peered at me from beneath his brist-
ly brows.

"Mama's having another baby," I said baldly.

"Oh." Gramps' monosyllable was comprehensive.

"And Pa thinks he's going to lose his job, and
everybody's worried, and the more worried we are, the
nastier we get to each other."

"Um," Gramps said. "Families are like that sometimes."

"If this is what families are like, I'm sick of families!
I'm sick of always hurting people or being hurt!" Tears
were starting to drown my vision; and much as I value
sensitivity, I hate like the Devil having anybody see me

really cry. I turned my head away and stared at the river. "Mama doesn't want another baby, on top of all her other worries. She and Pa had an awful row a couple of weeks ago." I hadn't meant to say that, but it came out all the same. "I thought things would get better afterwards, but they haven't at all."

Gramps nodded. "Ayuh, when things get spoke in a big blowup, it's kind of like when a crab loses its shell. Durn shell had to come off, but for a while after, till the new one grows on, everything's kind of tender."

"That's it exactly. I guess we just need to get away from each other for awhile. Gramps, it's a good thing you were willing to have us come. Mama wanted to get rid of us as bad as we wanted to leave."

"Well," said Gramps. "Tish, you got to remember your Ma's like your grandmother; they've got that Puritan streak that makes 'em afraid of sayin' anything nice. They're like prickly pears on the outside, and most folks don't have the patience to get at the sweetness within. Tell you something, though, when a person like that does say somethin' nice about you, you know she really means it."

Unfortunately, right now I didn't think Mama could find anything nice about me—or vice versa. The more I thought about her, the angrier I got. And the more worried I got, too, which made me even angrier. It was a vicious circle.

Gramps has the gracious gift of silence, and having pried the problem out of me he was content to let it brood of itself without hovering noticeably over it. He had been right in saying we were all kind of tender; we needed space and privacy enough not to rub on each other, and this the farm provided in abundance. We hardly saw each other except at meals, which were highly informal affairs. Bron and I could help with the cooking or not, and since we didn't have to, we usually did.

"Kind of nice to have a woman's touch around again," Gramps said.

Marnie had a field day helping with the farm work and forgetting she was a girl. Peter wandered around with an encyclopedia in one hand and a magnifying glass in the other, making friends with bugs. Ben taught Missy to float, and after that we didn't even have to think about her falling in the river. And I worried about what was happening at home.

I got a letter from Celinda, regretting she hadn't been able to see me before we left. We had two letters from Pa in his usual epistolary style, which as Gramps said meant he used a lot of fancy words and said nothing. Mama didn't write. She wouldn't; she hoarded her grudges like a miser. *And so did I.*

I didn't like myself too much, although I couldn't put my finger on exactly why. I certainly didn't want to be anything other than what I was. *That's the Sterling stubbornness again.*

Oh, drat and blast. *That* was what was wrong with this summer, the wrong behind the luxury of being left alone with time on my hands. I kept having dialogues with myself—and not only in my head. I was devoting most of my lovely blessed free time to an orgy of reading and writing. Gramps' shelves were loaded with old books: the *Aeneid,* Sophocles, Chaucer, John Donne and Alexander Pope. Some of them would have been considered highly unsuitable by my teachers. I got drunk on them; they made me ashamed of the forced sentimentality of my own writing, and determined to do better. High in the branches of an old apple tree or floating in the rowboat in a hidden cove, with a musty volume and my own Journal, I wrote and crossed out and wrote again. And over and over, in Gramps' books or in my own scribbling, I kept running into myself. It was like the disconcerting moment when you turn a corner and see a stranger coming toward you; a stranger at once odd and half-familiar and somehow fearsome; and then you realize you're looking at yourself, reflected in some store's glass window. I didn't like it. But I kept on writing, and I kept on reading.

I was no prize to live with, Bron informed me during one of our rare dust-ups that exploded like summer lightning one stagnant afternoon. I was reading in the shuttered front parlor, on account of its being the coolest place around, when Bron came trailing in, wearing a thin combing-jacket over her petticoat, and cranked up the phonograph noisily. It began to wheeze out a lovesick wail. I banged my book down in irritation.

"Honestly, Bron! I'm trying to concentrate."

Bron looked at me. "I guess I have as much right here as you. Go read outside if you don't like it."

"It's cooler here. Anyway, I was here first."

Bron exploded. "Who do you think you are, queen of the roost? You're getting downright queer, reading all those books. You'll ruin your eyes, too, in this bad light." Her eyes fell on the book I was holding. "Letitia Sterling, Mama would skin you alive if she knew you were reading Omar Khayyam!"

"Mama doesn't care what I do any more, and I don't care! Anyway, the *Rubaiyat* makes a lot more sense than all that goopy Wordsworth and Shelley you're devouring. Not to mention the Byron, if you're talking about dirty books," I added scathingly, and Bron flushed. "I thought you had more sense than to moon around like a dime-novel heroine over that stupid Herbie Willis who isn't worth beans."

"Well, at least I'm worrying about practical things," Bronwyn retorted. "Not wallowing around in how sensitive and misunderstood I am, or how famous I'll be

some day. I'm struggling with whom I'm going to marry
and how I can help the family; all you're thinking about
is how nobody appreciates you. Well, let me tell you
we'd appreciate you more if you acted as if our opinions
mattered to you. You're getting as prickly-pear as
Mama, and it's no wonder nobody wants to be around
either of you!"

*"Bronwyn!"*

"Oh, let me alone!" Bronwyn snapped, and uncharac-
teristically burst into tears. She slammed the lid of the
gramophone down and stormed out, and I tried to lose
myself in Omar Khayyam again, but it didn't work.

I kept expecting Gramps to put his two cents' worth
in pretty soon, but he didn't, although I almost wished
he would. I could feel his two knowing eyes surveying us
from under those beetling brows from time to time.

On Saturday night he was fifteen minutes late for supper, and his appearance made us goggle. Ben nearly fell
off his chair.

"As I live and breathe, Gramps, are you going courting?"

"Feller likes to get duded up now and then just to
shock folks," Gramps said complacently. He had assumed a red-and-white shirt with a blindingly white stiff
collar, a brocade cravat with an ornate pearl stickpin,
and embroidered purple suspenders. Considering as
how Gramps hates putting on a tie even to go to church,
this was really something. Marnie's jaw dropped, Bron
looked stupefied, and Missy crawled into his lap and
breathed, "Gramps, you're beautiful!"

"Didn't I tell you there's a dance over at the Grange
tonight?" Gramps said innocently. He beetled his eyes at
Bron, who was still trailing around like a lovesick maid-
en. "Better get movin' and get dolled up. Young'uns
too. It's a benefit for the church, and I allus believe in
supportin' Christian charity."

I put two and two together, remembered the minister's blue eyes, and mentally applauded Gramps' maneuver. Bron perked up considerably getting dressed for the dance. The younger ones, thrilled at the novelty of attending an evening social, were as wound up as a pair of June bugs. It took, we discovered, quite a while to get the farm dirt off us all.

Bron started to put on an everyday flowered cotton, stopped, said, "Oh, what if it is just a country social, we might as well do Gramps proud," and put on her graduation dress.

"Bron? Do you suppose I could put up my hair?"

"Go ahead! Gramps won't know the difference, and there's nobody else to scold," Bron said recklessly. "You can borrow my old corset if you won't tell Mama."

"Bron!" I glowed at her.

Bron's voice was half-smothered in the cloud of white silk mull. "I'm sorry I've been nasty lately. I didn't mean it."

"I didn't either. Bron, let's make a pact. No more fighting. I've felt just rotten."

Bron gave me a quick brief hug. "Come on, and I'll help you with your hair."

With my hair up and a real waistline, I didn't look so ordinary at all in my graduation dress.

Excitement fizzed like soda water, all the way over to the Grange. Old Mag looked rakish in her tasseled flynet, and Gramps had tucked some Queen Anne's Lace behind her ears. Ben and Peter, shining from scrubbing beneath the pump, had their hair slicked down so tightly it shone like satin. Marnie's cheeks glowed as bright as her red dotted swiss.

The Grange building proved to be a huge old barn built into the side of a hill. One whole side of the lower level opened out onto a carpet of emerald grass. The

dancers spilled outside, too, and as darkness fell
Japanese lanterns flickered from beams and from
branches of great old trees. A pianist and a fiddler were
established on a platform in the tie-up. There were old-
fashioned settees and benches lined up along the walls
for grandparents and aunts, but the old folks didn't sit
out many dances, not here! Gramps, I discovered, could
cut pigeon wings with the best of them. His face grew
red; presently he removed coat and collar and his suspenders shone forth in all their splendor. Everybody
danced together, young and old alike, and it was a sight
to see Gramps steering Missy, her face one enormous
grin, through the intricacies of Money Musk.

They played all the old dances—Soldier's Joy,
Sultan's Polka, The Tempest, Rochester Schottische.
The moon rose high, deep amber, behind a fringe of
pines behind the hill. As the young ones grew tired, they
drowsed off to sleep on the settees. I swept breathlessly
through set after set. Through the network of weaving
bodies, I caught sight of the fact that the young minister
had discovered Bron. Gramps was beaming like an
elderly cherub. My hair was starting to fall down, and
my head was pounding. I was whirling through the Sail-
ors' Reel when I heard somebody say, "Why, Tish!" I
looked up, startled, and there was Kenny Latham!

"What are you doing here?" I gasped.

"Staying with my uncle." The music swung me on to
my next partner, a stout perspiring farmer, leaving Kenny only time to shout, "See you at the refreshment table
after!" over his shoulder. Through the rest of the set, we
kept smiling at each other, and between meetings in do
si do, grand right and left and ladies' chain, I kept steal-
ing surreptitious glances. Kenny looked different, somehow; leaner and browner. He had grown some, too, and
he was wearing long pants instead of knickerbockers.

When the set ended, he came directly over and steered

me by the elbow to the refreshment table. I hadn't imagined he could be so masterful. I was glad I was wearing Bron's corset and had put up my hair. Kenny served me lemonade, and we sipped it, smiling at each other.

"You look different," Kenny said.

"That's right."

"You've put up your hair." He looked it over critically. "It's very becoming. But you look good with it down, falling around your face like it did at graduation. Like a Botticelli *Primavera*."

Imagine a boy knowing about Botticelli! Come to think of it, imagine his noticing me at graduation. I nearly dropped my punch cup. "Kenny—"

"Hush." Kenny looked around quickly and lowered his voice. "Look, Tish, the crowd here calls me Kenneth, or Ken. So don't say anything about me being called Kenny at home will you?"

"Of course not—Kenneth. And you don't tell anybody Tish is short for Letitia." We grinned at each other. "But what on earth are you *doing* here?"

"I'm staying with my uncle in the next township. His hired man up and quit, right in the busiest season, so I came out to help."

"Your brother didn't?"

"Doug," said Kenneth, "prefers hopping freights to ball games." It occurred to me that Kenneth didn't think any more highly of his brother than I did, which made me warm to him even more. "How about you? How come you're here?"

"We're visiting my grandfather. Mama's—not feeling well."

"Oh, I'm sorry." Kenneth glanced around. "They're forming for the next set, but first, may I come and see you? I'm in the fields all day, of course," he said proudly. "But I have evenings free."

I nodded, feeling enormously grown-up.

None of us were particularly enchanted when Gramps rounded us up and said it was time to start for home. The night was filled with fireflies and country sounds, and the twinkling light from the swinging lanterns on the wagon's sides. Bron was bemused, and she hummed while she undressed, the way she had done when she first started going out with Herbie. I felt like humming myself.

Life in Pennsylvania grew considerably livelier after that. Kenneth was in church the next morning. Bron had come, too, and we both had masculine escorts going home. Ben had met a bunch of local boys at the dance, and started palling around with them, with Marnie tagging along too, naturally. The young minister, whose name was Mr. Stanyon, began taking Bron for buggy rides. He asked Bron to sing a solo in church the following Sunday, and Bron stopped reading Wordsworth and started practicing scales. I wondered what Mama would say about those unchaperoned buggy rides, but I kept my mouth shut lest it occur to somebody that she might not think too highly, either, of my "walking out" with a young man at my tender age.

Kenneth was definitely, I decided, turning into a young man. It wasn't just the long pants. His voice had deepened, and grown firmer. Outdoor life agreed with him, that was plain, and so did being out from under his mother's shadow. He came riding over the six miles in the evenings, tired though he was from a day of manual labor, and we would walk out to the grape arbor and talk and talk until the moon rose high. We talked about books, mostly; to my astonishment I discovered he had read nearly everything I had and more. I had just finished the *Aeneid;* he had read that and the *Inferno*. I mentioned Sophocles; he countered with an Aeschylus-Euripides comparison. "And have you read the Racine version of the Hippolytus myth? I can lend you a copy.

Perhaps if Bernhardt tours the states again this winter, we could go see it."

I felt like a foreigner who had finally discovered someone else who spoke his language.

Gramps, who doesn't care a hoot or a holler for the proprieties, beamed on Bron and me benignly. Ben began making big-brotherly noises, so I negotiated a pact: he wouldn't trouble our parents with unnecessary worries over Bron and me, and I wouldn't trouble them with the knowledge of how much he was smoking.

August grew more and more golden; I felt more and more grown-up, and free, and happy; and we still hadn't heard from Mama. Then all in a row, several things happened.

The first was that Gramps' neighbors on the next farm, a cozy elderly couple, had us all for dinner. The whole time we were there they kept telling us about Mr. Stanyon—what a fine young man he was, and how inconvenient it was for a minister to be a bachelor—and looking at Bron. The next night Bron came in from buggying-riding with Mr. Stanyon, looking flustered. She pulled the pins from her hair, stared at herself in the mirror, said, "Oh, tarnation, anyhow!" and plopped down on the foot of the bed and started to cry.

I sat up, wide awake. I had only gotten in a few minutes earlier myself. "Bron, what's the matter?"

"I'm—just keyed up, I guess." Bron pushed her hair back with a wobbly smile. "I wish Mama were here."

"Bron—he didn't propose, did he?"

"No, not yet." Bron turned to me seriously. "There's a vacancy for a grade school teacher in the district. He says I could get the position with my high school diploma."

"Live here—in Pennsylvania?"

"I love it here," Bron said. "It's so—peaceful, compared to home."

I nodded.

"I wish I knew what was happening at home," Bron said slowly. "About Mama—and Pa's job. I don't know which way I'd be helping more, staying here and sending money home, or being there myself to help Mama. I wish Pa or Mama were here. It's not the kind of thing you can talk out in letters."

"Ask Gramps."

"I did. Just now. He says I have to make my own decisions, and that of course he'd be tickled pink to have me living here." Bron paused. "There's another thing. If I do stay, it will be the equivalent of telling Arthur to go ahead and propose."

"Do you want him to?"

"I don't know. I don't know whether I'm in love with him or not. Oh, why does life have to be so complicated!"

The next thing that happened was Kenneth's telling me the next evening that he was thinking of staying in Pennsylvania himself. "My uncle'd like to have me stay. He could use the help. I've always felt closer to my uncle than to my dad."

"Not—go to high school?"

"I'd go here. There's a fine one in the district. I like it here, Tish. I feel more *me* here. Freer."

I nodded, remembering how Kenneth was always just "Doug Latham's kid brother" at home.

"It's suffocating at home," Kenneth said almost savagely. Then, "Why, Tish! What's the matter? Have I said something wrong?"

Because all at once I was crying. I shook my head and blinked hard. "No. You've said something *right*. About suffocation—and families—and feeling different here." I stopped and swallowed, while Kenneth waited. "I wish I could stay here, too."

"Why don't you?" Kenneth said calmly.

"I wonder if I could! Mama—Mama wouldn't miss me. She'd probably be relieved." I stopped again. "I'm worried about Mama. She's not well, and we had an awful row before I left, and she hasn't written once."

"Well," Kenneth said, "I suppose it takes the more perceptive person to make the first move." That was disconcertingly close to some of the things I'd said myself to Pa. And *perceptive* had much more depths than *sensitive*.

I broached the matter of staying in Pennsylvania to Gramps the next day. He only said that of course he'd be pleased to have me, and as to whether it'd be right or wrong, why that was something I'd have to work out for myself. I was disturbed to discover, after all my vaunted longing for independence, that achieving it could be a very lonely thing.

The culminating touch was the letter I received the next day from Celinda. "I saw your mother downtown yesterday," she wrote. "She looks very tired, and I think she's lost some weight. She sounded kind of lonely. I guess she misses having you all around to talk to. Your father's been working extra hours, too. Pa says he's seen him coming home way after suppertime, nights. Mama says the more she sees of your mother, the more she understands where you get your stubbornness from."

I took the letter out to the grape arbor and reread it, and it occurred to me that in her quiet way Celinda was already a far more skillful writer than I. She hadn't uttered one criticism, or made a single suggestion, but she had succeeded in waking again that dialogue within me.

I remembered Pa telling me long ago that when he had to make an important decision he used to make lists in different columns of all the things involved, like blindfold Justice weighing the factors pro and con in a court of law. Involuntarily, as I walked half-seeing through the violets and rushes along the river bank, the columns of evidence began forming behind my eyes.

I was happy here in Pennsylvania, far happier than I was at home. It wasn't just the freedom. It was the sense of being more a person, more myself.

"Think we'd all be happier if you lived somewhere else," Ma had said.

I wanted to stay here, and not only for the summer. "Well, why don't you?" Kenneth had said. It was all right with Gramps; he'd told me so; the decision was up to me.

A small brown sparrow scolded briskly from a tree branch, and I could hear my mother's voice. "I'm tired of trying—carrying another child when I don't know how to cope with the ones I have already."

"Your Ma's fundamentally incapable of taking things easy," Pa had said. That was why he had sent us away, to make things easier by our not being there.

Bron didn't know which way she could help Mama more, by being away or by being at home.

Face it, I wasn't really thinking of what would help Mama, I was thinking of what was more bearable for me. Bron's voice re-echoed: "All you're thinking about is how sensitive and misunderstood you are and how nobody appreciates you."

"Head in the clouds so much you're good for nothing," said Mama.

My vaunted sensitivity had been a thing to wallow in and to count the bruises therefrom. Had it ever, for me, been a thing to use for others? Not very often.

Out on the river a stocky blond boy was fishing. The slant of his head reminded me of Kenneth.

In a short week there had sprung up between us the sort of friendship I had never known, had never quite imagined. He filled a need in me that my own family, or even Celinda, for all their dearness, could not meet.

Kenneth was going to be staying here all summer, perhaps all next year.

"I suppose it takes the more perceptive person to make the first move," Kenneth had said. That was just about what I'd said to Pa, the night I talked him into coming home. And he had come.

Mama was Mama—too old and stubborn-set in her ways to change. She would always be quicker to point out flaws than to appreciate our trying. *"That Puritan streak—afraid of sayin' anything nice—like prickly pears on the outside, and most folks don't have the patience to get at the sweetness."*

"If parents refuse to act like adults, *somebody* has to take the initiative," Bron had told me.

Drat and blast you, Celinda, I thought; you know me too well. I took her letter out again and sat down on a treek trunk that bent far out over the quiet water.

"Your mother looks very tired. She sounded kind of lonely." *It's not good for a woman her age to be having another kid.* "I guess she misses having you around." *We never thought of our parents as having needs.*

Talk, as Mr. Stanyon had that Sunday, about having deep elemental conflicts within us! This one was a dilly.

*"When we really love and are loved, we are no longer free to act as we please, because we can't shake off the knowledge that whatever we do affects those we love and who love us."*

I got up and started walking back toward the farm. High overhead above the river, pale green tree branches met and soared in a Gothic arch.

*"This is what family means . . . mutual love and responsibility, and the discipline of love."* Not childhood discipline, which someone else superimposes. I had left that behind me now, as Gramps had made clear. Growing up meant the freedom—or the responsibility—of disciplin-

ing oneself. Or of being disciplined by the love one felt.

I met my grandfather coming across the corral, a half-grown calf capering at his heels. He squinted at me, waved, and smiled. "Wondered where you'd gone to. It's time for lunch!"

"I'm starved!" I said, just discovering that this was true. I ran to meet him. He put out his arms to catch me, and I found that I was laughing.

"Gramps," I said, "after lunch, can we ride into town and telegraph to Pa that I'm coming home on tomorrow's train? I think Mama needs me."

# CHAPTER V

## *September*

So I went home to Mama, and before the month was over I was pondering whether I might have a vocation as an actress. I had never before been called upon to put on so convincing an act. I mean insofar as camouflaging my reasons for coming home ahead of the others, and keeping the lid on my temper when Mama cast self-centered aspersions on my motives. I knew well enough that although Mama might be playing the martyr bit herself, she couldn't stomach the notion of anyone making sacrifices for her; it would make her feel bad about a lot of things, and it was far better for me to keep my big mouth shut and put up with misinterpretations.

That was the bad part; that, and being conscious of the fact that Kenneth was still in Pennsylvania and might stay there. I was surprised to find how much I missed him. It was good to see Celinda again, but I couldn't discuss art and literature with Celinda the way I could with Ken, with excitement crackling back and forth between us. Celinda was awestruck at my interest in such things, but she didn't really understand them. Anyway, Celinda went down to Ocean Grove with her parents for the Methodist Camp Meeting shortly after I came home, so most of my time was spent with Mama. And that was the good part of the summer.

Celinda had been right in suspecting Mama was lonely. It dawned on me that there isn't anybody you can say is Mama's best friend, not the way Celinda is with me. I guess she'd been too busy to notice that before. Of course Aunt Kate was right next door, but I couldn't picture Aunt Kate as anyone's best friend, even if she and Mama didn't feel about each other as they so indubitably do. Our Aunt Annie, who's Mama's own sister, lives way up in Stamford, Connecticut, so Mama doesn't get to see her very often. Of course Mama had Pa, but come to think of it she didn't get to see him very often, either. I wondered if they ever really talked.

Pa was working late again. He'd really made an effort not to, the first week we kids were gone, Mama told me. "Came home and got all duded up in a fresh white suit and we ate at that fancy outdoor place two nights running. Took the excursion boat up the river on Saturday, too! Thought he could fool me into thinking his heart was in it and not worried sick about the time and money. Then I found out he was sneaking back down to the study after I'd fallen asleep, to finish getting the day's court notes transcribed. So I convinced him to stay downtown till he got it finished, 'stead of us gallivanting around on foolishness."

"Mama! You didn't say that!"

" 'Course not; got some diplomacy!" Mama's black eyes twinkled. "Told him it was a shame to buy those beautiful meals when Whatsitsname wasn't letting me enjoy them, and couldn't we take a rain check till next summer."

"How come Pa has so much work to do all of a sudden? He never used to stay late."

"Court's been extra jammed with cases. The new judge moves them along faster than Judge Simms used to, your father says. He says the old man really should have retired years ago. The new man moves cases along so lickety-split, folks can't keep up with them."

"I'll bet Pa can!"

" 'Course he can! Mr. Albright says he's the fastest shorthand-writer in the city." Mama sounded proud. "It's just getting the transcripts typewritten for the next day's session that's the problem. Your father really ought to have an assistant to type, but with the whole job situation hanging fire, he's leery of taking one on."

There had been no more developments on that score, Mama told me. The new judge hadn't said anything, and Pa didn't want to ask for fear of putting ideas in his head. "Mr. Albright thinks your father ought to do what he's always talked about, open a secretarial school. Shouldn't be surprised if Mr. Albright invested some money in it if he did."

"Do you think Pa might do it?"

Mama cocked her head. "Hard to say. He's thinking on it. Big gamble for a man of your father's age and responsibilities to start in business for himself, but then changing positions would be a gamble too."

This was the biggest change I noticed since coming home, Mama talking woman-to-woman as if I were grown up. Now that the younger kids, not to mention Cicero, weren't tearing things up, she didn't have as much excuse to knock herself out on housework. She'd lost weight, since she and food weren't agreeing with each other too well, but she felt pretty good so long as she spent most of her time horizontal, which Pa and Dr. Tuttle had convinced her was only respectable for a woman her age who was having a baby.

In the afternoons we'd go out on the side porch, which is shaded and breezy even on the hottest day and delirious with the scent of climbing roses. Mama would plop on the wicker sofa, and I in the swing or rocker, she

with the hand-sewing she was doing as a sop to her conscience, and I with a book from Pa's shelves. Mama was
furbishing up our fall wardrobes, always in need of re-
pairs, before starting to make a layette for Whatsitsname.

"Gave away all our baby things when Missy outgrew
them. Should have known better," she said ruefully.

I started reading *Peck's Bad Boy* aloud, and Mama
would throw back her head and laugh. I'd forgotten
what a nice laugh Mama had. And the tame catbird Peter had trained would swoop down onto the porch railing and scold us both, and we'd laugh some more.

Mama was making Bronwyn a white mull waist out of
material left over from her graduation dress, appliqued
with scraps of delicate lace. "In case Mr. Albright takes
her to any more concerts at the Opera House. He's
asked your Pa three times when she's coming home."

I didn't answer, and Mama darted me a look.
"What's all this about a minister fellow in Pennsylvania?
Bron's real close-mouthed, but your grandfather
dropped a hint."

"He's very nice. He's got gorgeous blue eyes and the
cutest buggy. I think he likes her a lot."

"Hmm," Mama said.

I felt uncomfortable. But I couldn't beat around the
bush, not when Mama was looking at me woman-to-
woman over her sewing and asking bluntly, "Is
Bronwyn serious about him? Enough to stay in Pennsylvania because of him?"

"I don't know." I looked at Mama. "She's been asked
to consider staying there to teach. But she doesn't know
whether she'd be more helpful to you being here, or
sending money home."

"*And*," said Mama, "she's not sure whether she's in
love with the preacher or with the blue eyes and the
buggy."

I hadn't expected Mama to be that perceptive.

Perhaps as a result of that conversation, Pa wrote a letter to Bron a few days later. Pretty soon I heard that Bron had decided to come back home again, at least for the fall. Mr. Albright came calling one evening, and inquired for the fourth time when Bron was returning, and I saw Pa and Mama exchange glances. It seemed kind of pathetic, his mooning over Bron like that when he must be nearly as old as Pa.

So the rest of August passed, a dreamy interlude. The first of September came, putting an official end to summer, although the weather still was golden. Pa borrowed Mr. Albright's surrey again and went to the depot to meet our returning family. The younger ones were as brown as Indians. Peter was loaded down with glass jars containing additions to his insect collection, many of them still alive, and for days afterwards we were finding crickets and grasshoppers in the craziest locations. He also had a shoebox, which he guarded as if it contained crown jewels.

"Don't touch it! Cornelius is very nervous," he warned Missy constantly. Cornelius proved to be a blacksnake named for Gramps, and Mama only yelled for five minutes before capitulating with the proviso that Cornelius never be permitted out of Peter's room, which was sure proof she had mellowed over the summer.

We all had, I thought. I myself felt immeasurably older. I found inordinate satisfaction in the discovery that all my recent story plots had revolved around renunciation, responsibility and self-sacrifice, instead of the old themes of sensitivity and lack of understanding.

Bron had come home wearing a puffy pompadour from which small curls escaped to frame her face, which had a new, madonna-like look of tender exaltation. Maybe Mr. Stanyon had been making more progress than we thought. I tried to pump Bron on that, but she was just plain uncommunicative, same as she was about Mr. Albright, who came calling the night they all returned and promptly booked Bron for a concert the following Saturday night. Bron serenely ignored the family's merry comments made after Mr. Albright took his departure, but later, when I went up to bed, I found her revolving before the mirror in the new white mull waist.

I watched her for a minute. "Something did happen in Pennsylvania after I left, didn't it?"

"Why?"

"You look different. It comes from the inside, somehow."

Bron studied her lovely image in the glass with grave dispassion. "I suppose I have changed. I'm out of school now, with more responsibilities." She looked at me. "You've changed, too, Tish, you know."

I caught a glimpse of my reflection over Bron's shoulder and depression settled like a mosquito cloud. "I wish the outside would catch up with the inside. I hate starting high school looking Marnie's age!" Then I remembered Kenneth's Botticelli *Primavera* comment, and flushed.

Bron was watching me closely. "I saw a hair style in a magazine that would look good on you," she said at last. "I'll do it for you tomorrow."

Bron turned me out with soft loops around my face and a turned-up braid. Mama felt enough better to go on a shopping expedition, and miraculously proved she was thinking of me as an adult by bringing me home a genuine grown-up corset. Thus armed, on Monday morning I started high school and met up with Hodel Resnikov.

I was scarcely aware of the significance of this encounter at the time, being preoccupied with matters of more immediate magnitude. Our high school is an im-

posing edifice, marble-trimmed in front where tax-
payers' money shows to best advantage, and plain brick
behind. Ben, in the kind way of brothers, discarded me
on the front steps to go off with Doug Latham and his
other cronies, and I made my way to the Girls'
Cloakroom where I encountered Celinda, looking
breathless and overpowered.

"I'll never learn to find my way around this place,"
she groaned.

"You'll get used to it," Mary Lou Hodge said patron-
izingly. She patted her pompadour with complacent
consciousness of her own sophomore eminence, and I
was glad that Bron had done my hair that morning.

"Why don't you try putting your hair up, Celinda?"
Mary Lou suggested with her customary sweetness. "It
might help a little. I think it's perfectly silly to insist on
looking like a child when one is in high school. By the
way, Letitia, didn't Ben come with you today? I hear he
and Doug Latham nearly got killed jumping off that
freight train Saturday." I stared at her appalled, hoping
fervently that that particular news item would not reach
Mama, while Mary Lou rattled felinely on. "Did you
hear the principal says he's going to expel anyone he
catches smoking? I'll just bet—" She broke off abruptly.
"My dears, look at that freak!"

"What?" "Where?" Celinda and I both swiveled
around. The cloakroom was rapidly filling now, and a
girl none of us had seen before was hanging her hat on
a hook beside the door. She was tall and angular, with
oddly sallow skin, and quite frankly the queerest looking clothes I'd ever laid eyes on in all my born days.
Even Aunt Kate, who thinks short sleeves are indecent
and agrees with Mrs. Dodds about low necks being in-
struments of the devil, had never put together an outfit
so outlandish and old-ladyish as this. The skimpy skirt,
of some coarse dark stuff, dragged against the girl's

heavy shoes, and the high shapeless bodice was bare even of buttons or tucks. Her hair hung in two black braids down her back. Celinda's face softened the way it always does over any waif or stray, and Mary Lou giggled.

"She must be one of those new foreigners. My father says this neighborhood is definitely going downhill, since all these undesirable elements are coming in."

"Oh, hush!" Celinda hissed, two pink spots appearing in her cheeks. But it was too late. The girl's back had stiffened. She turned, and her lustrous black eyes swept Mary Lou up and down with such insolent scorn that I felt like applauding. Without a word she walked out of the room with the hauteur of a Russian princess.

Celinda let her breath out sharply.

Mary Lou reddened, and bristled, and managed to murmur a few more phrases about undesirables and our sacred neighborhood. I felt like voicing my opinion that the most undesirable element in it was Mary Lou herself, but I only said icily, "Hadn't we better get seats in the Assembly Room?" I led the way out the door and down the corridor, and there coming down the hall toward me was Kenneth Latham.

I stopped, and he stopped, and we stood smiling at each other, and I knew my cheeks matched the scarlet ribbon Bron had poised like a butterfly atop my turned-up braid.

"When did you get back?" I asked finally.

"Last night. I'd have come over to your place, but I thought it was too late." We grinned at each other again. "I couldn't make up my mind whether I should come back or stay with my uncle. But I got to thinking, the high schools are better here, and it's important for a fellow to have a good education, even if he should decide to be a farmer. Besides, all my friends are here." The assembly bell rang at this juncture, and he followed me into the Assembly Hall and sat down beside me quite as a matter of course. Celinda, on my other side, said, "Well!" profoundly, and I felt my face turn red again, and that's why I say I had more important things to think about on my first day of school than Hodel Resnikov.

That strange awareness of change continued, and it was more than corsets and new hairdos, more even than Kenneth, although he was inextricably woven into it. The new feeling of closeness with Mama lingered, to my joy, despite the rest of the family's being home again and the resumption of the customary chaos of our family life. Bronwyn got a job with the telephone company, and she also took cooking dinner off of Mama's hands. She was a good cook, too, although a bit fancy for Mama's taste, but that didn't matter since Whatsitsname was still interfering with Mama's digestion.

Bronwyn went to another concert with Mr. Albright, and she started getting letters regularly from Mr. Stanyon in Pennsylvania. She didn't tell me anything about them, though, any more than did her reaction to the news I brought home that Herbie had left for Harvard. She didn't tell anybody her reaction to Mr. Albright, either, and Mama was getting mighty curious.

Mr. Albright was dropping by the house a good deal. We weren't having much company on account of Mama was starting to get self-conscious about her appearance, but Mr. Albright was such an old friend of Pa's that he didn't count. Ostensibly his visits were to confer on Pa's employment situation, but we all noticed he spent as much time in the back swing with Bronwyn as he did in the study with our father.

"I'd give a piece to know what's really going on out there," Mama said to me when we were drinking tea together after school. "Give something to know what's going on in the study, too," she added.

"Has Pa said anything more about his job?"

"Not lately. Mr. Albright's still at him to open that school, but he's not decided. Going to Chicago this weekend, to see about maybe teaching in a business school out there instead of starting one of his own."

The thought of maybe moving to Chicago made me feel suddenly bleak. High school was losing its strangeness for me; I was settling in. Kenneth had fallen into the habit of walking me to classes and home from school. Often he would linger at the gate, both of us lost in our conversation, until the light paled and Bron came home, and Mama would call to me from the doorway to come and help with supper. Talking with Kenneth was to me like unexpected rain is to parched and thirsty ground. He kept me on my toes keeping up with him, too. I searched the school library for translations of Aeschylus and Euripides. His mention of Racine sent me hunting a copy of *Phaedra*, and I thought the librarian would fall over in a faint.

I loathed doing Latin translations, and as far as algebra and science are concerned they are subjects we shall not go into, but my English Lit. and ancient history classes were a revelation. For the first time I found in a classroom the same excitement I find in poring over volumes on my own. Mr. Grimes, the ancient history teacher, is young and brilliant; he has traveled in many of the countries we are studying; he is obviously as much in love with his subject as I am with writing. He was thrilled to find in his classes a student who could talk his language and on his level. But to my inordinate chagrin, that student was not I. It was Hodel Resnikov.

This discovery came about in the first week of school, when we were "doing" the ancient Greeks. Mr. Grimes asked whether anyone in the room had ever read Sophocles, and I happily embarked on one of my better monologues, mentally congratulating myself on the reading I did during the summer, when Hodel raised her hand.

"The inference in that speech is quite different in the original." And in her quiet, heavily accented English, she proceeded to dissect one whole passage, for all the world like Mr. Derbyshire dissecting Scripture on a Sunday morning.

"You've read *Oedipus* in *Greek?*" Mr. Grimes goggled at her, and several of the class craned their necks.

Hodel's eyes widened. "Of course. Always. I find most English translations are so imprecise."

Hodel was nothing if not precise, a virtue which Mrs. Owens, the English teacher, considered that I lacked. Hodel, it developed, despite her heavy accent, wrote a beautifully correct English, and her reading equalled mine. She immediately established herself in first place in our history and English classes, with me a breathless second.

My chagrin at this development was mitigated by my receiving, the second week of school, an invitation to the Browning Society's September Tea. The Browning Society is the most prestigious literary group in school. Bronwyn had been thrilled when she had received a bid at the beginning of her junior year. Being a writer, I had taken it for granted that I would be bidden, too, but I had hardly expected it quite so soon in my high school career.

"It's probably because you're my sister," Bronwyn said, inspecting the invitation that evening. "Engraved invitations. They are getting high-toned! They often invite the legacies in right away and get it over with." She saw my face and added swiftly, "I didn't mean they wouldn't want you for yourself. Being a writer, you were sure to have been asked, even if you weren't my sister."

But I was doing mental calculations in my head. "Bron, if old members have that much influence, what's the chance of your getting Celinda a bid, too? She feels so out of things in high school. It would mean a lot to her to be with me."

Bron laughed. "Poor Cee might feel like a fish out of water in that high-toned atmosphere. Oh, well, I'll see what I can do, but don't get your hopes up."

Apparently Bronwyn had more influence than she thought. A few days later Celinda came rushing over after school, breathlessly clutching her precious invitation. "I can't imagine why they asked me! I'm not a writer!"

I waggled my eyebrows violently at Marnie to keep her mouth shut about my conversation with Bron. "Mrs. Owens said your last composition was very good. You know she did. Even if you did die when she read it out loud. Anyway, Bron says it's not all literature and writing. They drink tea, and visit, and read poetry aloud."

"I'm scared! I'm scared to death!" Celinda wailed, but her eyes were shining.

"Me, too," I said ungrammatically. "That crowd's so high-faluting. We'll be eclipsed in wardrobe by Mary Lou Hodge and in intellect by Hodel Resnikov." Hodel's reputation as a scholar had reached even the senior class, so her joining the Browning Society was a foregone conclusion. Mary Lou had been inducted last spring in one of those mistakes that can happen to the best-regulated clubs; her inclusion, according to school gossip, was attributable to her sister Viney's being an earlier membership error and to Mary Lou's having had a poem printed in the Literary Quarterly the previous April. According to Ben, that poem had been pure plagiarism from start to finish, but Mary Lou had somehow gotten away with it since only the kids knew and they wouldn't tattle despite their disgust.

The tea was held in the school library on Friday afternoon, right after classes were dismissed. This meant that those privileged few who had been favored with invitations turned up in their schoolday best. I wore a new plaid chambray dress that Mama had made me, trimmed with rows of hand smocking, and Bronwyn did up my hair.

"Don't you and Cee get your hopes up too high," she warned. "Today's only a tea party at which they look you over. It's not a membership bid yet. Lots of girls don't get that in their freshman year." But Bronwyn knew as well as I that even the Browning Society hardly had the gall to invite someone to a look-over and then withhold a bid.

Celinda met me on the corner wearing her white Sunday dress. I stared at her.

"How on earth did you get your mother's permission?"

"I sneaked out the back door," Celinda admitted shamelessly. "Do I look all right?" Her eyes were enormous in her pale face, and she kept clasping and unclasping her hands.

I hadn't the heart to tell her she might be killing her chances by overdressing, and when we reached the school and I got a look at Mary Lou, I was glad I'd kept my mouth shut. Mary Lou was attired, I do not lie, in white silk mull trimmed with so many ruffles and ribbons she looked like a walking lampshade. No one else went to quite that extreme, but all the same it was easy to tell who was going to the tea. Even the boys looked sprucer, with stiffly starched shirts and pants pressed to knife-edge sharpness. Teachers found it hard to get classes down to business; heads kept turning, there were subdued rustles and covert whispers of gossip and admiration. The attention did Celinda good; by noon there was color in her cheeks and she looked almost pretty.

Mr. Grimes, despite the fact that he'd been roped in

as the Browning Society's male advisor for the year, was annoyed at the class's inattention. "I'd be more impressed if I could believe people were concerned with the literary rather than the social aspects of the occasion," he said meaningly, thumbing through a terribly thin pile of homework compositions which had just been handed in. Since mine was among the missing essays, I blushed and spent most of the period staring at my lap, and forgot to see what Hodel was wearing that day.

Excitement spiralled to a crescendo as the day progressed. By that last class, Mrs. Owens gave up even trying to keep order. "I've put your composition assignment on the board. If you don't do it now, finish it for homework," she said resignedly. But her eyes were twinkling.

At last the three o'clock bell released us. I rushed to the cloakroom where I encountered Celinda, looking scared again, and Mary Lou flouncing her ruffles and biting her lips to make them red. "You may as well come with me," she said ungraciously, and swept us toward the library.

The library, actually a book-lined classroom with study tables instead of desks, was dim and shady. Two of the study tables had been pushed together and covered with somebody's embroidered cloth and trays of sandwiches. A stylishly dressed senior was dispensing cups of punch, and another senior, armed with the invitation list, was greeting new arrivals at the door and passing them on to shake hands with the faculty advisors. I felt like Alice just stepped through the looking-glass. Then across the room I spied Kenneth coming toward me with cups of punch, and I'm ashamed to admit I abandoned Celinda to the tender mercies of Mary Lou and Mrs. Owens.

Ken, who was nothing if not resourceful, had also snagged a plate of sandwiches and two chairs in a secluded bay. The soft-summer-fragrant air drifted in through the window and somewhere in the background dimness a gramophone was playing. Pretty soon Ken and I were deep in one of our literary discussions, and I was having a very good time. I'd forgotten to be nervous, I'd forgotten about having deserted Celinda, in point of fact I'd forgotten anyone else was there. Finally Kenneth, who didn't like group socializing any more than I did, said, "I guess we'd better go be polite," and we stood up and started back toward the center of the room. At that moment, by some accident of timing, several things happened.

The first was that the gramophone stopped playing. The senior girl who'd been talking to Hodel Resnikov went to rewind it, and a tall boy, who'd been buttonholed by Mary Lou, sighted escape and excused himself to help. Mary Lou, looking irritated, turned to speak to Mr. Grimes, who stood by Hodel. At least her words were addressed to him, though it was all too clear they were directed elsewhere. In the lull of conversation and gramophone, they carried clearly.

". . . interested in comparative cultures," Mary Lou was saying. "Is it true the lack of interest in the arts among Eastern Jews is the result of the prohibition against graven images, or is their lack of taste a racial characteristic?"

The intellectual-sounding part of that gobbledegook was a mishmash of a recent history lecture, but the venom was pure Mary Lou. Somewhere near me I heard Celinda gasp. For the first time I noticed what Hodel was wearing, which was the same shapeless black sack she'd worn every day since school began. Mr. Grimes looked as if he couldn't believe his ears; Mrs. Owens made an ineffectual movement as if uncertain whether she should intrude. Hodel, as on that earlier occasion, seemed to become ten feet tall. Her dark eyes swept

Mary Lou disdainfully. Then she turned to Mr. Grimes and her voice sounded for all the world like Peter discussing one of the insects in his collection.

"I had heard," she said, "that there were persons in this country who were more concerned with what they put *on* their heads than with what was *in* them."

Mary Lou flushed right up to her ridiculous, far-too-overtrimmed new fall hat. There was an electric silence, then all at once Mr. Grimes threw back his head and roared. He laughed until the tears ran from his eyes, and in that blessed, tension-relieving laughter, Hodel bowed formally and walked across the room and out the door. She was very dignified, very much in command, and also very much alone. And suddenly, without even thinking about it, I knew what I had to do.

"See you," I gabbled frantically to Kenneth and Celinda, grabbed my purse, and without bothering to stop for books or homework I ran out of the building in Hodel's wake. Fast as I was, Hodel was already nearly a block away. To anyone else I would have yelled, "Wait up," but you just didn't holler in public to Hodel Resnikov. I ran to catch up, and reached her red-faced and breathless and realizing awkwardly that I didn't know what to say. To my relief, I recognized library books underneath Hodel's arm.

"You going to the library? So am I. I have to do some fast research for that essay that was due to Mr. Grimes today. I meant to go down yesterday afternoon, but I never got around to it. I was so rushed with—things." I didn't want to admit I'd spent the whole afternoon conferring with Celinda on what we should wear to the Browning fiasco. I was chattering like a frantic fool, but to my relief for the first time since I'd met her, Hodel actually smiled.

"I, too. We had better do some hard work today, yes?

I am afraid Mr. Grimes was quite disappointed in us both."

"*You* didn't do the assignment?" I gaped in astonishment, and Hodel's eyes twinkled, then sobered.

"At home we had a family discussion that took—how you say it? Preceeding? Precedent?"

"Precedence."

Hodel nodded. "My mother, she is very old country. She does not understand her children wasting time with Gentile social affairs."

It was a view of the Browning Society that I had never considered.

"But the Browning Society's not a social club," I pointed out. "It's literary. Only the best students get to join."

"That is what I told Mama," Hodel agreed. "Intellectual. It improve the mind, yes?"

At that moment the image of Mary Lou Hodge, that most excellent scholar, improving her mind in her ridiculous hat, struck both of us at once. I let out a whoop, and Hodel's dignity dissolved in a peal of laughter. We ran down the hill in a gale of giggles, oblivious of the heat, our appearance and the passing traffic. When we reached the corner we collapsed on a convenient carriage-block and wiped our eyes. My hair had fallen down as usual, and Hodel's braids had come loose. Hodel inspected us both critically and grinned.

"It is a good thing my mama and your Miss Hodge cannot see us now."

"She's not my Miss Hodge. She's a pain in the neck and the bane of my existence. Nobody can stand her, in case you haven't noticed."

"I have noticed. Especially in your brother, and his friend Douglas, and his brother Kenneth." Hodel had observed more than I'd given her credit for. "That is why," Hodel said precisely, "Mary Lou behave like a whore."

"Hodel Resnikov!"

Hodel looked at me in astonishment. "The word is wrong? It is a correct word. It is in our Scriptures."

I decided maybe I'd been missing something in not reading more of the Old Testament. "It's a perfectly good word for Mary Lou," I said firmly. "Just don't use it in school, is all." I bundled my hair up haphazardly and stuck some pins in it at random. "Want me to pin yours up?" I asked Hodel daringly. "It's much cooler this way."

Hodel shook her head regretfully. "Mama would not like. Mama thinks she is very modern now, not making us always wear a kerchief over. Among my people, a girl always wear her hair down her back until she marries."

"Then what?"

"Then her hair is cut off and she wear a wig. A sign of dignity."

"Suppose she never marries?"

Hodel looked scandalized. "Everybody marry. The mamas and the papas, they make sure of it. They go to the *Yente*, the matchmaker."

"Even in this country?"

"Of course." Hodel's eyes widened. "If parents love their children, they take care they are provided for and happy, yes? Here, in the city, it is harder. A man must work hard, wait to marry, until he have an occupation and an income. Thirty, maybe. For the girls, sixteen." To my surprise, a faint pink colored Hodel's sallow cheeks and she looked at the ground. "Already Rev Meir, from our synagogue, has asked for me. He is a very brilliant man, very learned."

Hodel was going too fast for me. But what about love, I wanted to ask. Then I stole a glance at Hodel's averted face, and didn't have to.

"Rev Meir is an exceptional man," Hodel said carefully. "He appreciate an intelligent woman." She sounded exactly the way I had felt when I met Kenneth, out at Grandpa Stryker's. "He is willing to wait until I finish school. He persuade Mama last night to let me go to the Browning Society."

She stopped, and I wondered what version Rev Meir was going to get of the afternoon's events. Then she straightened briskly.

"Come, then. We must work hard at the library, or Mr. Grimes, he will be very angry with us, yes?"

So that was my initial encounter with Hodel Resnikov, human being, and the beginning of my being labeled by the school as Champion of the Underdog.

# CHAPTER VI

## *September*

It did not take long for me to learn the reactions of other denizens of the classroom jungle to my performance of the afternoon. For a starter, Celinda telephoned that evening after supper. This in itself was a rare occurrence. Her parents emphatically did not encourage her use of that pernicious instrument.

"What happened?" Celinda demanded, breathless as usual. "You tore out of the meeting like a bat out of Hell."

From her language I knew her parents were not within earshot. Neither were mine, so we were free to talk. I related the whole of my astonishing conversation with Hodel, and we spent a luxurious hour discussing all of its ramifications, which explains why I was up till two a.m. finishing that fool essay, which was already one day overdue.

I handed it in after class, rather abashedly, and to my surprise Mr. Grimes accepted it with quizzical approval. "I'm going to overlook the lateness, since I've already seen you demonstrate an appreciation of comparative cultures."

It was my first hint that my precipitate departure from

the meeting had been noted, and correctly interpreted, beyond my own intimate circle.

The next hint came at lunch. It was the custom for those of us who did not walk home to take our lunch bags to the huge all purpose room, which served for both gymnasium and study. Long ago I had been coached by Bron in the unwritten seating rules, which were as rigidly proscribed as the protocol of a medieval court. The choicest table, by the window and far removed from faculty, was the perquisite of the seniors. The remaining tables were the property of the various school cliques, according to prestige. Except for the unselfconscious seniors, the boys sat on one side, the girls on the other, like a Quaker meeting. Those few forlorn souls who had no special friends sat where they could find seats and ate in silence. Cee and I sat, of course, with our neighborhood crowd, and as luck would have it my seat was directly across from Mary Lou. Today she was gabbling on about the Sunday evening plans for Grace Church Young People's Society, and as usual giving the impression that any connection with religion was purely coincidental.

". . . Viney's friend is coming to show pictures of his trip to Europe. Gee, he's cute. He goes to Columbia, you know. And there's refreshments after." Mary Lou turned to me. "Are you coming, Tish? Or is it true you're turning Hebrew?"

I could have choked her on my liverwurst sandwich. "You ought to try reading Hebrew literature, since you're so interested in comparative cultures," I suggested sweetly. "It contains some excellent portrayals of human nature. Including yours."

"Try Jezebel," Celinda, who knows the Bible inside and out, muttered under her breath.

At that moment Hodel, who is decidedly one of the isolated souls I spoke of, entered the room and hesitated, eyes searching for a seat. There were the usual not-too-muffled snickers. I was so mad I stood and waved my arms incautiously. "Hodel! Over here!" There was a momentary blank silence, then our crowd began hastily looking around for a nonexistent empty chair as Hodel approached. Mary Lou stood up.

"That's all right, I was just leaving," she said nastily, and departed, to everyone's relief, and I was stuck for the rest of the lunch period trying to weave a decidedly uncooperative Hodel into the crowd's now-awkward conversation. It didn't help any that the old Hodel, arrogant and bristling, was back in full force. I could have kicked her. For once I was actually glad to have lunch hour over.

After that, somehow, it got to be a habit, as such things do. Mary Lou, who had study immediately before lunch, would queen it briefly, finish eating, and leave, to be replaced by Hodel, and embarrassingly awkward attempts at friendliness, and Hodel's version of the prickly pear outside wall. I tried, I really tried, to hold onto all I'd learned during the summer about love and making allowances and looking beneath the surface, but it wasn't easy. It especially wasn't easy knowing that Mary Lou was out on the playground in the warm September sunshine, cooing admiringly as the boys played sandlot ball. Kenneth was very good at baseball. And I couldn't help noticing that as Mary Lou's curves had increased over the summer, the boys' disparagement of her had decreased.

It got to be a habit, too, for Hodel and me to walk down to the Library together several afternoons a week. These were equivocal experiences. Hodel was different at these times, softer and more human, as she had been the afternoon of the Browning debacle. My work improved, too, from the discipline and the instinctive competition. Gentle Miss Oliphant, the branch librarian, beamed at us; she and Hodel were old friends, apparently.

"Naturally. I come here every day all summer," Hodel said.

I wondered how come I'd never noticed her, but I knew the answer. Hodel, like me when I'm in a mood, was a loner. And I'd been too preoccupied with family and self-pity most of the summer to notice anything that wasn't directly underneath my nose.

The other side of the coin was that I missed having Celinda along. Cee, after a few tentative attempts, had crept silently away from Hodel's arrogance, her contemptuous put-downs of anyone not as brilliant as she herself. I could keep up with Hodel, albeit a bit dizzy from the scramble; Celinda couldn't, and she shrank from Hodel's unconcealed scorn.

"I can't help it, I can't take it," Celinda said, ashamed but resolute. "I listen to her for half an hour and I'm scared to open my mouth in class for a week. I can't afford what she does to me."

"She does it to me, too."

"Yes, but you can take it," Celinda said with the frankness of long friendship. "She doesn't hit you where you live. Or else you've got more self-confidence. Or more kindness."

I did feel rather exalted at times, thinking of how much I'd improved since last year. But let's face it, I'd rather have been going to the library afternoons with Kenneth than with either of the girls. I could have managed it, too, I was pretty sure. The fact that I sensed Kenneth admired what I was doing sustained me.

"Half the school," Celinda told me, "thinks you're being a perfect saint."

"What about the other half?"

"They think you're an idiot," Celinda admitted.

I wasn't always sure which side of the argument I

agreed with, myself.

So September jounced along, in the usual New York end-of-summer heat. Scholastically, classes began to shape up as we settled down to business. At home, life was much as always. Mama was past the queasy-stomach stage, and only partly into the one of hiding from public gaze. We hadn't heard any more about Pa's job, and I felt shy of asking. Bron was occupied with the Telephone Company and Mr. Albright, and seemed to have forgotten about the dashing Rev. Stanyon as well as Herbie Willis. Ben was preoccupied with sports and not yet into too much trouble at school, except for cutting classes a few afternoons during irresistible baseball weather. Peter was wrapped up in his insects, and Marnie off on her own affairs. I walked to school with Celinda, and to classes with Kenneth. Celinda's mother hadn't let her come to Young People's yet; Mrs. Dodds considered the Episcopal Church too popish, but Celinda was working on it. And in the meantime, I walked to and from with Kenneth's exclusive company—Ben, who was supposed to be providing nominal chaperonage, generally cut off in search of Doug and the fellows as soon as he'd escaped from Mama's eye.

All in all, even in spite of the effort involved in being Hodel's champion, life was not half bad.

Toward the end of September came a spell of cold, rainy days, which meant I was able to wear my new amber-brown serge to the Browning Society's Installation Tea. This was held after school on the last Friday of the month. Celinda and I had several anxious hours before the official invitations arrived, two days beforehand. Celinda looked at hers about three times during the walk to school that morning.

"I told you it would come. They don't invite anyone to that first meeting unless they're sure."

"It's all right for you and Hodel," Celinda said grimly. "You're geniuses. I'm not." And she took out the invitation yet another time.

I made a point of checking Hodel's appearance out during history class, and my heart sank. Not only was she wearing the usual black rag, but her prickly pear facade was up at least two miles high. I determined to have a talk with her during lunch on the subject of letting me pin up her hair. Mother or no mother, Hodel was carrying filial obedience too far, at least as far as the Browning Society was concerned.

I sailed into lunch with my mind made up, but Hodel did not appear. I didn't know whether to be disappointed or relieved. I didn't get too much work done in class that afternoon; nobody did. Fortunately, Mrs. Owens was too preoccupied herself to notice. Three o'clock having arrived, Celinda and I met in the cloakroom and went off together to brave the Installation.

If the prospective-members tea party had been formal, it couldn't hold a candle to this. Candles in fact were there in abundance, especially during the installation ceremony, together with so many flowers I felt as if I were at a wake. It must have cost some money, I thought, the practical side of my mind adding things up even as the sensitive side of me was responding half-swooning to the candle flames, the suffocating sweetness of hothouse roses, the formal Shakespearean wording of the ritual. I heard myself promising to labor in the groves of academe, to uphold the high personal, moral and intellectual standards of the Society, to strive to be worthy of its lofty name. Then hands were pinning the coveted little gold pin to my bosom; the president, Mrs. Owens and Mr. Grimes were shaking my hand. Then there was music; somebody sang a song based on Browning, not as well as Bronwyn could have sung it, and somebody else read aloud from "Rabbi Ben Ezra."

*Then, welcome each rebuff/That turns earth's
  smoothness rough,
Each sting that bids nor sit nor stand but go!
Be our joys three-parts pain! Strive, and hold cheap
  the strain;
Learn, not account the pang; dare, never grudge the
  throe!*

The words shimmered inside my brain.

Afterwards there was more music, and tea and punch, and little cakes, and Celinda, looking overwhelmed and awed, and Kenneth, signaling me back to our private alcove. Safely out of sight, we collapsed into chairs and grinned at each other.

"Five more minutes," Kenneth said, "and I would have petrified into one of those fake marble statues. Gee, I hope all the meetings aren't going to be like this."

"Bron says they always trot out all the formality to impress the new kids. Later in the year it gets to be more fun."

"You're lucky to have a sister who knows her way around this kind of thing," Ken said ruefully. "The stuff my brother's an expert on isn't much help to me."

"They being the same things *my* older brother's also an expert on, I know what you mean. Ken, is it true they hooked classes yesterday and hopped a freight into the city?"

"After many years of being my brother's keeper, I've learned it's better not to know too much about his affairs." Kenneth grinned. "However, judging from the fact that Doug arrived home around nine p.m. with soot on his shirt and a tear in his pants, I deduce your assumption is correct. By the way, how come you're not playing brother's keeper this afternoon?"

"Huh?"

"Hodel Resnikov. I wondered why she isn't here."

Ken looked at me and his face altered. "Tish, don't you know?"

I felt ashamed. "I didn't notice. I've been in a fog—I just assumed . . . ."

Kenneth stood up. "Come on. Let's go find out." He steered me purposefully back into the main part of the room.

The correct person to ask, of course, was the president of the Browning Society, but he was eighteen, six foot four, and the editor-in-chief of the Literary Quarterly. Mr. Grimes and Mrs. Owens were more approachable. To my surprise, Mrs. Owens looked embarrassed. She turned uncertainly to Mr. Grimes, and Kenneth repeated his question.

Mr. Grimes was more direct. "Hodel isn't here because she wasn't asked to join."

"Not asked . . . ." I stared from him to Mrs. Owens stupidly. "But I thought it was automatic . . . ."

"We are only faculty advisors," Mrs. Owens said, too quietly, and it dawned on me that she, like Mr. Grimes, was very, very angry. "You had better ask someone on the membership committee."

"Here's one," Mr. Grimes said deliberately. Ane he plucked the elaborate sleeve of Mary Lou Hodge, who was busily engaged in making eyes at the president. Ken repeated his question, levelly, yet another time. I noticed the little muscle in his temple had begun to twitch.

Mary Lou flushed and tossed her head. "Well, really, Kenneth. I'd expect you to recognize why, even if Tish's too dumb. Those kind of people could never fit into a place like this. They make no effort to improve themselves so they can belong. Why, I don't think that girl is even clean!"

I remembered Hodel's ramrod pride, her courage, her fierce integrity. My eyes blazed. "At least she had too much honor to sign her name to a story she didn't write, and then count on kids' loyalty to keep them from spilling the beans!" I turned to the august president. "If this is the kind of moral and intellectual standards I've just promised to strive for, I've changed my mind. I don't want to sink so low." My fingers trembling, I managed to get the little pin off my dress and drop it into his hand. Then, head high, I got myself out of the room, through the cloakroom for my coat and hat, and out into the street before the tears broke through. In anger and disillusion, I bawled all the way down the hill as my feet ran me unconsciously and inevitably to the library. When I reached there, it seemed natural they should have done so. I wiped my eyes and went in to face Hodel, seated at our usual table with an enormous pile of books, her back as stiff as any Czarina.

"What are you doing here?" she demanded, angrily.

I sat down opposite her and reached for a book, relieved to find my voice could sound calm although my stomach quaked. "Doing my research for Grimes' latest paper, same as you. We're in the same class, remember?"

"Why are you not at the tea?" Inexorably she forced my eyes to meet hers, shuttered and antagonistic.

"Because," I said deliberately, "I finally learned what you already knew, that there's more integrity and scholarship and honor down here than in the society of a lot of Gentile snobs."

For a minute there was the suspicion of wetness in Hodel's dark eyes, then I thought I saw her chin quiver slightly. She pushed a pile of books toward me briskly. "The material you need for the report is in these. I have already skimmed through. We have work to do, yes?"

We worked together in silence until darkness had fallen and it was very late. I jumped up. "Gloryoski, Mama'll kill me. I'm supposed to be home by five-thirty unless I call ahead. Won't your mother be angry?"

Hodel shrugged. "She is always angry when I am out

anywhere. But Rev Meir will make her understand."
She hesitated, then, in a disconcertingly uncharacteristic
gesture, reached her hand across the table toward me.
"Letitia—thank you."

"For what?"

"For what you did today. You needn't say, I can
guess; I am no fool. I want you should know I appreciate, although it was not necessary."

"It was, for *me*," I said grimly. I looked at Hodel, so
fiercely independent, and found myself saying im-
pulsively, "Look, why don't you come home with me for
dinner? Mama won't mind. There's always room for one
more."

Hodel shook her head. "I cannot. It is not kosher for
us to eat Gentile food." She stopped, then straightened
with an odd look. "Instead, why not you come home
with me?"

"Why—if you want me." Curiosity, and the need to
establish friendship, overcame my instinctive hesitation.

"I want it," Hodel said firmly, and led the way toward
the library door.

"I'll have to phone and tell Mama." Miss Oliphant
was usually good-natured about letting me use the library phone for such a purpose, and fortunately Marnie
answered, sparing me Mama's comments on the lateness
of the hour. I relayed the message and hung up quickly.

"Don't you want to call your mother and warn her
that I'm coming?"

"We have no telephone." Hodel steered me out into
the street. I assumed we'd take the trolley car, but Hodel
seemed to take it for granted that we'd walk. She led me
around back of the library into unfamiliar territory.
Hodel was wrapped in one of her black Russian silences,
and I began to wish I hadn't been so precipitate.

Soon, imperceptibly, the feeling of the neighborhood
changed. Houses and streets seemed narrower and

darker. I wondered how I was going to find my way back home. The few people we passed seemed different, too. Their clothes looked shapeless and old-fashioned, the men's beards and their broad-brimmed hats looked strange. But it was the expression in their eyes when they looked at me that disconcerted me the most. I shivered. It seemed an eternity before Hodel's voice said, "We are here," and she led me up a flight of steps.

Hodel's house, like the others, was tall and narrow. I trailed in Hodel's wake through a bleak entry, up long steep stairs and down a dark corridor. Hodel knocked on a cheaply varnished door. I noticed she seemed to have grown taller, as if she were holding herself together through sheer will. Then a chain rasped and a door opened a crack to reveal a thin, dark, vulnerable child's face.

"My sister Tamar," Hodel said, and followed it with a spate of foreign words. The child looked frightened and scuttled off. She was replaced almost at once by an older, stockier edition of Hodel herself.

"Mama, this is my friend Letitia Sterling. I have brought her home to dinner." Hodel spoke first in English, as a courtesy, then in the other tongue. She was repeating, I knew, for I recognized my name among the foreign words. I recognized something else as well. Hodel was addressing her mother in the same tone of bravado and fear that Ben and Marnie use when they're brazening something out.

If Hodel at times was a Russian princess, Mrs. Resnikov was the Empress herself. Black eyes like Hodel's swept me with the same insolent scorn and, yes, hostility. Her words struck at Hodel in a terse staccato, then she turned imperiously away. I knew what she had said, even before Hodel had laboriously searched for the correct and formal English words.

"My mother—I have told you, she is yet very old-fashioned. She has never had a Gentile at our table."

And doesn't want to, I finished silently. Hodel's head was very high, and I knew I had to get out of there, had to spare her the humbling shame of apologizing for the unforgivable. "That's all right," I said awkwardly. "Mama wasn't that thrilled about me going out—she's expected me at home to help . . . maybe some other time . . . ." And I got out, fast, without looking back.

Once in the street, I drew a deep breath of the chill night air. I hadn't the faintest idea of how to get home, but I knew if I followed the trolley tracks I couldn't go far wrong. I pulled my old coat tighter around me and plunged off, almost running. Soon I *was* running through the deserted alien streets, not daring to look up, conscious of hostile eyes that stared from behind the dim lank curtains, the shuttered windows. I ran till my heart hurt me, and my breath was burning sobs, and the leaden knot in my stomach lurched within me.

It's funny how disconnected things come back to you at such a time, come back to form an inexorably connected pattern at the bottom of your mind. Never judge somebody till you've walked two weeks in his moccasins, Gramps often said. Hodel's people had come to America because they'd been unwanted in their native land. There had been pogroms, Mr. Grimes had said; "The Jews have traditionally been aliens and wanderers, a scapegoat people, that's how they came to pick up character traits many Gentiles judge them for harshly now." Pa had said once, grimly, that if Christians really acted like Christians they'd find out what it was like to be despised and rejected of men. Was that what I'd been doing? *Was* it? Or had I been attracted more to the role of saint and martyr than to Hodel herself as a person and a friend? Was friendship offered out of guilt and condescension and an aura of self-congratulation worse or better than the snubbing of a Mary Lou Hodge?

I stumbled into a carriage block and sank down until the black mists cleared, and when I lefted my heavy eyes I was gazing blessedly at the reassuring lights from the stained glass windows of my own Grace Church. I wanted to run inside and lose myself in some shadowy pew until the disturbing tumble of thoughts within me had sorted themselves out. Instead I walked up the quiet streets beneath their protective overhanging branches of great canopy trees, past the gracious houses with their encircling porches and trampled, spreading lawns. I opened the familiar gate and walked up the path, around back past the trellis where a few late roses still clung, sending out a whiff of poignant fragrance.

The whole family was in the kitchen when I opened the back door. Pa was poring over his paper by the fire, with Mama opposite him knitting baby clothes. Bron was making fudge, and Peter and Missy were spread-eagled looking at the funnies. The warmth and love and security reached out and drew me in.

Mama looked up. "Thought you were eating out." For a wonder she didn't sound mad.

"I was. But I wanted to come home." That was no lie, even if it wasn't all of the truth. Some day I would tell Pa and Mama the rest of the story—some day a long time off. First I had some things I had to settle within myself.

I was the one, just now, who'd been pre-judged, dis-criminated against, unwanted. I was the one who for the whole past month had been trying to practice for-bearance, Christianity and love. Why then did I feel dir-ty, feel shamed, feel as if I had looked deep within my-self and stumbled upon some terrible Truth I could not bear to know?

# CHAPTER VII

## *October*

To kids around our neighborhood, October's the real beginning of fall. September's still a yearning backward to the golden days of summer, to the freedom and laziness and staying out late. It's an invitation to dawdling over work, and—in Ben and Marnie's case, at least—to cutting school whenever they thought they could get away with it and occasionally when they couldn't. But October meant business. It meant early morning frosts that painted treetops orange and gold, and presently a multicolored carpet that swirled with a satisfying crackle around our feet as we tramped from lawn to lawn. It meant marshmallow toasting parties in our yard or down at Lathams', and trying to persuade Cicero that the piles of leaves had not been raked expressly for his private pleasure. And to the little kids it meant first and foremost the approach of Hallowe'en.

The soggy wet spell that ended September turned, the first week of October, into gorgeous Indian summer. The crowd rushed the season with a bonfire in our yard on Friday night. It wasn't planned, just one of those spontaneous things. It grew out of the fact that Ben, who was supposed to rake up the garden debris that afternoon, hadn't shown up in time to do it, and neither Marnie nor I felt like getting stuck with the job without some inspiration and incentive. So we developed the idea with Celinda, who'd walked me home and stayed to help rake, and spread the word to Jimmy Breidenbach, Marnie's new bosom friend, when he came around seeking some batting practice. He was a stocky, bespectacled boy with a round Irish face and thatch of red hair, who seemed chiefly enamoured of Marnie's willingness to pitch for him at any and all hours. For good measure we passed the invitation on to Anne Cameron and Stella Molloy, new girls from down the street, when they came by pushing Stella's baby brother in his stroller, and even to Junius Albright when he ambled by with his nose in a book. I told Kenneth when he stopped by on his way home from the library. With a base like that laid down, we knew, all the kids in the neighborhood would hear and arrive in our driveway by seven o'clock.

Kenneth had brought me a book for Mr. Grimes' latest history assignment. I took one look at the size of it and groaned. "He must think we're high school seniors instead of freshmen!"

"It's interesting, but it's hard," Kenneth said. "There's lots more in the reference books. Maybe we could go down to the library to study Monday night."

"There's a meeting of the King's Daughters down at church." That was the junior-grade version of the Ladies' Aid, which I was now old enough to join.

"Maybe I can finish the book I'm using by tomorrow, and you can borrow it over Sunday."

"When? Bronwyn's roped me into helping her teach Sunday School, and I have to write a composition for Mrs. Owens before we go to Young People's at night." I attacked my raking grimly, remembering the last English paper I had gotten back. Mrs. Owens was satisfactorily impressed with my writing ability, but she ex-

hibited an amazing intolerance for misplaced meta-
phors, fuzzy pronouns and run-on sentences.

"Sounds like you're getting mighty social," Kenneth
said mildly.

"Ken Latham, they're all church activities, and you
know it!" Despite myself, I blushed, and I knew he saw
it. Bronwyn had been a leading light in both groups
named, and I knew from her how much fun they could
be. Besides, even if you discounted the religion, which I
certainly did not, those groups were where the action
was in our neighborhood. If you were involved in them,
and in sports or Browning Society in school, you were
really somebody. And I had been discovering lately that
I had too much of the family's old Dutch stubbornness
in me to be satisfied with being less than somebody in
anything I tried.

"Mama," Marnie contributed, "says Tish is biting off
more than she can chew. Especially since she's determined to be the Brightest Kid in Class."

"Well, *somebody's* got to uphold the family reputation around the schools," I retorted pointedly.

"What you mean is that now Hodel Resnikov's quit
school, you've got a chance again to be a shining light
and you're not about to let it slip away." Marnie had an
alarming ability to ferret out odd bits of information
and add them up correctly. I looked away, my face red-
dening.

After that day in September, Hodel had not come
back to school. I learned from Mr. Grimes that her parents had decided it was better for her not to be con-
taminated with Gentile ideas. Mr. Grimes was upset
about it, I knew. But Hodel's departure did leave me
undisputed scholastic leader in history and English, a
position I worked hard to deserve.

"Speaking of Hodel," Kenneth said, "there was a
meeting of the Browning Society this afternoon."

"Was there?"

"It voted to suspend operations until after 'a period of study to evaluate goals, objectives and procedures.' And Mr. Grimes is doing a little research into plagiarism. One up for our side." It was nice of Kenneth to put it that way. Even though I'd been too proud to ask, I'd found out already that my dramatic exit had had about as much kick as a wet firecracker on the Fourth of July. The president and a couple of other seniors had managed to gloss things over smoothly. But a few days later Mr. Grimes and Mrs. Owens had had a little chat with the principal, followed by another, longer one with the club officers, and it was this, I knew, that had really led to today's decision. I also knew, in my secret heart, that when the reorganization eventually did take place, I would once again be a member. I told myself it was because I'd be able to accomplish more from within than without. I wasn't sure whether I exactly liked myself, but there it was.

Kenneth was looking at me. "You really are in a happy mood today."

"It's been a long day," I said waspishly. My head was beginning to ache, and I wished to goodness that Marnie would take her appalling frankness and go inside. Above all else, I wished Ben would show up in time for us to have a private conference before he encountered Mama. Ben was in for a heap of trouble, and I didn't know what I ought to do about it.

My first inkling had come during math class when I had received a summons to the principal's office. I'd gone downstairs, my insides shaking, to find Mr. Grimes and the junior class homeroom teacher in the office with Mr. Moore, who had come straight to the point. "Tish, we brought you down here to ask you about your brother Ben. He's been out sick quite a lot lately, hasn't he?"

Oh-oh. My mind flashed back a few weeks to the rumor I'd forgotten to follow up on about Ben and Doug cutting school to hook a freight train to the city. "Yes, he—has," I answered lamely. "He always is in the fall."

"He was out quite a bit last spring, also, as I recall."

"No doubt it's a seasonal fever," Mr. Grimes said smoothly. His eyes were quizzical. I knew perfectly well we were both thinking the same thing—seasonal ball game fever.

"Is that why Ben's out today?"

"But he was here before the nine o'clock bell," the homeroom teacher insisted. "He spoke to me very politely in the hall."

If that wasn't just like Ben, remembering his manners and losing his common sense. Mr. Grimes, I noticed, was amused.

"We called your house, but got no answer," Mr. Moore was saying, "so obviously he was not home ill. That's why we sent for you."

I thanked my stars that Mama had been out in the yard or over at Breidenbach's and had not received the call. But meanwhile I was stuck. "He—had a bad headache this morning. Maybe that's why he left." Against all protocol, I stood up, "Please, Mr. Moore, I have a Latin test . . . ."

"All right, Tish, thank you. Tell your mother we will be in touch with her." Mr. Moore nodded a dismissal, and I ran upstairs, cussing my brother every step of the way. I flunked Sourpuss Sadie's test, and I was reduced to asking Mary Lou at lunch whether she'd heard any current rumors as to the whereabouts of Ben and Doug, which explained why I was in no mood for Marnie and Kenneth's pleasantries that afternoon.

Ben ambled home, looking nonchalant and carefree, just as we were sitting down to supper, which meant I had no chance for a private confab. He handed Mama a bouquet of brown-eyed Susans and bittersweet berries. "Supposed to be raking the lawn, remember?" Mama snorted, but she was smiling. Ben can charm the paper off the walls when he has a mind to. I hoped he would have as much luck with Mr. Moore.

The Breidenbach kids wandered over before we left the table—Jimmy's a connoisseur of Mama's desserts—and everybody else piled in not long after. And Mama said, "Tarnation fool kids, can't tell time, get on out all of you, I'll do the dishes," but her lips were twitching because we'd both seen Pa surreptitiously reaching for a dish towel. So Bron got her guitar and came out with us too, and pretty soon the Bryant Avenue social circle was in full swing. Bron started out playing all the spoony ballads she prefers, but after awhile Viney Hodge, of all people, wandered down to join us for the purpose of dropping a few bits of information to prove she was in regular correspondence with Herbie Willis, and Bron's chin came up and she started playing all the new ragtime songs.

Then who should come strolling briskly up the path but Mr. Albright, supposedly to see Pa, but it was obvious he really wanted to talk with Bron. Bron tried to keep him outside long enough for Pa not to get caught helping with the dishes, and Mr. Albright tried to get Bron to leave the kids and go inside, and it was really pretty funny. Bron really likes Mr. Albright, and she doesn't give two hoots about Herbie Willis any more, but she can't stand being patronized by the Hodges. And let's face it, at that moment there was nothing impressive about a middle-aged beau whose teen-aged son was right there under our noses, prominent Adam's apple, big ears and all. Bron was getting mad, which made her look exceptionally pretty, but after awhile Mr. Albright gave up and went inside, and Viney drawled,

"Really, Bron, I had no idea you were having such an active social life." Bronwyn reddened, and Viney straightened and squealed, "Who's *that* attractive man?" We all turned around, and there hesitating at the gate was Mr. Grimes!

Celinda looked at me and rolled her eyes. Ben, I noticed, had instantly assumed his devil-may-care manner that had danger signals shooting out all over it. I decided I'd better act like a hostess. Bron and Viney, of course, were very much the young ladies, and the school kids looked self-conscious, but Mr. Grimes, eyes twinkling, was completely at ease. "Thought I'd stop by to see how Ben was surviving from that headache that kept him out of history—and practice—this afternoon."

Doug Latham, standing behind Ben, guffawed. Mr. Grimes shot him a look, and the laugh choked off abruptly. "Maybe," Mr. Grimes said, "we ought to take a walk around the block to discuss that headache," and before anyone knew quite was was happening, he had marched Ben smoothly down the path and they were arm-in-arming it down the twilight street. Ben looked as if he didn't know quite what had struck him, and Ken said, "Hmm," comprehensively. Viney mùrmured, "It looks as if we graduated from high school a year too soon."

At that moment a hack came rolling up the street, in the opposite direction from Ben and Mr. Grimes. It slowed to a stop at our front gate. "Great jumping Jehosophat," Marnie breathed reverently. Gramps had arrived for a visit in his customary unexpected manner.

He couldn't, I decided, have chosen a more auspicious time. At the very least his presence would dampen the parental wrath that was about to fall on Ben. Gramps, as usual, was riding not inside but up front with the cabman. He was duded up in his best suit in honor of the trip, but in the course of traveling had removed coat, collar and tie, so his galluses shone forth in purple splendor. Over the years Gramps had acquired the status of favorite local character, a role he played to the hilt. The kids who knew him well swarmed down to greet him, while Bron went in to break the news to Mama.

"Easy now! Don't jounce the baby!" Gramps was superintending the unloading of the cab's occupant, a huge hogshead of fresh cider from the farm. Every year he brought a new one with him, and took back the empty container from the year before. The kids, who well knew the quality of Gramps' homemade cider, were helping with alacrity. In the midst of the excitement Mr. Grimes and Ben returned from their walk and melted unobtrusively into the crowd. Ben, I noticed, looked exhilarated and argumentative, but the devil-may-care manner was gone.

Everyone swarmed inside for cider and Mama's home-made apple cake. It didn't seem to occur to my parents to wonder why Mr. Grimes was there. Presently, after Pa had glanced at the clock a few times and ostentatiously wound his watch, the kids started taking the hint and drifting off. Finally only Mr. Albright and Mr. Grimes were left, and it became obvious that each was determined to outstay the other. At last Mr. Grimes broke the deadlock by deliberately sitting down on the couch, and Ben looked startled. Apparently he'd counted on the presence of others being an inhibiting factor on Mr. Grimes, but it wasn't going to work. I sat down, too, and prepared to enjoy the fun, since I couldn't seem to do anything to prevent it.

"The fact is," Mr. Grimes announced with disarming candor, "I stopped by in the hope of saving Mr. Moore the trouble of a call."

At the name "Mr. Moore," Mama's ears perked up, and with one accord she and Pa both turned to look at Ben.

"It's all a lot of fuss about nothing," Ben said hastily. "I got a headache so I started home. Then I was afraid I'd get Ma worried over nothing, so I went and slept it off in the park."

"The ball park?" Pa asked mildly. Mama was starting to build up a good head of steam, and he waved his pipe at her. "Calm down, Evie, let's let the boy speak for himself."

"It wouldn't matter so much if it were the first time," Mr. Grimes said. "But these—er, headaches, seem to be occurring with alarming frequency of late."

"It's not as if I were missing anything important," Ben burst out. "Half of what we get in classes in a lot of horse manure!"

Marnie snickered. Mama jerked upright. Before she could explode, Mr. Grimes retorted coolly, "True. But do you think you're in any position to discriminate when you're not even in class to be able to tell?"

"Speakin' as a farmer," Gramps commented, lighting his evil-smelling pipe, "horse manure's the best stuff to make some things grow." He looked at Ben. "Heap sight better than anything produced by a stubborn-headed mule."

Mama decided things had gone far enough. "Ben! You and Marnie go down cellar and bring up more cider and a bowl of apples. And mind you get the new cider; the old stuff's turned enough to make your hair stand on end."

I thought it was time I got out of there, too, and let the grown-ups have at it. Bron and I went to the kitchen to cut more apple cake. We were a good long time at it, and when we went back Ben and Marnie had already replenished the cider, and the parlor was taking on the looks of a rip snorting old family party. The adults all liked each other, that was easy to see. It was also easy to see that Mr. Grimes had noticed Bron was something

pretty special, and that Mr. Albright didn't like it and
was irked that he had no right to object. I wasn't used to
seeing either of them in such a human situation, and it
tickled me.

"All it needs," Bron whispered, "is for Herbie Willis
to walk in now."

"Fat chance."

Bron giggled. "I didn't tell you. I got a letter from him
yesterday. From Harvard. Apparently he wants to re-
kindle the flame. I didn't tell Viney." Sparkling with
mischief, she swooped down on Mr. Grimes and Mr.
Albright with more cake and cider. Ben, I noticed, was
diligently keeping Pa's supply replenished. I guessed
he'd decided it was time to polish the apple a little. It
was his typical luck that things were working out so
charmingly. The presence of Gramps and Mr. Albright
kept the occasion from turning into the kind of parent-
teacher conference he deserved, and by tomorrow my
parents would be over the worst of their wrath; if Ben
maneuvered things well, he could avoid discussing the
subject for a few more days, and in any event that old
individualist Gramps was around to stand up for him.
Mr. Grimes himself seemed inclined to do so, too. I
heard snatches of dialogue about intellectual curiosity
not being sufficiently challenged, about special assignments and admission to an advanced philosophy class.
The devil-may-care look was triumphant in Ben's eyes,
and in Marnie's, too. I wondered how many classes
she'd been cutting lately.

It was real late before Mr. Grimes and Mr. Albright
despaired of outstaying each other and left together. It
was even later before we got Gramps unpacked and
bedded down, amid Mama's repeated admonitions not
to set fire to the sheets. Gramps considers being able to
smoke in bed is one of the few advantages of

widowerhood, and he wasn't taking any sass from Mama.

It seemed as if we'd been asleep only a few minutes when I was jerked upright by Mama's frantic voice from our bedroom doorway. "Girls, wake up! Your Pa's terrible sick, and I'm afraid to leave him. Bron, run downstairs and phone Dr. Tuttle to come directly. Tish, find the quinine and the spirits of nitre. Your Pa's delirious. Sure he has brain fever."

We all flew. I heard Bron arguing with the telephone operator that Dr. Tuttle had to be waked up, even if he had just gotten home from delivering a baby. Everybody was awake by now, and the whole family converged on our parents' room, including Gramps, resplendent in a red and orange striped nightshirt and a purple nightcap.

Pa was tossing and turning on a rumpled bed, hanging onto the bedpost and moaning. "Evie, get that light out, the light's so bright! *Evie!* Sit on the bed! The bed's bouncing on the ceiling!"

"We're here, Pa! We'll hold it down." Ben and Marnie plunked themselves on the lower edge, looking scared. Gramps pottered up for a clinical look, said "Hmm," comprehensively, and sat down in the big chair and lit his pipe.

"Father, how can you! Smoke will make him sicker! Oh, do something, somebody! Tried to get quinine in him, but he won't take it." Mama sounded like a hen with her head off.

"Pipe down, Evie, and hold the bed like Edward told you to," Gramps said calmly. "Better not do anything till the doctor gets here, anyhow. It don't look too serious."

"Not serious! Poor man been working too hard. Worried sick. Another mouth to feed at a time like this. Know it's brain fever, something's snapped. Yes, Edward, I'm coming!" For Pa was yelling again that the bed was bouncing against the ceiling.

Missy was wailing with fear, and I scooped her up to cuddle. "Bron, what do you suppose it is?" I whispered.

"I don't know. We've all been selfish beasts, not thinking about Pa's troubles at all. Oh, why doesn't the doctor get here! I wonder if I ought to call Sidney. He's Pa's best friend."

Worried as I was, I noticed that Bron was now calling Mr. Albright by his first name. It gave me another chill. Pa was thrashing around again and moaning, asking Mama why she couldn't hold the bed down, and Mama was trying ineffectually to sponge his head. Marnie's face had turned the waxy yellow of altar candles, and Missy was still clinging to me and sobbing. Gramps was still calmly smoking. Mama was muttering about how insensitive he was, and how he couldn't appreciate somebody with a mind like Pa's, and how worried she was about the pressures Pa was under. I wished Pa could have heard her; it would have made him feel good.

At last the front door banged, and Dr. Tuttle came bustling up. "All right, everybody, back off. Now, Evie, what's up?" Mama tried to tell him, between Pa's moans and Missy's sobs and howls from Cicero who was trying to push in between Pa and Mama to offer sympathy. Dr. Tuttle shoved him off briskly, peered at Pa's eyes and felt his head, and straightened quizzically.

"Evie," he said at last, "there's nothing the matter with this man except he's drunk!"

Mama gasped. "Sam Tuttle, he is not!"

"Was goin' to suggest the same thing, but waited for a medical opinion," Gramps said virtuously. "Figgered ruther it was you than me that Evie clobbers."

"Edward's a teetotaler. He's a Vestryman!"

"They're not necessarily synonymous." The doctor's eyes twinkled. He was a former Vestryman himself.

"Evie, like it or not you'd better face the fact I do know a case of the DT's when I see it. And this one's a beaut." He inspected Pa with professional relish. "Probably hitting him extra hard 'cause he's not used to it. What in thunder do you suppose he drank?"

Gramps puffed his pipe. "Don't want to incriminate nobody, but I reckon somebody familiar with the situation better check the level of last year's cider barrel. Must have the kick of a mule by this time."

Mama whirled, eyes snapping. "Ben, you *didn't!*"

"Mama, I swear we never thought . . . ." Ben's face was the color of Marnie's. He swallowed hard. "You said it would curl the hair, and we sort of wondered—since Pa'd never tried it . . . it was sort of an experiment . . . ." His voice trailed off, and Marnie added miserably, "We thought it would be funny."

"Funny!" Mama's nostrils dilated, ready to breathe fire.

"Now, Evie." Dr. Tuttle's voice was soothing, though his lips twitched. "It won't hurt Ed none. Just let him sleep it off. Maybe I'd better give *you* some soothing syrup. He'll be all right, though his head'll probably be fit to beat the band tomorrow." He looked back with evident enjoyment at Pa, who was still moaning about beds on ceilings. "Sure is a memorable sight."

Mama clenched her fists and stamped both feet. "Oooh, you, Sam Tuttle . . . !" All of a sudden she dissolved into gales of laughter. She laughed till she was gasping, holding her sides. Bronwyn, looking alarmed, hustled her off to our room to spend the rest of the night. Gramps, as expert, and Ben, as penitent, were going to sit up with Pa. And thus ended the aftermath of the first parent-teacher conference of the new school year.

Pa had a little talk with Ben and Marnie on Sunday afternoon, after his head had shrunk down again to its normal size. The rest of the family was pointedly not invited, but we could piece together a good bit of it from occasional raised voices emanating from the study. Ben got the worst of it, because of cutting school. That, in Pa's book, was a very serious matter. "It's not just that you're disgracing the family name, it's a tarnfool stupid thing to do besides. In the long run it's yourself you're hurting."

Ben tried to interrupt with his well-advertised opinion of the classes he'd missed, but Pa wasn't having any. "For sure you're not going to get anything out of classes if you don't put anything in. I don't care how bad you think the classes are, if you can't manage to learn *something* from them you're a dang sight stupider than any son of mine has a right to be."

Mama, who like me just happened to be hanging around the kitchen, which was right next door, snorted at that. " 'Fraid those two are going to think their chief stupidity was getting caught!"

Both Ben and Marnie were grounded for a good bleak period into the future, and just in case time hung heavy on their hands they were also provided with a list of chores around the house and yard. Both emerged from the conference trying unsuccessfully to not look deflated and shaken, and Marnie was in a foul mood for the rest of the day. She felt that she was being persecuted, despite the fact that her sentence was of shorter duration. "Ben gets to be out afternoons and Saturdays just because he's on the football team. Pa doesn't want to hurt Mr. Grimes and the team by depriving them of Ben's precious presence. Ha! And look at Mr. Grimes falling all over himself to get Ben into special classes just because he wants to make an impression on Bron!"

I thought that wasn't fair to Mr. Grimes. "He didn't even know Bron existed when he came over here. He was just interested in helping Ben."

"Sure, everybody always is! I'm just the goat around here," Marnie pronounced dramatically. "Ben even sweettalked Pa into letting *him* go to Young People's tonight, because it's religious and not just social. Fat lot Ben's interested in the religion part!"

"You couldn't go to Young People's anyway. You're only in eighth grade," I pointed out, but Marnie wasn't in the mood for logic.

"That's not fair either. Jimmy Breidenbach's no older than I am, but he's in ninth grade so he gets to do everything."

"Well, he's not going to Young People's tonight. He goes to St. Catherine's, and you know it." I made the mistake of laughing, which got Marnie mad. She flounced off, and I went to my room to primp for Young People's, wishing as I looked at my mirror reflection that I would hurry up and start looking more like a high school girl myself. It was infuriating to have your outside and your inside not match up.

I hate to admit it, but Marnie's right about the mixed motives that lead the Protestant part of the crowd to flock to Grace Church on Sunday nights. Ben's were probably part wanting to impress Pa with piety and part recognizing a good excuse to escape from prison. Doug Latham was there frankly for the food. Just as the Methodists in our neighborhood are famous for their church suppers and the Catholics for their St. Patrick's Day dinner, the Episcopalians are noted for their evening refreshments. Young People's is also known as an excellent place to meet and mingle with the opposite sex with full parental approval. Even Celinda occasionally got to come now, when there was no prayer meeting being held at her own dour church. She wasn't there that night, but Kenneth was, and afterwards he walked me home through the warm autumn night. Up in the sky a regular harvest moon was shining.

"Hard to realize it's almost Hallowe'en," he remarked.

"Peter and Missy have been planning their Hallowe'en costumes for weeks."

"Be kind of fun to get dressed up and go out too. Pretend we're still kids."

I was momentarily startled. Last year we'd all gone out on Hallowe'en quite as a matter of course. But we'd still been in grammar school then. I started to say I didn't feel that much older. Then Ken's hand touched my elbow to help me up the curb. I was wearing a short-sleeved shirtwaist, and when the rough tweed of his jacket sleeve brushed against my bare arm, a tremor ran up it. For a moment I actually felt scared and lonely, and I went into the house in silence.

I felt rather queer, but I didn't write about it in my diary, usual repository of such confidences. I didn't tell Celinda, either, and I didn't talk to Bron, which I might have done if Bron hadn't been struggling with a problem of her own. Herbie Willis had written a second time. He was coming down from Harvard for a weekend and wanted to know if he might call. "I don't know what to tell him!" Bron wailed. We were up in our room, and I was winding my hair on rags and trying to concentrate on Latin declensions when Bron sprang this on me.

"Do you want to see him?" I asked.

"I honestly don't care one way or the other," Bron said frankly. "We *are* old friends, and I'm not mad at him any more, so there's no reason to hurt his feelings. Besides, it'd be one in the eye of Viney if he came."

"Then let him come."

"There's something more." Bron hesitated. "Sidney's invited me to have dinner at his house on Saturday. He asked me tonight, when he was leaving. He was over talking to Pa about that secretarial school idea of theirs.

His sister keeps house for him, you know, so she'd be chaperone."

We looked at each other. The idea of Bronwyn eating at Mr. Albright's own table in the presence of Sourpuss Sadie and Jughead Junius had awesome overtones. Suddenly Bronwyn flung her hairbrush on the bureau. "Oh, why does life have to be so complicated! That Mr. Grimes came over this evening, too. While you were out. He and Sidney tried to outstay each other again."

So Marnie had been right about that. One of the irritating things about Marnie was that she usually was right. To do Mr. Grimes justice, though, he really did seem interested in Ben as a human being, and Ben, praise be, seemed to reciprocate. That week they began walking home from football practice together. Ben's comparisons of school and horse manure didn't bother Mr. Grimes, and once Ben found out he couldn't shock him, they settled down to a kind of intellectual wrangling that apparently stimulated and entertained them both. Usually they'd still be at it when they reached the house and would linger at the gate, gnawing away at their topic, till Mama called Ben in to dinner.

They were going hot and heavy on "Is Homework Necessary?" when Bron came home from work on Thursday night. Mr. Grimes, who earlier had refused an invitation in, looked disposed to change his mind, but Bron just greeted them absently and came on into the kitchen, looking tired.

"Home early," Mama observed.

"Sidney picked me up in the buggy." Bron hung her hat on the back of the rocker and ran her fingers through her hair. "Well, I got out of the Saturday night mess, anyway," she said. "I invited Sidney here for dinner instead. I told him I wanted to cook for him, which wasn't a bright thing to say either, I suppose. I didn't know how else to get out of it."

"You'll have to cook; Pa and I won't be here." We both gasped, and Mama actually blushed. "Your Pa phoned. Wants to go up to Stamford Saturday morning, about a job. Stay overnight with Annie and Will. Insisted I come, too, in spite of Whatsitsname."

"Mama, of course you'll go! Isn't it good the weather's turned cool, your autumn coat's cut full and you'll hardly show at all. Anyway, Aunt Annie's your own sister." Bron stopped short. "What will I do about Sidney!"

"Gramps will be here. Come to think of it, Mr. Albright could chaperone himself. Middle-aged family man."

That wasn't, I thought, exactly tactful of Mama. Bron looked wan.

It was a good thing that Mr. Grimes' interest was exerting a positive influence on Ben, because for the next days everything else around our house was at sixes and sevens. Mama kept having second thoughts on the propriety of a middle-aged expectant lady traveling on a public conveyance until Pa, looking irritated, almost put his foot in his mouth with a remark against poor little Whatsitsname. He caught himself in time, thank goodness, and retreated behind his newspaper irascibly. He was looking for something he could explode at safely, because he was mad as hops. Gramps had spilled the cider story to a crony at the firehouse, and the story had made the rounds till it had caught up with Pa at the barbershop on Friday afternoon. Since several prominent acquaintances of Pa's had been present, Pa had not been amused.

The safest thing to explode at proved to be Marnie, whose teacher had telephoned that day with several uncomplimentary remarks. Marnie was already smarting because she'd found out Jimmy Breidenback was invited to a party at Anne Cameron's that Saturday night, to which Mama wasn't allowing her to go because of being grounded. It ended with Marnie in tears, stamping her feet and yelling, "Hell and damn, I'm the goat around here, nobody cares two hoots about me," and Pa saying, "Tish has the copyright on that line of dialogue," which got me mad, and I tell you it was a three ring circus till we got Pa and Mama safely stashed in the buggy on Saturday morning. Mr. Albright was driving them to the railroad station, and even that couldn't happen till we'd pried away Cicero, who was determined to go along, and Missy, who'd turned fractious and was whining and wailing and clinging to Mama's skirts. Finally Pa yelled, "Tarnation, Sid, get us out of here!" and Mr. Albright clucked to old Bessie and away they rolled.

"I'll see you at six," he said to Bron, departing.

That sent Bronwyn flying to the kitchen. By mid-afternoon, between stirring up messes on every burner of the stove and forays to the dining room to set the table with Mama's best china and Grandma Stryker's crystal, she was flushed and frenzied. She wasn't helped by the fact that Ben had capitalized on our parents' absence to not come straight home from the football game the way he was supposed to. She'd been counting on Ben to tend to some minor errands and keep the kids in line. As it was, Peter had innocently spread his latest insect project all over the parlor not half an hour after I'd finished picking up. Missy had gone to take a look at Peter's snake, which had been growing like leaps and bounds, and had left the cage door open. The snake, naturally, had departed for parts unknown. Missy herself was being a babyish nuisance, whining and clutching. Finally Bronwyn had exploded.

"For pity's sake, Marnie, can't you get her out of here for me? Take her for a walk or something."

"I didn't think I was allowed out of the house,"

Marnie said smartly, still seething about having to miss the party that night.

"I don't care where you go," Bron said recklessly, "so long as you keep Melissa out of my hair till dinner time. Take Peter, too. You can buy them an ice cream soda. There's money in my purse."

Marnie, who knows a good thing when she hears it, grabbed money and kids and departed precipitately. I cleaned the parlor again and went on a scavenging expedition from attic to cellar, but I still couldn't find that snake. Finally I settled down in the bedroom to get in a little solid work on the latest paper with which Mrs. Owens had afflicted us, feeling considerably martyred because it was a perfectly gorgeous autumn day outside. Before I knew it, Bronwyn appeared in the doorway, looking the way I felt.

"It's ten minutes to six, I'm not dressed, Marnie hasn't brought the kids home yet, and Lord only knows where Ben is." Bron ripped her bedraggled shirtwaist off savagely. "Why do I get myself into things like this!"

The absentees put in their appearance a few seconds after Mr. Albright's arrival. Mr. Albright, looking positively elegant in a new suit with a pearl stickpin in his cravat, had brought Bron a bouquet of flowers. Ben, on the other hand, was still attired in his football jersey, and Missy was tearstained and grimy. "She got sick from the soda," Peter contributed. Bron's lips tightened. Ben and Marnie looked at each other, grabbed the kids, and vanished in the direction of the bathroom. When they reappeared, all four of them looked clean, neat and reasonably discreet.

"It's a good thing," Bron muttered grimly, dishing up, "that Sidney is, as Mama says, a family man."

It was not an auspicious start for the evening. Gramps ambled in late, in his shirtsleeves, naturally, and monopolized the conversation at dinner. Halfway through it, Missy got sick again. Marnie, who had a cast-iron stomach, coped with that. At this point, to my inordinate relief, Ken walked in to escort me to the party. Mama would never have let me go with him alone, but what she didn't know wouldn't hurt us. We fled the house.

It was a good party, and I was glad for Anne's sake. Tall, dark and quiet, she was inclined to be shy and afraid she didn't fit in with the crowd. But everybody was there and obviously having fun, even Celinda and that prize wallflower Junius Albright. Stella Molloy was giving Mary Lou competition in the boy department, I was overjoyed to see. Jimmy Breidenbach was being the life of the party doing imitations of noted school personalities. I could see why Marnie was mad she wasn't there.

Somebody, inspired by Jimmy's imitations, suggested that we all go out on Hallowe'en disguised as such celebrities as Sourpuss Sadie and Mr. Moore, an idea which struck everyone as absolutely brilliant. We were developing this rollicking idea over refreshments when Mrs. Cameron came into the room.

"Tish Sterling is wanted on the telephone."

What on earth? I followed Mrs. Cameron to the kitchen. Bron's voice came to me over the wire, in a tense whisper as if she was afraid of being overheard. "Tish, I hate to ask this, but can you come home?"

"What's the matter?"

"Herbie's here. Remember his letter? He came over without phoning, and he just won't leave. He and Sidney are determined to outsit each other. And Gramps isn't home. He went off to the firehouse, the rat, before Herbie arrived, and he's out on the truck somewhere."

"I'll be right there." *Darn,* I thought, and went off to break the news to Kenneth. "Mama's away, and my little sister's been sick," was the explanation I gave the crowd. I told Ken the real story as we walked home, and Ken was amused.

"Want me to come in? See if I can help?" he asked when we reached our gate. I did, but I didn't think it would be a good idea. I said goodnight, far more hastily than I wanted to, and hurried in.

The sight that greeted me was memorable. Bron, by some lack of foresight, had seated herself in the center of the horsehair sofa, and Herbie and Mr. Albright had captured the spaces on either side. Ben, who had caught onto that fact that Bron didn't want to be left alone, was sprawled in Pa's chair, embarked on an endless monologue about the day's ball game. Both of the gentlemen looked annoyed and determined. When Bron saw me, she rose with alacrity. "Tish, will you help me fix refreshments?" she called, and fled. Her two beaus rose till she left the room, then seated themselves again, very firmly.

Bron shut the kitchen door behind us and leaned against it. "Thank goodness! Tish, what am I going to do? If Gramps were here, it wouldn't be so bad, but he walked out, the skunk! Said Sidney was too far over the hill to need a chaperone! At least Sidney has the sense not to leave me alone with Herbie, but *how* am I going to get Herbie to leave?" She took a deep breath. "If only he wouldn't sit so close beside me!"

"What's that got to do with it?"

"Oh, don't ask stupid questions," Bron said irritably, and started pouring cider.

I saw what Bronwyn meant when we went back inside. Herbie was definitely taking undue advantage of the tight squeeze on the sofa. He was also definitely trying to impress her by being the big Harvard man. He had asked permission to smoke. He was wearing spats. And he had grown a mustache! Every time he leaned toward the ashtray his arm pressed against Bronwyn's thin silk sleeve. Bronwyn sat rigid, and I saw Mr. Albright's lips tighten.

Finally Mr. Albright took out his gold watch, looked at it, and rose. "It's very late, and we both have Sunday School to teach tomorrow. Willis, you live in my direction. I'll walk along with you." Herbie gave him a black look, shifted position, and showed no sign of leaving. Mr. Albright, having made his move, just stood. Bronwyn shot me an agonized glance. Then, like a *deus ex machina*, came a few ragged trumpet notes from the top of the stairs.

Peter came first, waving aloft the trumpet. "We're trying out our Hallowe'en costumes," he explained unnecessarily. He was attired in Gramps' ripe old overalls —land knows why Gramps had brought them to New York, but there they were. An unlit cob pipe dangled from Peter's lips. The overalls, being a good foot too long, flapped behind him as he marched, and were occasionally snapped at by Cicero, who was next in line. Cicero was sporting Pa's best hat and Gramps' purple suspenders. He was followed by Missy, an unlikely cherub in one of Marnie's best dresses. Missy loves dressing up, and tonight she had adorned herself in my Roman sash, Bron's party shoes, and all the beads and bangles she could lay her hands on. Her face looked as if she's painted it with red water colors.

Bringing up the rear—for a second I heard Bron draw her breath in sharply—came Marnie in Bron's coral party dress. She had twisted her hair up on top of her head and skewered it with Mama's tortoise comb. She had laced herself into Bron's best corset—I recognized the lace frill peeping above the dress's drooping neckline. Obviously she was still mad about the party, for her eyes were glittering, her cheeks were flushed, and she looked very, very pretty. She positively slinked down the stairs at Missy's heels.

"I," she announced throatily, "am portraying Miss Mary Lou Hodge." She brushed against Mr. Albright in the doorway, undulated over onto Herbie's arm of the sofa, and batted her eyelashes at him. Bron looked fit to kill her. Ben roared. Cicero collided into everybody and plopped down in front of the fireplace to gnaw on Gramps' suspenders. Missy tripped in her high heels, started to cry, and stumbled over to butt against Bron's stomach.

"I don't feel good," she wailed. "Why is it so hot?"

"It's all right, baby." Bron scooped her up to cuddle. Over Missy's damp head, Bron's eyes met Marnie's accusingly.

"Don't look at me," Marnie said defensively. "I tried to get her to bed. She wouldn't go. She's been cross all day. And it *is* awful hot in here!"

"Oh, Lord!" Bron dipped her handkerchief in the cider and scrubbed at Missy's face as Missy wailed and burrowed. "If I could just get this stupid paint off her face, I could tell whether she has a fever."

"It isn't paint," Marnie said absently. She leaned against the wall and rubbed her arm across her eyes. "Why did Ben put so much coal on the furnace?"

"Bronwyn, let me see her." Mr. Albright peered at Missy underneath the light. "That doesn't look like paint, it's more like a rash," he said decisively, just as Ben was saying, "But, I didn't *put* coal on the furnace," and then, "Holy jumping Jehosophat! What's the matter with *her?*"

We swiveled around just as Marnie silently slid into a little heap on the floor, coral dress and all. She looked much younger, lying there with her eyes closed, and vulnerable. The room erupted into action. Ben lifted Marnie to the couch.

"You'd better get a doctor," Mr. Albright said tersely.

Herbie jumped with alacrity. "I'll call. Who do you want, Doc Tuttle?" I have to give Herbie credit, he recognized an emergency and dropped the phony act. The last thing I saw, as I lugged Missy upstairs, was Bronwyn starting to cry against Mr. Albright's broad and reassuring shirtfront.

In no time, Dr. Tuttle was bustling in, grumbling, "Hope it's more of an emergency than last time." He took one look at Missy and his joking manner vanished. "How long's she been feverish?" he demanded sharply.

"She's been fussing all day." Marnie, who'd revived and insisted on walking upstairs herself, leaned against the bedroom doorframe wearily.

"Shouldn't wonder. Looks like scarlet fever." Dr. Tuttle peered around. "Where's your ma? Connecticut? Somebody's better phone her not to come home. Nursing scarlet fever could be no joke in her condition."

"I'll call them," Mr. Albright went out quietly, followed by Bron.

Herbie started for the door. "I'll go find your grandfather."

Dr. Tuttle stopped him. "You're not going anywhere, nobody is. Scarlet fever's a communicable disease. You're under quarantine. Sorry, that'll affect you, too, Sidney," he added when Mr. Albright and Bronwyn reappeared.

Mr. Albright nodded. "I figured so. I've already called my sister."

"I told Aunt Kate," Bron said. "She phoned to see if Pa was home yet." She looked white and trembling and about ready to collapse. Dr. Tuttle steered everyone firmly toward the door.

"What you all need more than anything is a good night's sleep. The girls can settle Melissa. Just sponge her off and try to keep her cool. I'll get your grandfather located and send up some medicine, and I'll be up again first thing tomorrow morning." The bedroom door shut behind them all.

"I'll take care of Missy," Marnie said in a small voice, "if you want to get the others settled, Bron. I'm sorry if I embarrassed you tonight. I don't know what gets into me."

"It wasn't your fault," Bron said tiredly. "It's just been one of those days." Suddenly she began to laugh. She laughed till the tears came, and Marnie and I were shaking her in alarm. "Sidney and Herbie quarantined together for three weeks! Can you imagine what it will be like? It's a mercy Ken didn't come in with you, Tish. We'd have had a full house!"

I wondered what it would have been like. Anne's party seemed ages ago in another world.

Together we got Melissa bathed and tucked in bed. Now that things had quieted down, she was beginning to feel better and enjoy the attention. "I'm going to be you for Hallowe'en, Bron," she murmured. "Didn't we look pretty? Bron, why's it so hot?"

"Because you've got bumps on your face, baby. Close your eyes and try to sleep."

Missy wasn't having any of that; her eyes were firmly open. "Marnie's got bumps, too," she announced with satisfaction.

Bron's own eyes, which had been drooping, flew open. "Oh, Lord, Marnie, don't you get the fever." She inspected Marnie closely. "You look beat, but I don't see any bumps."

"There are too. There." Missy pointed graphically. We all looked at Marnie, leaning against the wall in Bron's coral dress. The neckline was falling off of Marnie, too, the way it had on me. But it didn't look the same.

Marnie looked down at herself. "Oh," she said. "Well. It's about time." It was disgusting, she's a year younger than I am, and she had more shape than me already. I was glad Ken hadn't seen her in that dress, and I didn't like myself any for the things I was thinking.

"Herbie noticed, too," Bron said. "I saw the way he was looking down your neck, the skunk. I suppose I'd better go get them tended to. They'll have to bunk together in Pa and Mama's room!" She started to laugh again, hysterically. "Oh, how I wish Mama could be here! But if she had been, none of it would have happened. Only how on earth are we ever going to manage!"

"Bron, stop it!" Marnie grabbed her and slapped her face. Only now Bron was sobbing and couldn't seem to stop. Marnie's eyes were scared, and I had a sick feeling at the bottom of my stomach.

At that moment the bedroom door opened, and there in the doorway, like the most unlikely saviour figure ever, stood Aunt Kate. She carried a valise, and for the first time I could see her resemblance to Pa.

"Get Bron to bed, Tish, and then you girls'd better get some sleep yourselves. Your grandfather's already got the menfolk bedded down. Better give her a shot of medicinal brandy so she'll sleep. There's some in my bag. I'll stay with Melissa. I've already had the fever. Land sakes, child, don't take on so! What else's a family for?"

# CHAPTER VIII

## *October*

Having Aunt Kate and Mr. Albright in the house turned out to be manna from heaven. One in the sickroom, one downstairs, they kept us on an even keel.

Marnie did have the fever, too, and had the worst of it, on account of she was older, Dr. Tuttle said. We didn't get to know much of what went on in the sickroom, because the door was shut and firmly sealed off with sheets dipped in disinfectant. Aunt Kate was sleeping on a cot inside. We had to leave medicines and meals outside the door for her to get, and we had to boil all their plates and silver after use.

Bron, who'd hastily read up on scarlet fever in Mama's doctor book, grew white and frightened. "It's worse when you're older, especially if the fever gets so high they can't break it. We keep forgetting Marnie's not a little kid. And poor little Punkin, no wonder she was whiney and fractious all day. I thought she was just being a pest. Oh, I'm a selfish beast!"

"No point in kicking yourself about spilt milk," Mr. Albright said quietly. His fingers closed dispassionately around Bron's wrist, and I could see my sister, who had been trembling, grow calm. I was beginning to realize why more and more Bron was coming to look on Mr. Albright as a Rock of Gibraltar.

On the first Sunday of quarantine, when we were still adjusting to being a little world of our own, he telephoned Pa in Connecticut and they fixed it up that while Mr. Albright was at our house, Pa would stay at his and be looked after by Sourpuss Sadie. Pa insisted Mama stay in Stamford with Aunt Annie.

"Give her a good rest and a visit, and the further away she is the less she'll be able to worry."

Pa and Mr. Albright worked out a sort of reciprocal trade agreement. Mr. Albright looked after us and kept Pa posted; Pa tried to ginger up Junius and tended to some of Mr. Albright's legal errands. During the daytime Mr. Albright used the kitchen as his law office, conducting most of his business and holding conferences by phone. Bron, who couldn't go to work, of course, offered to type his notes for him, and after that they spent a great deal of time together, which made Herbie furious. I couldn't help feeling sorry for poor Herbie. To give him credit, he really behaved himself and stopped trying to be the big college man.

I telephoned Celinda that first Sunday, just as soon as I thought she'd be home from church, to break the news. I dearly wanted to phone Kenneth also, but I felt queer about it. But Ben called Doug, and almost immediately afterwards I was called to the phone and it was Ken.

"Tish, I just heard. How awful for your family. What can I do?"

Hold me up, was what I would like to have said, but I wasn't about to. "Get my school assignments for me? And takes notes in the classes we have together? Celinda's bringing over my books."

Except for Dr. Tuttle, no one who once entered the house could leave, and nothing could be taken out, but that didn't mean things couldn't be sent in. So Celinda duly deposited my schoolbooks, and a long letter, on the doorstep on Monday afternoon. The whole crowd rallied round, and so did Pa, and hardly a day went by that some useful, or comforting, or amusing object did not arrive. We were grateful for these distractions, for after the first two days, when we were still numb with the newness of it all, life was strained. There we were, two beloved if often irritating sisters very sick indeed, our parents absent, and not a single thing that we could do. We were sealed in a little world of our own, with the presence of Herbie and Mr. Albright giving added awkwardness. Things were improved a little by a rearrangement of sleeping quarters so that Ben and Herbie bunked together; Gramps made the heroic sacrifice of giving up smoking in bed so that he and Mr. Albright could share. But after a week we were all getting on each other's nerves. We were starved for other ideas, other faces, and outside our windows all the last golden days of autumn were slipping unattainably away.

Celinda telephoned me every afternoon, and Kenneth every evening. Kenneth kept my mind stretched and my spirits up; Celinda supplied the gossip. She reported that Viney was absolutely furious about Herbie's being quarantined. "She seems to think he engineered the whole thing himself!" She kept me supplied with full details on the Hallowe'en party Stella was having. I remembered that Stella was a very pretty girl as well as a very smart one, and I didn't like one bit the idea of Kenneth's being at that party without me. But whenever I felt like indulging in an orgy of self-pity, I recalled that life was harder on Bron than it was on me. It certainly wasn't easy having one's beaus living under the same roof, especially such divergent types as these. It was awkward seeing them across the breakfast table before you were ready to face the day, and even more so going up the same flight of stairs to bed at night. I had to admire the way they were all behaving. "Like patricians," Kenneth would have said. Ken and I were sharing an orgy of reading up on ancient Rome.

Bron had decided that we should spend the afternoons staying out of each others' hair, and should dress up for dinner to keep our spirits high. Afterwards, we'd all gather around the parlor table for a study session. Sometimes Mr. Albright, or Bron or I would read aloud. Or Bron would play the piano and she and Mr. Albright would sing; he had a fine baritone voice. It was really his calm decisiveness that was keeping the lid from blowing off the house.

"Having you here is just like having Pa," I told him one evening after he'd been helping me with Latin. It was the finest compliment that I could give him, but he gave me a startled look.

"Thank you, Tish. That's very nice indeed." His voice sounded flat. I saw him glance across the parlor to where Bron's and Herbie's heads were bent close together over his college book.

After that Mr. Albright didn't seem to sing quite so often. By the end of our second week of quarantine, everyone was getting wound up tight. Peter, the quietest of the family, discreetly stuck to his books and his insect collection; Gramps had brought him some new specimens and was helping him soften and mount the butterflies he'd caught last summer. Ben took refuge in the garret with apples, a tame rat and sometimes Herbie for companions. I got drunk on books, and wound up with my head one continuous dull ache. Ken had sent me over a copy of *Phaedra*, which I'd tried unsuccessfully to get myself, but it didn't hold my interest. Personally, I thought Phaedra was an absolute sap to carry on like that over Hippolytus when it was obvious that she didn't really love him or how could she have treated him like that?

When I tried to discuss it with Bron one night she retorted, "Love has nothing to do with it. Oh, you don't know anything," and burst into tears.

Pa called nightly, and Mama wrote, and we worked at our appointed tasks and tried to keep from exploding at each other, and worried about what was going on in the closed-off room upstairs. None of us were permitted near the sickroom.

"Just thank your stars no one else came down with it," Dr. Tuttle said, "and leave it up to Kate. Kate can cope." But we couldn't help noticing that his face looked sober. The girls' room was next to ours, and at night sometimes we could hear them tossing and moaning, and the murmur of Aunt Kate's voice as she tried to soothe them. Bron and I, holding tight to each other in the darkness of the night, didn't dare let our eyes meet because we were afraid of what we both were thinking. I had looked into the doctor book and I knew that things weren't good. We hid the book away so Peter couldn't find it.

Aunt Kate knocked on the wall between the rooms one night just as we were finally getting back to sleep. "Bring up some ice from the ice box, Bronwyn. Bring all you can."

Bron was up in an instant, fear coloring her voice. "Aunt Kate, what is it?"

"Melissa's sleeping, but Marianna's fever's worse. No need to send for the doctor till morning, but she'll rest easier if I can get her cooled down some."

Bron and I staggered up the stairs with the old tin washtub filled with blocks of ice and left it outside the sheet-draped door. Back in our own room, we could hear Aunt Kate dragging it inside, and hear Marnie's parched voice moaning that she couldn't swallow, her throat hurt so and the bed was on fire. Marnie, who prided herself on being as stoical as any boy.

Bron tapped gently on the wall. "Aunt Kate, do you think it would calm her down if I sang?"

"Couldn't hurt none," Aunt Kate mumbled. So Bron got her guitar and sat on the bed with her back against the wall between our rooms, and played and sang until the dawn was a purple-pink streak of light beyond the maple tree outside our window.

Dr. Tuttle came early the next morning and was closeted in the sickroom for quite a while. "Later, I'll talk to you later," he brushed Gramps off testily as he hustled out. But when I was alone in the kitchen in mid-morning, peeling vegetables for soup for lunch, Bron came in and shut the door behind her. "Tish, when Dr. Tuttle was here—I stayed in our room and listened against the wall. Tish, he told Aunt Kate maybe we ought to get Mama home from Connecticut." Bronwyn was trembling.

"Bron, you don't—"

"*No!* We're not going to get upset. We daren't." Bron turned and pressed her forehead against the cabinet and clenched her fists as if willing herself to stop shaking.

The door opened quietly and it was Herbie, looking hesitant and anguished. "Bron, I saw you come in. What is it? Won't you let me help?"

He put his hand on her shoulder, but Bron flung a wild arm out to ward him off. "No! Don't touch me!" She bolted from the room, and after a moment of in-decision he left, too.

I went back somberly to lunch preparations. A lot of prayers, as well as vegetables, went into the pot that day.

In the late afternoon the doorbell rang. An assort-ment of cartons, surmounted by a grinning jack o'lantern, was piled on the porch. Pa had sent us up a Hallowe'en party. "Today's the thirty-first, I hadn't no-ticed. Missy was looking forward to Hallowe'en so much." Bron hugged the pumpkin against her until her voice steadied.

It was typical of Pa that he'd thought of a thing like

this in the midst of his own worries. There were decorations, party snappers, silly hats. There were jack o'lanterns, large and small, and games and presents. Pa had had help on these; I recognized Celinda's writing on the labels. There was a pumpkin pie made by Sourpuss Sadie, and a bucket of chocolate and orange ice cream.

Dinner had an aura of hectic gaiety. We all worked hard to make it like a party. The presents helped. Pa loved to write limericks, the sillier the better, and each gift contained one. Even the invalids received gifts, although these were sent unwrapped and could not be sent upstairs; after the fever had passed, Dr. Tuttle had said, everything in the room that could not be fumigated would have to be burned. But Pa had obviously, I thought with a lump in my throat, chosen those particular gifts to send a message. For Missy there was a tricycle for which she had been pestering for absolutely ages. For Marnie, new skates, the best to be had. The promise implicit in those gifts was like a banner waving.

Most of the other gifts were small mementoes. Junius and Sourpuss Sadie had sent packages to Mr. Albright. Viney had sent Herbie one, to Bron's amusement and his discomfiture. Celinda sent me an embroidered penwiper, and Ken a small volume of Browning's poetry. For Peter there was a beautiful book on butterflies with colored plates. After dinner he and Gramps settled down to look at it at the parlor table. Mr. Albright was teaching Ben to play chess, and Bron and Herbie had gotten out the checker set. I curled up in the rocker by the fire with my Browning and tried not to notice the bobbing lights as small, fantastically costumed figures carrying lanterns trudged by outside. The big red quarantine sign would keep them all away from our door.

Browning set up too many conflicting thoughts for me. They chased themselves in circles, like rats holding onto each others' tails. I let the book fall in my lap and sat, half-drowsing. Peter was showing Gramps a picture of a great golden butterfly, and I heard Gramps' calm voice saying, "That's a *Citheronia Regalis,*" and I willed my mind to take me back to the summertime meadow in the days when I had first become aware of Ken.

It was a peaceful scene, but gradually, like a counterpoint, the sound of footsteps overhead accelerated, and the creak of the bed as someone tossed and turned, and presently it began again, the nighttime noises, Missy's little voice sobbing for Mama and Marnie's parched, cracked moans.

Mr. Albright stood up decisively. "Let's have some music. Bronwyn, play for me, please." Herbert looked up hotly at the peremptory tone, but it was what Bron needed. She moved to the piano like a sleepwalker and played beautifully as always. Mr. Albright sang impressively, and Herbie taught us a bunch of college songs, and then Gramps started up with his repertoire of disgraceful barroom ballads to which he is addicted principally because they embarrass Mama. We made a lot of noise, and we almost fooled ourselves. Then Bronwyn hit a wrong note, and banged her hands down haphazardly on the keys, and bent her head.

"I can't play any more."

Mr. Albright went over silently and rubbed the back of her neck, and I noticed that this time she didn't draw away. I went upstairs and tried to work on my Journal, but I couldn't write. I put out the light and knelt down for a long time by the windowseat, but the words for a formal prayer just would not come. All I could think was just, "Oh, God, God, God." Bronwyn came in quietly and undressed, but she did not speak. Faintly, from somewhere outside, came a sound of music.

Bronwyn came over and touched my shoulder. "Look," she whispered. There, down on the side lawn,

was Stella's party come to serenade us. All the crowd
was there—Anne, Stella, Junius; Doug Latham with his
arm around Mary Lou's waist; Jimmy Breidenbach and
Ken and Stella's big brother Larry; Mary Lou's dear
friend Charlene Snead; all the kids we'd grown up with
or acquired as new high school friends. Even Celinda, I
noticed, had gotten permission to attend. They sang for
an hour, all the current songs and then the oldies, winding up with a bunch of the old gospel hymns that we sing
around church on Sunday nights. At last they left, calling out soft good-byes and messages of cheer. Bron,
without a word, hugged me hard. Outside in the street,
as the crowd crossed at the corner, I saw Kenneth stop
under the streetlight, turn, and give one last salute.

The house fell silent, except for the sound of Gramps'
snoring and the now-familiar sickroom noises. Missy's
crying finally trailed off to sleep, but Marnie's thrashing
and moaning seemed to grow worse as the hours passed.
The ticking of the grandfather's clock, down in the hall,
seemed unnaturally loud. In the hours after midnight
the wind rose, whirling dry leaves from the skeleton
trees and sending branches tapping against the window-
panes.

"Sounds like a storm's coming up," Bronwyn
breathed.

The wind rattled again. A branch of the maple tree
cracked and fell against the window, and Marnie
screamed. "There, it's all right. It's nothing." "It's coming, it's coming! . . ." We could hear Aunt Kate's
soothing murmur, and Marnie's voice as it spiraled in
hysteria, cracked, and descended again in a broken
moaning. ". . . hot, so hot. . . . The eyes! The eyes! . . ."

After an hour of this Bron rapped on the wall. "Aunt
Kate, isn't there *something* we can do?"

Aunt Kate hesitated, deliberating. "Contagion
period's about passed now, and if you were going to get

the fever you probably would have done so already. Dump all the ice you have into the bathtub, and then get in here. Her fever's bad, and I need another set of hands."

It was like a macabre repetition of the night before. We crept down to the back porch silently and dragged up the heavy cake of ice—in a sheet, this time, since the washtub was still inside. "Thank goodness the ice man came today," Bron whispered. Aunt Kate met us in the doorway, looking tired and gaunt. A dim light from the bedroom made her shadow look ten feet tall.

"Dump the ice in the bath, get that sheet good and wet, and bring it in, it's just what we need." She disappeared inside, and we obeyed. The room felt suffocatingly close and sickish sweet, as sickrooms do. Missy, like a flushed cherub, slept curled in a ball on Aunt Kate's cot. Dim light from the rose-shaded lamp and the jack o'lantern on the bureau cast flickering shadows over the bed where Marnie tossed restlessly. She had kicked off the covers, and her nightgown was plastered wetly against her hot body. Aunt Kate grabbed the cold sheet from Bron and wrapped Marnie in it tightly. "Hold it around her so she can't toss it off. Tish, get another sheet and soak it in water as cold as you can make it. Keep the bathtub filled. We'll put that one on her when this one gets heated up."

We kept it up in relays for an hour. Slap sheet in tub . . . squeeze it out . . . run it across the hall . . . back with the old one. Aunt Kate stood by the headboard, trying to bathe Marnie's face, but Marnie wouldn't lie still. She tossed and moaned, punching the pillow into a wet ball, crying out that the light was hurting. I tied a towel around the lampshade and that seemed to help.

It helps having something to do. I went through the routine doggedly, while every mean thing I'd ever thought about my sister ran through my head. I repeated every prayer I'd ever known. Marnie's thrashing seemed to be subsiding through sheer exhaustion, but she was delirious with fever. Her dark hair, tangled and matted, was heavy against her neck and there were purple shadows like bruises around her eyes. "She'd be cooler with the hair off," I heard myself saying. Bronwyn gasped in protest, but I said firmly, "Marnie's not sentimental, and you know it. She won't care," and ran next door for the scissors. With her hair chopped off above her shoulders she at least looked cooler. Bronwyn laid the discarded locks carefully away to give to Mama.

"Couldn't we at least open the window to air the room?"

Aunt Kate shook her head firmly. "Night air's poison in the sickroom. Marnie, no!" For Marnie was suddenly sitting bolt upright and pointing and screaming, "The eyes, the eyes! . . ."

"It's the jack o'lantern." I blew the candle out quickly. Aunt Kate took Marnie's temperature again, and shook the thermometer down quickly before we could look, but I had seen the expression on her face. "I wish I dared give her another dose of nitre, but it's too soon."

"The sheet business isn't working any more. It heats up right away," Bronwyn reported.

Aunt Kate struck her fist against her forehead. "Old fool! I just remembered something. Bron, Tish, get the bottom sheet unhitched. We'll put her right in the bathtub, ice and all." Marnie's pretty solid, but between us we managed to carry her in and submerge her up to her chin. Bron supported her head, oblivious to the fact that she was getting soaked herself, while I kept the cold water running.

"Have to send out for more ice if it doesn't work by morning." Aunt Kate smiled grimly. "Bathroom's turning out to be an advantage after all. I thought it was a tarnfool extravagance when your father put it in."

Gradually, imperceptibly, the moaning, the labored breathing diminished, then ceased. I looked at Marnie in panic and yanked on Aunt Kate's skirt.

"Aunt Kate! . . ."

Aunt Kate bent, put on her glasses, looked closely, and straightened. "The fever's broke. She'll sleep now." She walked to the window and pulled up the shade. Outside a faint pink light was beginning to form. "Looks like we made it to morning, after all."

*Thank God,* I whispered.

We carried Marnie back, changed sheets and nightgown, and got her settled quietly. Bronwyn hugged me and then, after a moment, Aunt Kate. Aunt Kate didn't even flinch.

"Better catch a few hours sleep," she said. "Let the menfolks worry about breakfast." We tiptoed out into a silent house—it seemed unbelievable everyone had slept through it all—and fell onto our bed.

When we awoke it was midmorning and the house was still. "I feel," Bronwyn said, "as if I could sleep for a week. I hope Gramps saw to breakfast."

"He did. Can't you smell his coffee?" There was no mistaking that particular strong aroma. Bron grinned, splashed water on her face, and started pulling on clothes. "Oh, drat, this dress shrank. I must have washed it differently than Mama." She was contemplating one of my favorites, a brown and coral plaid trimmed with heavy cotton lace run with brown ribbons. "Here, you try it. You've been getting taller lately."

I had, at that. The dress fitted fine, making allowances for a certain roominess which the ruffles of the yoke concealed. Bron inspected me critically. "It's too long, of course, at your age. Oh, what does it matter just this once? Keep it on, it's good for morale. And come let me try your hair a new way."

Our morale suitably lifted, we went down the back

stairs to the kitchen where we encountered Gramps. "Doc's been and gone. The fever's lifted, she'll pull through." He poured us cups of coffee strong enough to curl your hair. "Fed the boys a real farm breakfast and sent Kate up her toast and tea. We also," he added with conscious virtue, "washed up all the dishes. Boys are doing their studying in the parlor and Sidney wants to know, if you're not too tired, if you'd transcribe those notes you took down yesterday."

Bron, who had been looking weary, was suddenly radiant. She patted her pompadour, bit her lips redder, and hustled out. Gramps looked after her, said "Hmm," and ambled after. I cut a hunk of coffeecake and sipped the evil coffee, hoping it would put some starch in my spine.

A pile of clean dishes from last night and this morning was stacked on the kitchen table. I carried them into the pantry closet and put them away and stood resting my forehead against the shelf. Tiredness closed in on me. All I could think was, *Thank You, God.* I had never realized before how terribly much I loved my sisters.

Somebody came and stood in the doorway behind me, cutting off the light. As from a great distance, I heard Herbie's voice saying, "I've been trying to see you alone for days, but you've been avoiding me. Bronwyn, we've got to get things straightened out."

I opened my mouth to say I wasn't Bronwyn, but before I could get the words out, Herbie's hands turned me around firmly and he was kissing me, hard, on the mouth. For a second I was too startled to pull free, and anyway he was holding me too tight. I struggled against it, and then something happened. My body didn't seem to belong to me any more. It was like some stranger's, arching in against his till it felt like my heart was pounding inside his chest. My legs were behaving like I'd just gotten out of bed from some high fever, and my insides felt as though some strange flower had started to grow and unfold deep within me. When he released me, we stood staring at each other.

"*Tish!* I'm sorry! I thought! . . ." He turned and bolted.

I wandered into the kitchen slowly, feeling as if the bottom had dropped out of my stomach, and sat down shakily. I felt exactly as if he'd seen me naked. It wasn't right for me to have been kissed like that, not at four-teen. But it wasn't on Herbie that my feelings of shame and fear were focused. It was on myself.

Something I hadn't known inside of me had stopped resisting, had strained my body hard against his as if to become one flesh. Something hadn't wanted it to stop. And, as Bron had said earlier, love had nothing to do with it. I didn't like to think about what did.

# CHAPTER IX

## *November*

When it was all over, Pa liked to refer to November, 1900, as "The Comedy of Terrors." But that was decidedly after our eventful Thanksgiving had been celebrated and life had settled down again into its customary chaos. It was the month in which, as Pa said, he "sent his bark out into unknown waters like a new Columbus." And Aunt Kate discovered Women's Rights. And Bronwyn finally made her mind up about Mr. Albright.

The month's first clash of cymbals occurred when the quarantine sign finally came down from the door. This happened on Monday, the fifth of November, a bright, cold day. Dr. Tuttle came over in the early afternoon to inspect the invalids. Missy was pretty much back to her old self now, meaning full of beans. Marnie's sore throat, rash and fever were gone, but she was so pale and still that looking at her scared me. She'd lost so much weight that her newly noticeable figure and the dark smudges underneath her eyes made her look much older. But her disposition was still pure Marnie Sterling. She was mad that she was still stuck in bed, and madder yet that she didn't have the strength to sneak out, and she told Dr. Tuttle that if he stuck that tarnfool thermometer in her mouth one more time she was going to bite him. Dr. Tuttle laughed and looked at the thermometer, and said he guessed she'd survive, and then went downstairs and took away the sign. And three hours later Pa drove up to the front path with Mama in the carriage.

All of us, with the exception of Marnie, who was too weak, and Missy, who had to be forcibly restrained, went hurtling out of the house without bothering to stop for coats. Mama'd gotten pretty bulky during the past few weeks, but she came running up the path as if she were no older than Marnie and considerably spryer. And Cicero, in the middle of things and hysterical with excitement, started thinking he was a circus dog and pranced around on his hind legs, which made him five feet tall, and almost knocked Mama over on the steps. And Pa yelled, "Dangnation, somebody lock up that tarnation mutt before he kills us all! Don't you children care two hoots about your Ma's condition?" Marnie was hollering from the parlor where Gramps had parked her on the sofa, "Goldurn it, will you guys come on in here so I won't miss it all?" And oh, Lordy, it felt good to be a family again!

Mama got rather grey and quiet when she got a look at Marnie, and she hugged Missy very hard, but after a cup of tea and a quick tour through the house, noting little changes that had crept in in her absence, she was snorting and chipper and ready to light into fall housecleaning then and there. And it was as good as a play to watch her having to cope with feeling grateful toward Aunt Kate, and Aunt Kate trying to be gracious about accepting. She didn't mind having to feel grateful and apologetic to Mr. Albright. "Dratted shame you had to get caught in this. Don't know what the children would have done without you."

'I didn't mind," Mr. Albright responded, his eyes on Bronwyn.

Mama said, "Hmm," speculatively, and looked at me, and I had a feeling that in the very near future we were going to have a little heart-to-heart chat.

Herbie Willis had taken himself out of the house as fast as ever he could, and I don't know who was gladder about it, he or I. The last few days had been decidedly uncomfortable. I had told Bronwyn the bare facts about the mistaken identity, just in case Herbie mentioned it to her, and from the look on her face I suspected she was filling in all the disturbing details I'd left out. I also suspected she used the affair as a convenient pretext for washing Herbie out of her hair for good, because she was decidedly frosty to him after that, and so when Dr. Tuttle finally released us all, Herbie looked very glad to get away. As for me, after the first tumultuous reunion with my parents, I ran straight down to Celinda's. It felt a lot safer to be getting back with kids my own age.

Celinda saw me coming and ran out to meet me, her face alight. We hugged tempestuously, then she linked her arm through mine. "Let's go to our place in the park, where we can talk." The Dodds' discouraged Celinda's having guests at home, and I was just as glad, for it was a depressing place. Celinda's parents were fanatics about religion, among other things, and the kids referred to them, behind her back, as the "old black crows."

The park Celinda referred to was not a real one, but a group of vacant lots that curved around behind an old deserted house, reputed to be haunted. The kids played ball there in the summertime, and Easter ducklings swam on a little pond. Far to the rear, by a lot that was now all woodland, was a huge section of drainage pipe we'd discovered long ago. It had been our secret place for playing house as children; later, a refuge when we needed to be alone. The stones we'd used as benches were still in it, and we sat down on them, smiling at each other.

The walls of the pipe cut the wind, which already had a bite of winter to it, but the fading light shot in a golden beam that aureoled Celinda's pale hair. She was wearing a new winter coat, chosen as usual for wear, not flattery. "Wait'll you see Mary Lou's new one," Celinda said. "It's bright blue and green plaid, with velvet facings and a big lace collar. She wears it to school, of course. Doug Latham thinks she looks pretty spiffy, apparently." Celinda grinned at me breathlessly. "Golly gee, it's good to see you again!"

We had, of course, talked on the telephone nearly every one of the twenty-some-odd days of quarantine, but it wasn't the same thing, so now we rehashed item by item all the happenings and gossip. "How's Kenneth?" I said at last, trying to be casual.

"Good enough for Mary Lou to make a play for him at Young People's Sunday night," Celinda said, eyes twinkling. "But it didn't work. Tish, didn't you call him and tell him you were out?"

I turned red. "I thought about it, but I was scared. Anyway, Mama would skin me for calling up a boy."

"Call Stella," Celinda said practically. "Ken's probably over there anyway. Visiting her brother," she added, as my heart lurched. "Ken and Larry have gotten to be awfully good friends."

"I thought Larry was a senior."

"He is. But it doesn't seem to make any difference to them. I guess that's because they're both geniuses," Celinda said comfortably.

My return to school the next day was a triumph. I wore the plaid dress Bron had given me, and it did make me look older. Bronwyn did up my hair. I hoped I looked pale and romantically tragedy-touched, but I knew I was far too happy. When we reached the school, Ben was promptly carried off by his own cronies and the girls swooped down on me in the cloakroom. Even Mary Lou and her cohorts condescended to come around; and Celinda had been right about Mary Lou's new coat, it was pretty awful. It made her look like a Scarlet Woman, as if she wasn't well on her way to that already. But I had the satisfaction of seeing her check me up and down in the calculating way she usually reserved for real competition. I caught a glimpse of myself in the mirror, and I did look pretty good, and on this roseate knowledge I floated out into the hall as the first bell rang. And I heard somebody say, "Hello, Tish," and there was Ken, and if Mr. Grimes and Mrs. Owens, not to mention Sourpuss Sadie, hadn't been watching, we would have held hands.

"Golly, it's good to have you back." Kenneth seemed to have gotten taller, and his eyes were very bright. "How are your sisters?"

"Much better. They're going to be all right."

"I was going to come down last night, when I heard the quarantine was lifted, but I thought your parents would probably want just the family the first night. I'm working for my father in the store now, after school," he added proudly. "But do you suppose I could come down and see you tonight after supper?"

He said it right out loud in the crowded corridor, oblivious of the listening ears. "I don't see why not," I responded with what I hoped was admirable casualness, and walked off beside him to my first class, while inside I felt like turning cartwheels and shouting *alleluia!* right out loud.

Lunchtime was the crowd's first chance to congregate all together. Somebody had had the bright idea of sending out for Italian food, and Stella, who's always daring, had ordered it between classes, only when it came it was delivered to the office, and Mr. Moore's prissy secretary was scandalized, but he just laughed after giving us the necessary lecture, and said we could eat it in his office while he was out. So the boys came in, too, and we had a regular party in the principal's office, and got tomato sauce all over our faces, and nobody did much work that afternoon, and something tells me the old school will never be the same.

When the three o'clock bell rang, Kenneth went off to his job, but I stayed to talk with Mr. Grimes and Mrs. Owens about the work I'd missed, and Cee and Stella and Anne stayed, too, so we ended up in Mrs. Owens' cheerful classroom, having more of a social visit than a school conference. It was four o'clock when we finally left. When we reached my path, I bid the girls a blithe goodbye and ran up the steps to break the news to Mama about Ken's coming over.

The first thing I noticed when I burst in the front door was how quiet the house was. That was unusual. Ever since the fever crisis was past we'd been back to our usual cheerful din. Marnie's gotten worse, I thought, feeling the bottom drop out of my stomach. But when I entered the parlor I saw my sister lying in her usual place on the sofa, looking not sick but kind of scared. Then I saw Pa sitting in the big chair, a curious expression on his face. Mama was standing behind it, leaning against the back, her hand on his shoulder. Bronwyn was standing in the dining room doorway, a paring knife in her hand, as if she'd been interrupted in the middle of dinner preparations. Bron wasn't going back to her job for a few more days, till she helped with the fall house-cleaning.

"What's the matter?" I asked. My voice came out a whisper.

Pa turned to me with a whimsical smile. "Ever hear of the Sword of Damocles, Tish? The thread just got cut."

"Pa's lost his job," Bronwyn said flatly.

Oh, Lordy, I thought, and sat down hard.

"No need to look so," Mama snapped. "Not a shock. Knew it was coming. Just a question of when. Been making plans and provisions." But from her tone I knew she was worried. "Your Pa will make out just fine," she said staunchly, coming around beside him.

"I hope so, Evie. I do hope so." Inadvertently Pa looked at her middle, and Mama flushed and turned away, and we all thought the same thing. What a time for poor little Whatsitsname to be putting in an appearance.

"I'm going to call Sidney," Bronwyn said suddenly, and marched out with determination. I half expected my parents to protest, and the fact that they didn't jolted me a little. Pa drooped forward as if he were quite tired, and Mama's face had that private look, which meant it was time for us kids to butt out. Marnie, who couldn't leave, closed her eyes, and I followed Bron into the kitchen.

Bronwyn was cranking the telephone vigorously. In a minute she was engaged in a spirited argument with Mr. Albright's secretary. "No, I can't tell you what the call's about. It's a personal—well, yes, maybe it *is* a business matter." Her patience snapped. "Look, Miss Whoever-you-are, you just put your boss on fast and keep your nose out of his private affairs. Oh, Sidney—" Bron's voice changed again. "Thank goodness. Sidney, Pa's come home. It's finally happened, and I think we need you. You will? Good."

Bron hung up abruptly and turned to me. "Sidney's Pa's best friend," she said, as if to explain her action. I was pretty sure Mama'd noted the significant use of Mr. Albright's first name, but she didn't seem inclined to bother about it at present. When we went back to the parlor, she was leaning over Pa, rubbing his shoulders, her face grumpy, which meant she was in deep thought.

Pa had his chin in his hands, and he was staring at nothing somewhere across the room. Marnie held out her
hand to me silently, and I went over and scrunched
down beside her on the sofa. The air was heavy with our
unvoiced thoughts, and with something else too. I recognized it by the bitter taste in my dry mouth. Fear.

Pa looked beaten, and he looked old. And it wasn't in
the same way as last summer, because then he'd been
mad. Now he looked on the verge of giving up.

The door banged, and I thought it was Mr. Albright,
but it was only Ben clattering noisily in. Bron grabbed
him and dragged him into the kitchen, and when they
emerged a few minutes later he too looked stunned. And
there we sat, like sitting ducks in a shooting gallery. It
was awful, I thought. Somebody ought to say something
to cheer Pa up, but I couldn't have thought of a thing if
my life depended on it.

All of a sudden, somebody exploded, "Hell and
damn!" and everybody jumped, and the held-in tension
burst in the broken silence. It wasn't Marnie who'd broken it. It was Mama. She marched around in front of Pa
and planted her hands on her hips, and her eyes were
snapping. "What's the matter with us all? Bunch of nin-
nies! Acting like somebody'd died!"

Pa looked at her as if she'd taken leave of her senses,
and she stamped her foot. "Great opportunity. Been
saying so for months, only now it's come we're being too
chicken to recognize what it is. Edward Pierce Sterling,
long's I've known you, you've been talking 'bout how
you were going to run a school of your own some day.
Said nobody trained stenographers properly, and when
you had time you were going to show them a thing or
two. Well, now's your chance, and you're a-going to do
it!"

"Evie, I was younger then," Pa said patiently. "Now
I'm nearly fifty, we own a house, a family to support.

It's too risky starting a new business. I'm too old."

"Horsefeathers!" Mama retorted. "Not too old to be a new father in a few more months. Guess that proves something about us both, only we've been too dumb to recognize it. Stuck in the mud. Getting scared. Us! And you a Vestryman, Edward, I'm surprised at you. Where's our faith! Seems like the good Lord's given us a kick in the pants to start us in the direction we didn't have the gumption to head in on our own!"

I don't know which astonished us more, Mama's energy or her language. She'd have tarred Marnie for using some of those expressions. But right now she almost looked like Marnie herself, like somebody's given her a jolt of pep-up tonic, breathing fire and spoiling for a challenge.

Pa looked at her and all of a sudden he started to grin. "Evie, I haven't heard you sound like this in years."

"Forgot I could," Mama said, "but I'm enjoying it. Maybe we've all been needing a jolt. Getting old too soon!"

"You could be right, Evie," Pa admitted. "I've been thinking about the school idea, you know that. We visited that one in Connecticut. But they told me a man needs capital to last three years. Business rents are high in the city now; I've looked. Don't know what we'd live on while we're getting started."

"Same things we talked about last summer," Mama said. "Sell the house if we have to. Take in boarders."

"I have a good job now," Bron said. "They like me. I think I'll be getting a promotion soon. I could get more money right now working nights. And the telephone company's looking for trained operators to send to the Buffalo Exposition. I could apply for transfer."

"I told you months ago," Mr. Albright said calmly from the doorway, "I'd go in with you on a partnership. You've got the shorthand knowledge and can teach. I'll supply the money. I've got some put away."

Pa shook his head. "Sidney, you know that money's for Junius' college education."

"He won't be going for three more years. It might do him good to knock about a bit and earn his own way. You and I both did, and it didn't hurt us any. I didn't realize how queer that son of mine was getting till I lived here with your children and could compare. Come on, Ed," Mr. Albright said firmly. "Let's go for a walk and talk about it." And before we knew it the men were outside and marching down the street, oblivious to the rest of us left behind.

"Well!" Mama said. Her eyes were still snapping and she still had a good head of steam, but her legs didn't seem to be cooperating with her spirit. She sat down kind of abruptly.

" 'Well!' is right!" Bronwyn said proudly. "I told you Sidney would know how to cope. Mama, don't give me that look. You sit here and I'll fix dinner. Mama? What's the matter?"

For Mama had suddenly clutched her stomach with a startled look. Then her brow cleared and she laughed. "Tarnation, looks like this one's going to be a spunky one, too. Whatsitsname just kicked me!"

So all in all, the family's release from scarlet fever was eventful in more ways than one. Bronwyn roped me into helping her rustle up a festive dinner, and she talked Ben into cracking nuts for a cake. "Hang the expense!" she said recklessly, dipping into butter and sugar with a prodigal hand. "We need to celebrate! For a lot of reasons. I wonder whether we should ask Sidney to stay for supper?"

"Hasn't he been eating here enough lately?" Ben asked derisively, and Bron turned red.

Mr. Albright did stay for dinner, but we ate very late because the men stayed out so long on their walk, and

Bron had to hustle around keeping her dinner from getting burned. By the time we had finished eating, Mama, and Mr. Albright between them, had Pa all steamed up to go out looking at possible school locations the next morning.

"I'll start drawing up the partnership papers first thing," Mr. Albright said. "Before you change your mind!"

"I could go around to some of the other secretarial schools in the city," Bronwyn offered. "Pretend I'm interested in enrolling. Find out what they teach, and how much they charge, and so forth."

"We'll have snow in a few more weeks," Ben said. "I should be able to pick up some good money shoveling walks. That will help, won't it?"

"So can I," Marnie called from the parlor, "if I'm ever able to get up from this dumb sofa!"

"Don't start pestering about that yet," Mama said firmly. "Can help best just by concentrating on getting well." But she looked pleased and proud. Pa had perked up considerably, too. In fact, everything was happening so fast that we were fairly getting drunk on inspiration, and it was near seven-thirty before we got up from the dinner table and transferred our planning to the parlor. Since Marnie had the sofa, Bron was sitting by Mr. Albright on the little love seat, and she wasn't complaining a bit about *his* being squeezed up close.

The doorbell rang just as our ideas were approaching genius. "Go get it, will you, Tish?" Mama said, and I dashed out, annoyed at having to miss a word. And there on the doorstep, with a couple of books and an anticipatory expression, stood Ken. Incredible as it seemed, I had forgotten all about him. My face must have showed it, too, for he suddenly looked uncomfortable and embarrassed.

"You did say I could come."

"Oh—of course." I pulled him inside quickly and shut the door. "We've had a crisis that's turned into a family council. Come on in and say hello while I figure out where we can go." I no longer gave two hoots about what I was missing in the family council. I wanted what I'd been missing for weeks, the chance to talk with Ken alone. Telephoning just wasn't the same thing, and after more than three weeks, we had some rebuilding of bridges to do. My mind raced. It's long been established that the first family member to receive callers gets the parlor, the next the kitchen, and any stray kids play up in the attic. But the parlor was thoroughly occupied; the kitchen was a mess from dinner and Mama turns purple if anyone sees it in that condition; and I didn't particularly want to entertain Ken in the cobwebby attic, even if Mama would have permitted it, which she decidedly wouldn't. And it was too cold now to sit outdoors.

Ken, making the polite rounds shaking hands, cased the situation quickly. "Can't we go for a walk," he whispered from the corner of his mouth. I detached Mama from the mob and put in a fast petition.

Mama shook her head firmly. "Absolutely not. It's too cold. 'Sides, what would the neighbors think? Not proper."

"Mama! We wouldn't do anything!"

"How do you know?" Mama retorted practically. "Anyway, last thing we need right now is problems with your Aunt Kate's spyglass!" She looked at my face and relented slightly. "Tell you what. You can go visit somewhere so long's you take Ben with you. School night, but I'll stretch a point this once if you're back by nine-thirty." She went off to talk fraternal responsibility to Ben while I held a hurried conference with Ken.

"Molloys'," Ken said promptly. "It's a big house and there's always a mob there. They won't mind."

I went to the kitchen and cranked Stella's number vig-

orously. "Can we come over?" I asked without pre-
amble. "Ken's here, and there's a family conference
going on."

Stella got the point. "Come ahead. Anne's here.
We're helping the little kids make fudge. We're very
busy, and there's lots of room."

In the parlor, the family was back in the thick of
things. Ben was in the hall with Kenneth, pulling on his
coat. Mama'd done a job on him, and he wasn't happy.
"Thanks a whole heap," he glowered darkly. "Why
can't you kids get your private stuff finished in the daytime? I was planning to go out somewhere with Doug
tonight."

"You couldn't anyway," Ken said. "Mary Lou's already got him. He's explaining algebra to her, if you can
picture that."

"More fool he," Ben muttered, and loped off ahead of
us into the darkness, which couldn't have pleased me
more, since it gave Ken and me a chance to talk. We
hadn't accomplished too much, though, by the time we
reached Molloys'. It was hard picking up where we'd left
off weeks before. We'd both become self-conscious and
stiff, and I could have kicked us both more easily than
manufacture conversation. I wanted to, but the words
would not come out.

That was the situation when Stella threw open the
door. She looked very pretty even with a streak of chocolate on her face, and little brothers and sisters hanging
on her skirts, and I felt a pang of jealousy. But to my
surprise it wasn't at Kenneth she was looking. She
flashed me a comprehending grin and turned to Ben.
"Hi, there. Larry was hoping you'd come along. He
wants to talk to you. But don't stay upstairs too long, or
the little kids will eat all the fudge."

Stella's brother was tall, with the same expressive eyes
and an unruly thatch of dark hair. I knew him by sight,

but he was both a senior and a genius, which put him into a separate class of beings where I was concerned. I'd forgotten he was in Ben's philosophy class. He saluted Ken and greeted Ben with an outstretched book. "Good man! You tackled Grimes' philosophy propositions yet? I've run into an interesting problem in the second one." He bore Ben off upstairs, both of them talking a mile a minute about the relative merits of Plato and Aristotle.

"Anne and I have to watch the fudge so it doesn't burn. You two can go in the pantry and grease the pans." Stella fairly pushed us into the tall, narrow room, and the door swung shut behind her.

Kenneth grinned. "She may not be tactful, but she sure is efficient."

Somehow, that had broken the ice. Ken lounged against the storage wall, I perched on the edge of the flour barrel, and we talked a lot more than we greased the pans. As you might know, despite my good intentions, I even told him about Pa's plans for the secretarial school. Stella had to come in and rescue the pans for the fudge, and Mama had to telephone to remind me it was high time to come home.

Things happened fast after that. Bron went back to work the next day and came home, her face determined, to announce the telephone company had transferred her to night work. Mama hit the roof. "No daughter of mine's going to traipse around the city that hour of the night. Not safe. You march right to the telephone and tell them you quit."

"No," said Bronwyn.

Mama couldn't believe her ears. "What?"

"I said no," repeated Bronwyn calmly. "I *asked* for night duty, and I'm not backing out. It pays more. And I'll be home daytimes to help Pa if he needs me. We're all in this together, Mama. Didn't you always teach us a family had to pitch in and pull together?" She had

Mama there, and she had her even more with her final threat. "If you don't let me, I'll go ask Aunt Kate if she'll let me live over there. I guess she'll understand my wanting to help Pa, the way she did when Pa was young and just getting started."

To Pa, that night when Mama was out of earhot, Bron gave another reason. "I couldn't say it in front of her, but I want to be home with Mama while the kids are in school. The baby's due in less than three months, Pa, and you know what Mama's like. She'll be standing on stepladders trying to work off excess energy by scrubbing the ceiling, if somebody doesn't stop her."

Pa, who's more broadminded than Mama anyway, saw the point and gave in with the proviso that he was going to escort Bron to and from the telephone company every night. Bron submitted with only token argument, since she was more scared about being on the trolleys alone at night than she intended to admit.

Bron started working nights the very next evening, and the following afternoon she sallied forth in her best suit to pretend she was an applicant at the city's other secretarial schools. In her absence, Aunt Kate came to call. Mama's mood was not helped by Aunt Kate's opening remark. "Pretty sad pass we've come to when I have to rely on the local grapevine to find out my own brother's undertaking a new profession."

"Suppose," Mama said sweetly, seething, "you tell me exactly what you're talking about, Kate."

"I'm talking about the fact I had to learn of this schoolteaching notion from Emma Jane Latham at Ladies' Aid this afternoon," Aunt Kate snapped tartly. "I nearly died of embarrassment. It was perfectly obvious to those cats I didn't know a thing about it, even though I did my best to cover. Evie, I do think you might have had the courtesy to tell me first, even if Edward was too busy."

Mama was so mad she was hard put to remember she

was still feeling grateful to Aunt Kate for nursing Missy and Marnie. She relieved her feelings on me as soon as Aunt Kate was gone. "Have to tell everything you know to that fool boy? No conception of private family business!"

I thanked my stars that Kenneth had had the discretion not to mention at home the fact that Pa had lost his job. Mama would have killed me.

Don't ask me why, maybe because she'd had the satisfaction of getting Mama's dander up, or maybe because Pa'd gone over in the evening and soothed her down, but the next afternoon Aunt Kate telephoned as sweet as pie. She wanted Bronwyn to accompany her and Sourpuss Sadie to, of all things, a Suffragette Tea. Another old maid teacher who was supposed to go had backed out, and Aunt Kate was stuck with the ticket. Mama told me about it when I arrived home late from school. The afternoon was unexpectedly golden for November, so I had dawdled to socialize on Anne's side lawn.

"Did Bronwyn go?" I asked with interest.

"Yep. Doing her good deed for the week," Mama said wryly. "Suffrage. What in tarnation do you suppose Kate will take up next?"

Bron was dead asleep when I left for school next morning, but when I came home in the afternoon she was having tea with Pa and Mama in the kitchen. Or rather, Pa and Mama were sitting and sipping while Bron paced the floor. She was full of yesterday's meeting. A very famous suffragette had been the honored guest, and Bronwyn had been dazzled.

"Do you know that in the United States Constitution, women are classed with slaves, lunatics and children? It's barbaric! When they work they're paid half the salary of men in the same jobs. And most jobs they're not even allowed to have!"

"Don't holler at me about it," Pa said mildly. "I'm all for women being anything they want. Look at your Aunt Kate. She's sold real estate, run a boarding house. She did office work way back when hardly any women did, to help me through college. In fact, she's offered to come help me with the school. Be my registrar and bookkeeper."

"Edward Pierce Sterling, don't you dare!" Mama sat up very straight. "Need any help, you come to me, you hear?"

Pa apparently didn't want to get into discussing that, so he murmured something noncommittal, grabbed his cup, and beat an exit to his study. I turned to Bron.

"So you had fun at the meeting?"

Bron got off her soapbox and sat down at the table, blushing faintly. "It was queer. Being there with Aunt Kate and Miss Albright, as a—a social equal, sort of."

I knew what she meant. Mr. Albright had been after Bron again to come to his house for dinner, but so far she'd found excuses to avoid it.

"Hmm," Mama said, and looked at Bron, and Bron flushed again and got up and refilled her teacup very briskly.

"I forgot to tell you, Mama. Mr. Albright's offered to take turns with Pa, escorting me home from work at night, if you don't mind."

"Suppose it wouldn't hurt," Mama said deliberately. "Old as your Pa is, and a father, too."

"He's not so old," Bron flared. "I—oh, Mama, I haven't time to talk about it now! I have to get dressed for work."

She flounced out, and when I ambled upstairs casually I wasn't able to pump her either. In fact I was told in no uncertain terms to mind my own business.

So after that Mr. Albright alternated with Pa in bringing Bron home from work in the small hours of the morning. And a week later Aunt Kate invited herself for tea, and in a very solicitous voice posed the question of propriety to Mama. "He is a widower, Evie. It's known he has been taking Bronwyn out socially. Folks are apt to think she's setting her cap for him by getting him into a compromising situation. Do you think it's wise?"

"By folks you mean Sadie Albright," Mama said irritably. "Sure we can rely on you, Kate, to reassure her."

After that Pa and Mama had a couple of low-voiced conferences in the kitchen, which we kids weren't supposed to hear. Mama was on the spot. Mr. Albright was Pa's best friend, and highly respected. They couldn't insult him by suggesting the need for a chaperone. On the other hand, he indubitably *was* courting Bronwyn, who was impulsive, self-supporting and not an icicle. Mama compromised by beating around the bush with Bronwyn, trying to find out what her feelings were and at the same time advocating discretion. It was both funny and pathetic seeing Mama trying to be diplomatic. As for Bron, she attempted righteous indignation mixed with lofty disdain, and ended by angrily bursting into tears.

I wasn't about to tell Mama, but Bronwyn herself was finding having Mr. Albright escort her home a problem. I knew this because one night, when they arrived, I just happened to be out in the hall in an admirable location to hear the front porch conversation. It was a dilly. Mr. Albright was trying to talk her into giving up night work. Unfortunately the reasons he put forth were all colored with masculine chivalry and protection, and Bron was still on fire about equality for women. She stormed inside and slammed the door in the poor man's face.

Women's rights were definitely in the air. There was a big rally downtown, and Aunt Kate and Miss Albright attended, accompanied by Bron. Aunt Kate covered herself with glory by giving a lecture at church on "Feminists in the Bible." Sourpuss Sadie launched a suffragette club at school, with the blessing of Mr. Moore, who thereby brought the wrath of several parents down on his head. Despite the handicap of Miss Albright's sponsorship, the club prospered. At the next big area suffrage meeting, the members wore blue sashes over their white dresses and acted as ushers. A few of them even got their pictures in the papers. I wasn't particularly interested, and Celinda cringed at the very thought, but women's rights were right up Stella's alley.

Pa, when he spotted her in one of the newspaper pictures, just laughed. "Stella doesn't need to campaign for suffrage. That girl was born liberated!"

Aunt Kate even presumed to give Mama a lecture on women's rights, and Mama, who's pretty liberated herself, was torn between agreement and resentment. "Don't notice not having the vote's ever handicapped you none, Kate."

Aunt Kate preened. "Not every woman's got my strength of character, I grant you. That's why they need help. Take yourself, Evie. A woman should have the right not to be having a child at your age."

That did it. Mama might have her private thoughts about Whatsitsname's arrival, but she was not about to allow anybody else to voice them. She stood up, breathing fire. "Guess I have a right to whatever children I want! Right to decide who's welcome in my own house, too. You keep your nose out of our affairs, Kate Sterling, or you just stay home!"

So November moved along, and what with women's suffrage, and Pa and Mr. Albright in a ferment of school plans, and Mama in a flurry of fall housecleaning, we had a right lively time. Gramps had gone back to Pennsylvania as soon as the quarantine was lifted, and re-

fused to budge again till Christmas, but Aunt Annie and
Uncle Will wrote from Stamford with astonishing news.
They were coming down to visit for Thanksgiving, and
they had adopted twins! A boy and a girl, about Peter's
age!

The news threw Mama into an additional orgy of
home renovation. She even decided to upholster a couple of chairs. Bronwyn was involved in the fruitless task
of trying to get Mama to let *her* do the heavy work; she
was also acting as Pa's secretary, and going around with
him to inspect possible school locations, and brushing
up on her shorthand, and working nights for the telephone company, not to mention coping with the Mr.
Albright situation afterwards. This was also complicated by the fact that Mr. Grimes finally got around
to inviting her out. She went, too, and when Mr.
Albright found out he didn't look any too pleased. The
result was that Bron was losing weight, which made her
look more than ever like a romantic heroine, and did
nothing to improve her Sterling disposition.

We all needed a diversion, and an unexpected one arrived in the middle of the month. The Elks Club spon-
sored a traveling carnival as a money-making project for
their charity fund. Needless to say, the little kids began
clamoring to go just as soon as they heard the news. The
older crowd acted as if they were above it all, but I noticed that Ben and a lot of the other boys cut school the
afternoon of the carnival to go help the men set it up.
Even Kenneth went over, after school was out, instead
of working at the store. As for Marnie, who was finally
being allowed out in limited circulation again, she didn't
turn up home till we were half through dinner. She was
covered with grease and dirt, minus her coat, and sub-
limely happy, and Mama near had a fit.

It had been decided that the family would attend the
carnival in a body, accompanied by such hangers-on as

Ken, Jimmy Breidenbach and Mr. Albright, and that Mama would bring the little kids home after an hour while Pa stayed on with the rest of us. Bron had the evening off from work, and she was in a reckless mood and looking very pretty. As soon as we reached the carnival, Peter and Missy began pestering for rides, and candied apples, and cotton candy, and Ben went off with Doug, and Marnie and Jimmy disappeared on mischief of their own. Ken and I bumped into the Molloys and went around with them.

After awhile it started getting cold, so we adjourned to the refreshment tent for cocoa. There we found Bron and Mama, both of whom had problems. Pa had gone off with Peter and Missy, and Mama was impatient to get them home. Bronwyn had bumped into Mr. Grimes, who had given her a gaudy doll which he had won, and Mr. Albright did not look happy. Mr. Albright was obviously trying to detach Bron from the bosom of the family, and Bron just as obviously was trying to avoid it. He finally suggested a ride on the Ferris Wheel.

Bron shuddered. "I'm scared to death of those things," she admitted, and added, fatally, "I'm surprised you're interested in going on them at your age!"

Too late, she realized what she'd said. Mr. Albright looked grim and turned away. All of a sudden Mama slapped the table and stood up. "*I'm* not too old. Always wanted to try one of those things. Come on, Mr. A., you can take me up!"

Poor Mr. Albright was really in a spot, because delicacy forbade all the things he obviously wanted to say. And so when Pa finally returned, he saw his best friend and his *enceinte* wife atop a gaily lighted Ferris Wheel, while at its base his eldest daughter sat suffering from a bad case of foot-in-mouth disease.

I found *enceinte* in my French dictionary, and it's a dandy word for Mama's delicate condition, but when I used it in school my French teacher turned a little pale.

All in all, the carnival was not what you could call a success. Peter got lost, which perturbed him nowhere near as much as it did Mama. Missy got sick from cotton candy, and Marnie caught a chill, which sent her back to bed for a few days, to her great annoyance. And Bron was in a very equivocal state, which meant that sparks were flying.

"You're going to have to do something about Mr. Albright," I advised Bron when we finally got home to bed that night.

"Why does somebody always have to *do* something!" Bron exclaimed irritably. "Why can't things ever just go on the way they are!"

" 'Cause they don't, that's all. You know what Gramps always says, 'if you're not going forward you're going backward.' Anyway, we change things ourselves, whether we mean to or not. You gave the poor man quite a jolt yourself, tonight, you know."

"I know it." Bron's brow furrowed, and she started to brush her hair like mad.

"Bron? How do you feel about him, anyway?"

"I don't know. Oh, let me be, Tish! You're getting to sound as bad as Mama!"

Perhaps as a result of that night, Bron took action in a couple of ways. She saw to it that it was Pa who escorted her home from work every night that week. She didn't rush to answer the telephone whenever it rang. And she was pretty brief to Mr. Albright over the wire when he finally got hold of her to invite her to the Opera House on Saturday night.

Bron was in a strange mood all day Saturday. Even Ben and Mama noticed it, thrown together as we all were in the final orgy of housecleaning before Thanksgiving. "What's got into her?" Ben demanded as he tacked down carpets.

Mama shook her head. "Dunno. But I'd give a piece to, I can tell you that. Suppose we'll find out when she's good and ready."

Bron came down to dinner dressed for the Opera House in her coral party dress, and Ben amused himself by trying to bait her into revelations, but she didn't respond. Finally, when Mama started dishing up the cottage pudding, Bron straightened.

"I've been putting it off all day, but I've got to tell you now before Sidney gets here and I lose my nerve. Pa, Mama—" She took a deep breath. "I told you the Telephone Company was looking for people to send out to work in their big office at the Buffalo Exposition. I put in my application the beginning of the week, and I've been accepted."

Everybody just stared. Then Mama's breath came back in a burst. "To Buffalo? Young girl alone? Out of the question!"

"Mama, it's perfectly safe! The company's very particular about having young girls of good character and family. They're taking over a boarding house just for us, and there'll be chaperones. The pay is excellent, and it will be a wonderful experience."

"How come this sudden urge to travel?" Pa asked quizzically.

"It's a wonderful opportunity. It's an honor for me to be selected. I—just think it's a good idea, that's all."

"Mr. Albright know about it yet?" Ben asked shrewdly.

"No. I'm telling him tonight—there he is now!" Bron cried thankfully, and grabbed her coat, and escaped.

There was an interesting family discussion that night, but I bet it didn't hold a candle to the one that Bron and Mr. A. had. Bron got home very late, and the way she tore off her coral dress was indicative of her state of mind. I decided the most diplomatic thing to do was pretend that I was still asleep.

It was in this highly charged condition that our family arrived at church on Sunday morning. Pa must have warned Mama to stay off Bron's back, for Mama's silence fairly quivered. Aunt Kate took one look at us and practically expired from curiosity. Even Kenneth picked up the vibrations, but I had learned my lesson and kept my big mouth shut, which was awfully hard. After church Ken walked me home, and Mr. Albright tried to walk with Bron, but he didn't get the chance. She turned him off crisply, which was mean of her considering he was a Vestryman and half the congregation was looking on. I saw him slide a folded paper into her muff before he tipped his hat formally and strode off with Junius and Miss Albright, both agog, tagging behind him.

"Well!" Mama said, eyes snapping, once we were gathered round the dinner table. "What was that all about?"

"Look at that!" Bron wailed, and plunked down the paper Mr. Albright had passed. Pa and Mama observed a decent reticence, but Ben and Marnie, not hampered by delicacy, promptly read it aloud with suitable dramatics. It was a two-page poem, the refrain of each verse a variation on the same theme: "This poor old heart will fill with woe/If Bronwyn goes to Buffalo."

It was not the world's greatest poetry, but I admired the ingenuity. Even Ben whistled. "You have to give the old geezer credit, he's really in there trying!"

"He's not an old geezer!" Bronwyn blazed, and promptly burst into tears. She snatched the poem back and tucked it in her bosom.

Mama looked troubled. "Whole thing not a wise idea. Always thought so. Old enough to be your father." She realized she was on thin ice there and subsided abruptly. Pa looked from one to the other, and threw back his head and roared.

"I don't know what to tell you, Bronwyn," he said at last. "I feel like the fellow sitting on the fence between two catastrophes, not knowing which way to jump. I'll tell you this, though. *You're* sitting on a hornet's nest till you really know your own mind, and Sid Albright's not one of your tame puppies that gives up easily. He's too good a courtroom lawyer for that!"

As proof of this, Mr. Albright arrived for tea that afternoon, as cool as you please. Bron was flustered, and Mama was like a cat on a hot stove, but he just calmly picked up the argument where, apparently, they had left it off the night before when Bron slammed the door.

"I'm just trying to tell you that you should look at all the angles," he said patiently. "You want to help the family. The pay will be more there, but so will expenses. Besides, you promised to help your father set up the school. No one knows yet how long the Buffalo Exposition will run, it could last a year. And surely your mother would feel better having you with her at a time like this."

Mama's face was a study, and Bron looked torn.

"Besides," Mr. Albright pushed his advantage, "you're not used to working under those conditions, Bronwyn. I've seen how much this night work's taken out of you in two weeks, don't deny it. At least here you have a home, people to look after you if you get sick. You're free to quit your job if it proves too much. For a young girl like you to live alone among strangers, in a strange city, it's too much."

Unfortunately, Mr. Albright had forgotten he was talking to Bronwyn Sterling, the New Woman. All her temper exploded in a rush. "You think I'm too weak to take it, go ahead and say it! If I were a boy, you'd say wonderful, great initiative, go to it! I've heard you and Pa going on about the chances you both took when you were starting out, and how you wouldn't trade them for a farm! But because I'm a woman you take for granted I can't do it too. You think I'm not capable of holding down a responsible job, and taking the struggles, and making good! You're just a prejudiced male supremacist like all the rest!"

"I am not a male supremacist!" Mr. Albright yelled at her, just as if he were a member of the family. "Dangit, Bronwyn, you think I don't know you well enough by now to know you've got the brains and gumption to become anything you want? I'm not being prejudiced, I'm just being selfish! I don't want you to go to Buffalo because I'm going to be lonely here without you! I don't want you away from me that long, and I don't want to take the chance of your meeting someone else!"

There was an electric silence.

"Well," Bronwyn said, the wind knocked out of her sails. "That's different. Why didn't you say so in the first place?"

"Because you never gave me a chance to," Mr. Albright retorted. "Because I want to look noble just as much as you do. And if you're so all-fired determined to see the Buffalo Exposition, *I'll* take you to it."

"Why, Mr. Albright," Bron said shakily, "is that a proposal?"

"You bet your boots it is," Mr. Albright said grimly. "I'm making it in front of everybody so you can't wiggle out of hearing it, and because I may never get as good a chance again. How about it, Bronwyn?"

Everybody in the room held his breath.

Bronwyn got very busy tidying up the tea things. "I really do want to see the Exposition," she said in a small voice.

Pa cleared his throat, "Now that's settled, guess the rest of us have things to do. Evie, come on, I'll take you for a drive. And isn't it time you young ones left for church?"

It wasn't, but we left anyway, accompanied by Ben's whistling rendition of the appropriate music from *Lohengrin*. We stopped by Molloys' and told them the fascinating tale, and then went on down to the Parish House where I acquired an even wider audience, and for once nobody at Young People's was paying much attention to the continuing saga of Doug and Mary Lou.

After that, excitement mushroomed in all directions. In the morning Mama had the satisfaction of rendering Aunt Kate speechless with the news. Mr. Albright wanted to be married fast. "At Christmas," he said firmly, "before Bronwyn takes it into her head to change her mind." Pa decided Thanksgiving was the logical time to make the formal announcement, as if the whole neighborhood didn't know about it anyway. It was arranged that the Albrights would come to us for Thanksgiving dinner, along with Aunt Kate and the Stamford relations, and in the evening we would hold a formal reception and collation. Mama went into a tailspin of preparation, and we all thanked our stars that the house-cleaning was finished. By the time Thanksgiving Eve service at the church came along, we were all weak from labor and emotion—naturally; in our family, neither tongues nor tempers had been idle either.

In the late morning of Thanksgiving Day, Aunt Annie and Uncle Will arrived, bringing pumpkin pies and also their new family members, Leslie and Alice, who looked more than a little overwhelmed by the family furore. Peter rescued them and bore them off to the sanctity of the attic, and then the Albright contingent arrived, and Aunt Kate, and we sat down to a very strange Thanksgiving dinner. It felt decidedly queer to have my Latin teacher sitting across the table from me, not to mention Junius, who pulled on his ragged forelock and looked embarrassed. Aunt Annie and Uncle Will, thank goodness, kept conversation going, and afterwards Aunt

Annie sent Mama upstairs to rest her feet, and she came out in the kitchen with us to do the dishes; and before you knew it, dark was falling and people were arriving.

Bron and Mr. Albright had gone for a walk, during which he had presented her with a diamond the size of which rendered everybody speechless. Pa pulled a sheaf of yellow paper from his pocket and announced he had written a poem in honor of the happy occasion. You can deduce the nature of this opus from the fact that it was written in Spenserian stanzas, it started with the creation of the world, and it took five whole pages to get up to the point where he himself met Mama. After the reading, when everyone had sufficiently recovered, we moved to the dining room for chicken salad and hot biscuits and cake, amid a dazzle of cut glass and candlelight and Grandma Stryker's silver. Afterwards we gravitated back into the parlor, and sooner or later everyone gathered around the piano as always. Aunt Annie was playing with real bounce, and we launched zestfully into all the harvest and Thanksgiving hymns. Presently there was a clamor for Mr. Albright to sing the solo he had sung the night before at church.

> *Now thank we all our God, With heart and hand and voices,*
> *Who wondrous things hath done . . . .*

I was thinking contentedly what an appropriate song it was, and how lovely everything was turning out, when I happened to glance at Bronwyn, who had slipped over to stand beside our crowd in the dining room arch. She looked as though somebody'd kicked her in the stomach; her face was white, and she was staring into the future with horror-struck eyes.

"What's the matter?" I whispered swiftly. "Are you sick? You haven't changed your mind, Bron, have you?"

Bron snapped out of her trance and looked at me dazedly. "About Sidney? Certainly not! But it just hit me. Oh, Lordy, Tish, do you realize? *I'm going to be stepmother to Jughead Junius!*"

# CHAPTER X

## *December*

So Bron was going to have a Christmas wedding, and within a week everyone concerned was in a state.

Mama was still bothered by the difference in their ages, so the day after Thanksgiving she cornered Bron for one of those embarrassing woman-to-woman chats. I got caught in the middle of it, because Mama chose a time when she had Bron trapped in the kitchen with her, washing dishes from the party, and I was in the dish closet putting things away. It was really funny; here was Mama trying for once to get rid of me instead of forcing me to help, and Bron just as determined to hang onto me as a buffer between them. Finally Mama gave up, set her shoulders and launched into her little speech.

Mama pointed out that Bron would still be young when Mr. Albright was getting old; that if they had children he would be well into his sixties when their first child graduated from school. Bron retorted that Mr. Albright was still young enough to ride on Ferris wheels, and that Mama was in no position to imply he was over the hill already, after the speech she'd made to Pa about the forties being the prime of life. She also added that there'd be no more age difference between Sidney and

their prospective children than there was going to be between Pa and Whatsitsname, and that if Pa and Mama
weren't too old for that sort of thing, then why was
Sidney? At which Mama, who always gets jittery when
the birds and the bees are mentioned, decided it was
time to change the subject.

"Don't see how you expect to get everything for a
wedding in one month," she grumbled. "Right on top of
Christmas. Hardly anything in your hope chest.
Trousseau to get ready, not to mention marking linens.
Take a good year to do it proper. Me in this fool condition. Like to know where the money's coming from with
your Pa not working. Make him feel dreadful if he can't
give you a proper wedding."

You have to hand it to Mama, she was really hitting
all the bases.

"Oh, come on, Mama," Bron said patiently. "We
don't need a big wedding, nobody expects it. And as for
linens and china, aren't you forgetting Sidney has a
houseful of them already?"

Mama sniffed. "Shouldn't think you'd like starting
housekeeping with another woman's leftovers."

Bron's eyes darkened and her lips pressed tight together, and even Mama knew it was time to shut up.

"Anyway," Bron said brightly, "we can talk about the
wedding and what we need to buy when we're at
Sidney's on Sunday. You know Miss Albright insisted
we all come to dinner." Bron grimaced. Mama's reaction to the engagement couldn't hold a candle to
Sourpuss Sadie's. She had retreated into austere silence
that implied she could speak volumes if she only chose.

Fortunately she hadn't chosen to so far, and Mama
was squelched not only by Pa but also by the presence of
Aunt Annie's family. Aunt Annie made no bones about
the fact she thought that Bron and Mr. Albright were a
very romantic match. "And between you and me, Evie,"

I heard her telling Mama, "it could be the best thing ever happened in this family. That man's got a good head on his shoulders. Well off, too. Don't you let Edward be too proud to let him set him up in that secretarial school he's been talking about."

Pa's school was rapidly on the way to becoming a reality. Mr. Albright, we were discovering, was a whirlwind when he once got started. He brought over the papers he'd drawn up, forming a partnership between himself and Pa. And on Friday, while Bron was having it out with Mama about the birds and the bees, he hustled Pa downtown to have another look at the office space they'd been considering, and to sign the lease. On Saturday, while we were putting Aunt Annie and Uncle Will and the children on the train for Stamford, he and Bron managed to get off alone, and when they came back they had most of the wedding details already settled.

The wedding was to be on the afternoon of Christmas Eve, with a small home reception like the one we'd had Thanksgiving Day. "Catered," Bron said firmly. "Don't argue, Mama. I have enough money put by from my job to take care of it." Afterwards Bron and Mr. Albright would leave by train for the Parker House in Boston, from which, on the day after Christmas, they would embark on a three-week visit to Quebec, Montreal, Toronto and Buffalo.

"So she can see that Exposition she was so set on," Mr. Albright said, grinning. He was already, I swear, beginning to look about ten years younger.

Mama, of course, pretended to be annoyed that she was not consulted, but she was secretly relieved to have the wedding worries lifted clear out of her hands. As for Pa, he was just plain jubilant, not only about the wedding but about having the secretarial school business definitely settled at last.

All this meant that there was plenty to talk about when we went *en masse* to the Albright house for Sunday dinner. At least, Pa and Mr. Albright and Bron talked enough for all the rest of us, who were feeling kind of strange. Junius just sat around looking embarrassed, and Sourpuss Sadie, refusing offers of help, got the dinner on the table in frigid dignity. The embroidered damask table linen was gorgeous, but she was not a very good cook.

"Sarah made those," Sadie said when Mama admired a napkin. "Sidney's *first* wife. Spent two years making all her linens by hand. Always took such care of her lovely things . . . would hate to think of them being ruined by somebody's careless handling."

Bron's eyes shot sparks. "She didn't talk like that when Sarah was alive," she muttered to me grimly. "Sidney says she was always running her down for being extravagant, using her good things for everyday."

Pa hastily changed the subject to the secretarial school. He was going out the next day to order desks and chairs; he planned to begin running advertisements in the papers and interviewing prospective typewriting teachers. The grand opening was planned for the Wednesday after New Year's. Pa planned to teach business practice, Munson and Pitman shorthand, bookkeeping, filing and typewriting.

"And students interested in legal work will be coming down to my office," Mr. Albright said, "for a practical apprenticeship."

Miss Albright unbent to join the conversation. "Kate tells me she's coming down to act as your Registrar."

Now Mama's eyes shot sparks, as Pa looked uneasy. "Only at first," Mama said. "Till Whatsitsname's old enough to leave. Then *I'll* be doing it. Always did relish the idea of getting out of the house."

"And I'm coming down too," Bron put in quickly.

"Sidney and I have it all worked out. I'm to be Pa's secretary in the mornings. That will still leave me afternoons for housekeeping and cooking."

"Oh, I don't think you'll find there's much to do," Sadie said sweetly. "I've been managing it quite well by myself all these years."

A little alarm bell rang somewhere in a corner of my mind. I saw Bron and Mr. Albright exchange glances. "And of course," Bron went on too brightly, "sewing, and shopping." Her eyes flicked over the tall windows with their bare shutters. "New curtains."

"I've never allowed curtains in a house," Sadie said. "Unsanitary. Dust catchers."

"Sarah had green brocade draperies," Mr. Albright put in unexpectedly. "Made them herself. I always kind of liked them."

Mama decided it was time she helped Bron out. Fighting Miss Albright was exactly like battling Aunt Kate. "Tomorrow morning we'll go downtown and look at linens. Pick out material for your wedding dress, Bronwyn. And I saw some beautiful china advertised at Wanamaker's."

"Oh, I don't think you need spend any money on household things," Sadie said distinctly. "Especially now when you're short of cash. There are certainly enough *good* things here already for the four of us."

There was a ghastly silence, interrupted at last by Mr. Albright in matter-of-fact calmness. "Three people, Sadie," he said pleasantly. "My wife. My son. And me."

Bronwyn breathed again.

It took a full minute for Sadie to get her own breath back. "Do you mean to say you're putting me out of my home—after all I've given up for you all these years—all I've sacrificed . . . ."

"*My* home, Sadie," Mr. Albright said, just as pleasantly. "And nobody's putting you out. It's exactly what you want. I appreciate the sacrifice you've made these past ten years, giving up a home of your own to keep house for us. But you don't have to now, Sadie. You'll be free to live the way you like, do what you want. Land knows you've told us often enough you wished you could."

"But I didn't," Sadie said grimly. "I knew my duty. Which is more than you do, apparently. I brought up your motherless son. I've cooked and cleaned and kept house for you. Do you intend to turn all that over to a chit of a girl whose only concern's her pretty face?"

Mama looked like a mother tiger about to spring, but Bron breathed, "No, Mama! *Please!*" She was staring at her lap, and her face was very white.

"And your own son, Sidney. To a stepmother? Have you forgotten that we know what that's like?"

"I never thought our stepmother was so bad, Sadie," Mr. Albright said softly. "Come to think of it, maybe you were just plain jealous."

His voice was very quiet. It dawned on me that he was too angry to trust himself to speak. Everybody was. And then into the awful silence, unbelievably, stepped Junius. His jughandle ears were bright red and his voice was shaky, but it was definite all the same.

"I don't mind," said Junius.

Sadie stared at him. "What?"

"I said I don't mind. About a stepmother. Not if Father wants it. It couldn't be any worse than—" Junius stopped abruptly, his face matching his ears, but Sadie had gotten the message, loud and clear.

Pa drained his coffee cup and set it down firmly. "Think it's time we were going, Sidney. I'm sure you and your sister would rather talk this out in private."

"Oh, no." Miss Albright stood up very tall. "Oh, no. Far be it from me to drive you from my *brother's* house. *I'm* leaving. I'll be out of the house in an hour. You can send my bags after me later." She stalked out, banging the door behind her.

Bron fled into Mr. Albright's arms. "Oh, Sidney! It was even worse than I expected. I'm so glad it's over!"

Pa looked at the two of them and grinned. "Like I said, it's time the rest of us went home. Come on, Evie. I'm getting kind of worn out by all this excitement."

"Worn out!" Mama said, ruffling her feathers. "Better not be! Got a school to get opened and a wedding planned! And soon's they're over, it'll be time to get ready for Whatsitsname! Edward Sterling, you don't dare be tired!"

There's nothing like having somebody else *against* a thing to get Mama *for* it.

So Pa and Mama took the younger kids home, and Ben and I went down to church to Young People's where we filled Ken and Celinda and the other kids in on as much of the story as was repeatable outside our own four walls. We were so busy talking we let Mr. Derbyshire get away with roping us into putting on a church Christmas pageant on the Sunday before Christmas.

We found out the next day that Sourpuss Sadie had taken refuge with our Aunt Kate, who had promptly offered her a home. "It's a perfect arrangement," Pa said when he heard. "They'll have a field day telling each other how selfish we all are; but the minute one starts sympathizing with the other, they'll each fly to the defense of their own families and from then on, we'll be in the clear. They'll have a fine time fighting with each other then, and they'll both be off our necks."

Things moved fast after that. Always before, December had been marked off by Christmas preparations: the day we baked cookies, the day we made the door wreath, the day we bought the tree. This year there were other symbols of time progressing. On Monday Bron and Mama went downtown and bought material for the wedding dress, white silk muslin with a fine satin stripe. Mama was bound and determined to make that wedding dress herself, no matter what. She also bought grey georgette chiffon and lace to concoct herself a dress; it was going to be heavy on draperies and floating panels to conceal her expanded middle. Pa went out and bought Mama a gorgeous new grey coat that flared widely below a sealskin collar, and a matching sealskin muff, to wear in church during the ceremony. Now that the school business was definitely settled he was feeling so jubilant he was downright reckless. Already there had been several applications from prospective students, and he had hired a brisk young man to be the typing teacher. He intended to teach shorthand and dictation himself.

The engravers, spurred on by Mr. Albright, rushed the invitations through, and there were endless addressing sessions around the dining room table. We all got stuck for this except Marnie, who escaped as a result of blotting ink on two of her first three tries.

"Too bad I didn't think of that," Ben grumbled, making a face as he licked a stamp.

"Too bad we can't enclose our Christmas cards," I added. "Think of having to write all these same addresses twice!"

Ben shrugged. "Why don't we just forget about the cards? They don't have anything to do with the meaning of Christmas, anyway."

I stared at him. "Ben Sterling, of course we can't forget them. Why, they're a part of Christmas!"

"According to who?" Ben asked with maddening logic. "You know, when you come down to it, most of our Christmas celebrations are downright pagan customs."

"Now don't you two start fighting," Mama interrupted. "Don't have time. Nothing especially sacred about Christmas cookies, either, but I notice that don't stop you from wolfing them down." She looked pointedly at Ben's hand, reaching out toward the plate that she had just arranged.

Bron was still going to work nights for another two weeks before quitting her job, and during the day she divided her time between wedding preparations and helping Pa set up the school. Mr. Albright complained that he hardly ever got to see her, but Bron laughed at him.

"When could you! All your spare time's being swallowed up by Pa!"

Everybody was amused over the fact that Mr. Albright's best friend was about to become not only his business partner but his father-in-law as well.

When we got home from school in the afternoon, we never knew what we were going to find. Celinda came over whenever she could escape from her mother, and Anne and Stella formed the habit of dropping by almost every afternoon. They found the excitement at our place a lot more fun than the Christmas chores awaiting them at their own homes. Mama, who was no fool, soon pressed them into service, pulling out basting and putting in hems. She even hoodwinked Anne into helping polish silver. As for Marnie and Jimmy Breidenbach, who were bored with the sewing and too clumsy to be trusted with wedding activities, they had a fine time carrying out the family's Christmas preparations to suit themselves. The tree they came home with would have fit in the house only if Mama had let them cut a hole in the parlor ceiling.

"Have to cut the top off it," Mama said. "Get Ben to do it when he gets home. Where *is* that boy, anyway?"

"Probably over at my house," Stella said unexpectedly, "studying with Larry for their philosophy exam. He's been there a lot lately." She hesitated. "Is Ben mad or anything? When he was over yesterday, he hardly said two words to the family, and he looked like a thundercloud."

"Been like that at home, too, come to think of it," said Mama. "When he's *been* home. Give him a piece of my mind when I catch him. Neglecting his chores."

"He's probably worrying about the philosophy exam," Stella said quickly. "Larry says they're awfully hard. I heard them arguing about some theory or other, and I couldn't understand a word they were saying." Since Stella's brainpower was already legendary in the school, we appreciated the import of this statement.

"Suppose I daren't jump on him then," Mama said ruefully, contemplating the satin ribbons she was sewing on the wedding gown. "Hope that test's going to be over soon. Work for him to do."

"That's not all he's forgotten," I said. "He never showed up at Christmas pageant rehearsal yesterday afternoon either." Mama and I exchanged puzzled glances. It was a tradition in our family that however much you might sluff in family responsibilities, you were honor-bound to respect commitments made to others.

Ben didn't show up for the rehearsal on Sunday, either, and Mr. Derbyshire was not pleased. I suspected that when he'd first handed the pageant assignment to Young People's, he'd been expecting Bron to run it. That was before he knew about the wedding. Now of course it was out of the question, and Mr. Derbyshire was stuck with directing the thing himself. Normally he was a dear and dignified old soul, but under the holiday pressures, he was growing decidedly harried, and he was no end annoyed with Ben. Ben was scheduled to play Joseph, and he had now missed two rehearsals, and so, needless to say, had his dear pal Doug, who was supposed to be a king.

"This is most disturbing," Mr. Derbyshire kept saying, through the ravages of the rehearsal. "Most disturbing indeed."

"It's like Doug not to show up," Ken said when we discussed the situation during refreshment break between pageant rehearsal and Young People's meeting. "I never did think Doug would go through with it. But I'm kind of surprised at Ben."

I decided it would be strategic to have a little talk with Ben before Mama got wind of what was going on.

This was easier said than done. Ben, like the rest of us, knows how to be a slippery eel when he wants to avoid encounters. I finally cornered him in the coal room one night when he went down to stoke the furnace. Ben informed me in no uncertain terms that any truancy of his was none of my darn business.

"It'll be everybody's business if it gets back from Mr. Derbyshire to Pa and Mama. You know how Pa feels about church. And all Mama needs is something like that to make her really blow. She's running round like a hen with its head off, already."

"Pa's going to have to face the fact that not everybody agrees with his church sentiments, one of these days," Ben said tersely.

"What do you mean by that?"

"I don't mean anything. Why do you have to catch me up on everything? I just don't want to be in that stupid pageant, is all."

"Then why didn't you tell Mr. Derbyshire so?"

"I tried, believe me. It's impossible to say no to that man! He only hears what he wants to hear. Maybe that's how he manages . . . ." His voice trailed off.

"Manages what?" There was no answer. I shot an arrow into the dark. "Ben, does this have anything to do with being worried about philosophy class?"

I must have landed close to target. Ben whirled around. "And just where did you pick up that piece of information?"

"Stella said you'd been studying with her brother. She thought you seemed upset."

"Don't you females have anything better to do than sit around slinging the mud? You're getting as bad as Mary Lou Hodge!"

"Ben, that's not fair. Stella was worried. She wondered if you were mad at her or something."

The anger seemed to drain out of Ben. "I'm not mad at anybody. Except maybe myself. Oh, why can't you let me be!" He started swinging the coal shovel doggedly, and I beat a discreet and thoughtful retreat upstairs.

I forgot about Ben's behavior in the excitement of the rest of the week. Wedding presents were starting to arrive—silver candlesticks, vegetable dishes and a coffee service; bowls and pitchers of glittering cut crystal; laces and embroidered linens. A Wedgwood tea set came from Aunt Annie and Uncle Will; a chocolate service of translucent china, decorated with Japanese ladies in rickshaws, from Aunt Kate. Junius even sent a gift, a Chinese bowl, adorned with Chrysanthemums and a vivid-plumaged bird.

Mama, by dint of killing herself in her usual manner, had finished the wedding dress and it hung, wrapped in a sheet, in the spare-room closet. We were absolutely forbidden to show it to anyone. "Bad luck," Mama said firmly. This seemed kind of silly in view of the fact that most of the girls and our female relations had had a hand in its construction. Mama wasn't so stuffy about the rest of the trousseau, or the clothes for the wedding party. She had made me a maid-of-honor dress of green velvet, the most grown-up thing I'd ever owned, and similar ones of dark crimson for Marnie and Bron's friend Selma, who were bridesmaids. Since it was a Christmas wedding, we were going to wear white fur toques and muffs adorned with single red poinsettias. Mama and Bron had concocted the furpieces out of an outmoded lapin coat of Mama's. I modeled my ensemble for the girls after school on the Friday, before Christmas week, and they were duly admiring.

"It'll be lovely if we get a real white Christmas," Stella said. "Speaking of Christmas, Mama says she'll take us downtown shopping with her tomorrow if we want to go."

Since none of us was allowed yet to travel alone on the trolleys to lower Manhattan, the idea was accepted with acclaim. It also had the added advantage of getting me out of the house. The family temper was accelerating now that the wedding was only one week off, and I had had enough of the "do this, do that" which constituted Mama's current idea of holiday preparations.

Saturday was grey and lowering, threatening snow. Trolleys were crowded, and stores were thronged with shoppers. Christmas carols rang in the air. It was kind of nice to find Christmas at last; I hadn't realized how much the wedding had been drowning it out for me. Mrs. Molloy treated us all to lunch at Delmonico's, which added the crowning touch. By the time Anne and Stella and Celinda and I, clinging to straphandles and laden with bundles, squeezed into the trollery for the long trip home, we were all in decidedly silly moods.

"Good thing Christmas comes only once a year," Mrs. Molloy said, twinkling.

The snow had become heavy enough for the little kids to pelt us with snowballs when we reached the house, and it continued through the night. By morning a thin film of ice crusted the paths beaten by neighbors on their way to early Mass, and Pa decided Mama was not to risk the walk to church. "All we need at this point is for you to fall on the ice," he said firmly.

"Edward Sterling, I'd never do no such thing!" Mama protested. But she didn't protest too hard. I had an idea she was more weary than she was willing to let on.

"I'll stay home with you," Ben said quickly.

Mama sat up straight. "You will not. No invalid. Go to church where you belong."

"I said I'm not going," Ben said stubbornly, and vanished outside to shovel walks for the rest of us; Pa looked at Mama, and jammed his pipe in his mouth as if he'd like to say a lot of things that wouldn't sound too good on a Sunday morning.

In church the Advent candles burned in their wreath of pine, and we sang Christmas carols. I could feel the Christmas spirit starting to burst within me in small tentative firecrackers of joy. From across the aisle Kenneth winked at me during the sermon, and on our way out he managed to come up behind me. "Pretty posh," he said, referring to the fur muff I was carrying, which Mama would have killed me for using before the wedding had she been there to see. "Say, do you still have to work on the wedding stuff today? I was thinking we could get the crowd together. Go caroling when it's getting dark."

"We've got pageant rehearsal this afternoon, don't you remember?"

"Oh, rats," Ken said inelegantly. "I don't see why we have to go to so many, anyway. I'm just a shepherd. I don't say anything."

"I'm an angel. I have one whole line."

"Oh, well," Ken said, "it's only one more week. I suppose we can stand it. But I feel like a fool wrapped in that stupid sheet."

"Celinda's the one who's really having problems. Her parents don't see why she had to be in an Episcopal pageant anyway."

Ken grinned. "It's just like her parents to think their church has a monopoly on the Nativity!"

Mr. Derbyshire had cast Celinda as Mary, and at rehearsal that afternoon I could understand why. It was the look in her eyes—vulnerable, shadowed with sorrow, as if she "kept all these things and pondered them in her heart." That look came partly from her background and partly from pure terror; Celinda was panic-stricken at the idea of acting and had submitted only because Mr. Derbyshire had promised her a real live baby to hold. Celinda is crazy about babies.

"Too bad Whatsitsname isn't here yet so we could use him," Celinda said, practicing with a doll from the kindergarten classroom. Celinda was convinced Whatsitsname was going to be a boy, because girls outnumbered the boys in our family already.

"Too bad a certain other member of our family didn't choose to show up," I muttered grimly. Ben again was conspicuous by his absence, the more so because even Doug and Mary Lou were there. Everybody was, for there was only one more rehearsal, next Saturday afternoon. Doug was glowering, but he was present. As for Mary Lou, the sight of her as an angel would have convulsed me if I hadn't been so mad at Ben. Mr. Derbyshire was distressed, so much so that he sent me over to the rectory to telephone home, and that only made things worse, because I found Mama had been suffering from the delusion that Ben was down at church. What with calming Mama down and wracking my brains, I went back to rehearsal absolutely boiling.

"Calm down," Ken told me. "You're out of character for an angel."

"I don't feel angelic. I could cut his throat!"

"So could Mr. Derbyshire. He's run out of guys to corral, so if Ben won't do it, there just might be no Joseph."

That did it. When rehearsal, such as it was, was over, and the rest of the kids went out caroling in the interval before Young People's meeting, I plodded doggedly home. It was hard walking through the gathering drifts, but that only added fuel to my fire. When I reached the house, all was silent. Mama was taking a nap; Bron was over at Mr. Albright's, chaperoned by Pa; the little kids were out playing in the snow. So much the better!

I had a pretty good idea of where to start my hunt. The attic door was locked, but we kids had long known how to pick it silently, and when I sneaked the door open cautiously, a whiff of tobacco smoke confirmed my suspicions.

"Ben, I'm coming up, and I know you're there, so don't bother to hide." I locked the door behind me firmly. The last thing I wanted was Mama horning in.

Ben was lying on the broken sofa, smoking a cigarette, eating an apple and reading a penny-dreadful novel. He might as well have been wearing a sign saying, "Hands Off!" in letters two feet high.

"If you're planning to read me a lecture, you can just butt out, because I'm not in the mood." He buried his face in his book.

I sat down on a moth-eaten pillow and decided I'd better not mention the pageant straight off. "Pa was pretty mad about you cutting church this morning. He didn't say much, but you know how he gets." Ben didn't answer. I nodded at his book, the cover of which featured a bosomy lady tied to a railroad track on which a train was rapidly approaching. "I kind of gave him the impression you had to study for that philosophy exam."

"Philosophy!" Ben tossed the book away and stood up, jamming his hands in his pockets. "I wish I'd never heard of that darn class."

This was something new. "I thought you loved it. You like Mr. Grimes . . . ."

"I do. I did. Oh, Tish, get lost, will you!"

"Nope," I said firmly. "Not till you tell me what the dickens is going on. I'm sick and tired of covering up for you when I don't know what it is I'm covering."

"Nobody asked you to!"

"Tough. You're stuck with it. So you might as well tell me, 'cause I'm not leaving till you do." I let that sink in while I searched for clues. "Mr. Grimes. Philosophy class. You're mad at the world and you're avoiding going near the church. What's the missing link?" No answer. "Mr. Derbyshire is really going to be in a spot if you don't play Joseph, because he hasn't anyone else to do it."

"That's his hard luck. I didn't ask him for the part."

"You're going to feel pretty silly facing him at the wedding rehearsal next Saturday night, if you don't show up for pageant practice in the afternoon."

"Maybe," Ben said, "I won't be in the wedding party either."

I couldn't believe my ears. "You're the bride's brother. It would just kill Pa and Mama. You've got to be an usher."

"No, I don't," Ben said bluntly. "Not if I think it's phony. Pa will understand; that is, if it gets to the point where I've got to tell him."

It dawned on me slowly that we were talking about something a whole lot bigger than a Christmas pageant, bigger even than Bronwyn's wedding.

"Ben," I said, "it's the church, isn't it? You're avoiding all the things going on at church. Ben, why?"

"Because if you must know, I just don't want to go to church any more."

"Why not?"

"Because I don't believe in it," Ben said. "Because I'm not so sure that I'm a Christian."

I stared at him. "Of course you're a Christian. Everybody is!"

"That's a dumb thing to say, and you know it."

"Ben Sterling, you know perfectly well what I mean. We've been brought up to be Christians. You've been confirmed."

"That," Ben said ironically, "doesn't necessarily prove a thing." He rose and walked restlessly to the window, staring out at the Christmas-card street. "I'm not even sure I believe in God any more."

I was kind of surprised the heavens didn't fall. But they didn't, nothing happened except my stomach lurched and my back felt cold and the silence hung in the air between us like untouched bells.

"Ben," I said slowly when I could find my voice, "what happened? You never used to talk like this. You went to Sunday School and church, same as the rest of us. What's changed?" I looked at him. "You're not happy about it either. I can tell."

"I grew up, is what happened," Ben said angrily. "I learned too much. Did it ever occur to you that having brains like ours could be a curse? We *think* too much!"

"Maybe if you talk to Mr. Grimes . . . ."

"Mr. Grimes!" Ben gave a short laugh. "What do you think started me thinking? Him and his advanced philosophy classes! They opened my eyes. And I couldn't go back to blind faith now even if I wanted to." He looked at me. "Why am I telling you all this? No point in ripping off your rose-colored glasses. You keep going to church if you get anything from it, Tish. I wouldn't wish this on you."

"Maybe," I said carefully, "if you told me what happened in philosophy class, we could kind of work it out together."

Ben shrugged. "I don't want your disillusionment on my conscience. Anyway, you wouldn't understand."

"Try me," I said. And waited.

Ben looked at me, and rubbed his neck, and finally sat down beside me. "When we're little—we're told all this stuff. They teach it to us, before we're old enough to understand, and expect us to believe it. And we do. Only in life, as we get older, we're expected to question. To look at all sides of an issue. To ask for proof, and facts, before we decide what's truth. In everything except religion! There we're told a lot of—fairy tales, that won't hold up scientifically, and we're expected to swallow it whole. Only when you find out there *are* other sides to something, you just can't do that any more. Trying to find out what's really truth is like only being able to look at shadows of it cast on the wall of a cave!"

"Oh," I said. "You mean Plato's concept of reality."

I must admit that, even concerned as I was, I could not help but relish Ben's reaction. My brother was staring at me as if he'd just discovered his idiot sister was the genius of the century.

"Where on earth did you ever hear of that?"

"I get around," I said with dignity. "Kenneth and I read a lot, you know. We discuss philosophy with Mr. Grimes, too."

"Hasn't it ever shaken your beliefs?"

"It's made me think things through more," I answered honestly. "A lot of times, things I thought I knew I found I'd never really understood. But it was me who'd been wrong, not what I'd been taught. I've never been tempted to throw the baby out with the bath water."

"That's just what I am doing," Ben said. "The Christmas Baby, anyway. I just can't believe that stuff any more. Did you know nobody really knows when Jesus was supposed to have been born, anyway? The early church just took over the Roman Saturnalia, which was a real pagan orgy for the winter solstice. They took over Easter from the pagans, too, especially the Druids. Did you know that every culture has a death and resurrection myth? How can we be sure Christianity's not just another of them? And look at how we celebrate Christmas. How many people think of it as a religious festival? It's all spending money trying to impress people, and a lot of fancy pagan decorations, and often as not a whole lot of family fights. It's a great big gimme gimme contest!"

"Ben, that's not fair."

"I can't believe that stuff about virgin birth and angels and shepherds any more," Ben said. "Believe me, it would be a lot easier on me if I could. But I just can't. And I'm not going to sit in church if I can't believe it, not even to please Pa and Mama."

"I'll bet that lots of other people do."

"Because other people are a bunch of hypocrites doesn't mean I have to be one," Ben said, and went downstairs and started shoveling walks like mad, while I sat alone in the attic and wondered what I should have said.

Ben's argument had made a lot of sense. I didn't agree with it, but I could understand it. It upset me, too, only not in the way that Ben had feared. I didn't lose my faith, but I did start worrying whether I was stupid not to.

For good or ill, my faith—in God, in anything—was not a matter of logic. I believed, not because something could be proved, but because I *knew* it in my blood and bones. A lot of people had told me I was too gullible that way, or stubborn, or closed-minded. I started wondering whether I ought to listen to them.

I did go to Mr. Grimes the next day and ask for an explanation of Saturnalia and Easter, and what he told me made a lot of sense, about how pagans converting to Christianity had been reluctant to give up these yearly festivals in which lay deep family ties of loving and rejoicing, so the Christian church had taken them over and transformed them into celebrations of the Christian year. But it was Mr. Grimes' parting remark that struck the deepest. "Remember, Tish, a myth is not a fairy tale, contrary to popular belief. It's a story illustrating a deep-seated truth about man and God that's so important that the story, even if it's fact, is only the vehicle of the deeper truth."

I clung to that like a talisman, for Ben's question, "How can we *know?*" haunted me.

For the first time, I was beginning to understand the meaning of Pilate's, "What is Truth?"

# CHAPTER XI

## *December*

I wished to god that Ben's crisis of faith hadn't happened at that particular time of year—or, if it had to, that he hadn't shared it with me. I'd opened a Pandora's box I couldn't close the lid on, and all I really wanted to do was hide my head in the sand. And if that was being an ostrich, then that was just the way it was.

The week before Christmas was upon us now, a time that was always spectacular around our household. I should explain that Christmas in our house is decidedly not characterized by peace on earth, good will to men. There's something about the holiday pressures that bring out the Sterling tempers in us all, even Mama who's only a Sterling by marriage. Everybody wants to do his own private thing in everybody else's way; there are more fights per hour than at any other time of year, and it's all a part and parcel of what Christmas is to us, and we wouldn't have it any other way.

This year everything was heightened by the wedding and Mama's delicate condition, so we didn't have time for any proper fights, and when one started, we generally remembered we couldn't afford the indulgence and clamped the lid on tight. But as always, by some miracle

of the season, everything got done. The house was
cleaned, the silver polished, the gowns for the wedding
party and Bron's trousseau finished. Bron had quit her
job and was floating in a daze. Mama discovered she
hadn't done a thing about Christmas presents and was
indulging in an orgy of Christmas shopping. She was
having so much fun getting in a dither that she forgot to
be self-conscious about Whatsitsname. Whatitsname
was still kicking her at inconvenient intervals, but
Mama'd just give her middle an absentminded pat, tell
it to behave itself, and go on about her business. She
forgot herself and did that in Wanamaker's one afternoon, and the expression on the salesclerk's face near
put us in hysterics.

In school the Christmas spirit pervaded everything.
The music classes went caroling in the halls. One of the
English classes was rehearsing scenes from *A Christmas
Carol* for an assembly program. Nobody was doing
much work, which wasn't unusual, but for a change we
got away with it. With all except Miss Albright, that is.
Sourpuss Sadie scheduled a Latin test for the last half-
day of school.

"I think she's taking out her spite on us," Celinda
grumbled to me when that little item was announced.
Celinda knew all about how Miss Albright felt about
Bron's engagement.

We sang Christmas carols, and snow fell, and on
Thursday afternoon the kids came over to our house
and helped with the Christmas decorations—all but the
tree, for Missy was still under the impression that Santa
Claus took care of that. And through it all I realized that
I'd been growing up, these past months, more than I'd
realized; more than I wanted to, perhaps. I couldn't take
refuge in fantasy and illusion any more. Under the
carols, and the candles, and the Nativity scene on the
mantelpiece, and the way my heart hurt me when I saw

the happiness in Bron's eyes, Ben's words throbbed. *How can we know there's any meaning to it? How can we know there is a God?*

It didn't spoil my faith, but it sure as hell did spoil my joy.

Snow fell steadily all Thursday night, and on Friday we awakened to a world of ice. The trees were sheathed with it, their branches clinked together like tinkling crystal fingers above our heads as we set off for school, our breaths making frosty clouds before our faces. This was the last day of school before vacation, which would commence at one o'clock, and it consisted mainly of the Dickens' *Christmas Carol* assembly. I'd always loved that story, but today, as I sat there between Celinda and Stella, that little demon of doubt nibbled at my mind, making me wonder whether anything could be quite that simple.

When I mentioned this thought to Mrs. Owens after school, she just said drily, "Dickens didn't live a life exactly conducive of optimism, yet he still could write it." We didn't have English class on account of early dismissal, but the usual bunch of girls had ended up in Mrs. Owens' room for a last pre-holiday visit. We were still in the middle of comparing holiday plans when Ken stuck his head in and announced he was waiting to walk me home.

"Just like that, huh?" I demanded, flustered, for Cee and Stella were grinning knowingly.

"Just like that," Kenneth said calmly, and scooped up my notebook and pointed me toward the door.

"Oh, go ahead," Stella said good-naturedly. "We know you two are spooning." And I turned bright red, and Ken glowered, and we didn't say too much on the way to our respective cloakrooms.

A cold wind struck at us as we emerged from the building and seemed to drive the cobwebs from our

brains. "I'm sorry if I embarrassed you," Kenneth said.
I noticed that his ears were red. "I was getting tired of
waiting. I thought maybe we could go sleigh riding this
afternoon."

"Oh, Ken, I can't. Bron's having a tea party to show
off her wedding presents."

"Oh," Ken said, and we walked the next couple of
blocks in silence. When we got to my corner, he stopped
abruptly. "We never seem to see each other lately," he
blurted out. "You're always wrapped up in the wedding,
or Christmas, or stuff like that."

"Ken! You were over yesterday, helping us deco-
rate!"

"Sure, along with everybody else!" Ken hesitated.
"Look, you're not trying to avoid me, are you? Or mad
at me? It seems like you're a million miles away."

I stared at him open-mouthed, and for the first time I
got a clear idea of the damage my internal preoccupation had been causing.

The expression on my face must have given Ken his
answer, for his brow cleared. "I just wondered," he said.
"A fellow likes to know where he stands."

"I'm not mad," I said. "At least not at you. I'm just
—confused."

"About us?"

"No. Well, yes, maybe. But that's not the main
thing."

"What is?"

"I can't tell you." I stared at the snow and could feel
the walls rising between us, ten feet high.

"There you go again," Ken said. He looked at me.
"Does it by any chance have anything to do with Ben?"

I didn't answer. There were times when Ken could
read me all too well. "I thought so," he said. "Even
Doug says Ben's been acting weirdish lately."

"My brother is not weirdish!"

"Okay, okay, don't get all het up!" Ken answered mildly. "I'm not going to fight with you about it. Look, do I get to take you to the Glee Club Concert tonight or not?"

"You get to take me," I said grimly, "even if I have to hogtie Mama first to get permission.

And I was going to get Ben to the pageant and the wedding, I added mentally, if I had to hogtie him too. My uncertainty and depression were rapidly hardening into energy and action. But I would worry about Ben and his crisis of the soul tomorrow. First things came first, and I'd had enough of a shock to convince me I didn't want to let anything, not Ben nor Christmas nor the wedding nor my own confusion, do harm to my relationship with Ken. That, at least, was a rock that I could build on.

When I reached home, Bron's tea party was well in progress and the house was full of females, friends of hers and mine and of our parents. Ken's mother was there, and Aunt Kate, and Mrs. Breidenbach and Mrs. Molloy. The girls themselves were coming over later. I sneaked upstairs and redid my hair, admired myself in the plaid dress Bron had bequeathed to me, and went downstairs to play waiting maid for Mama.

Bronwyn was the center of attention, naturally, but when I went to the kitchen to refill the teapot she pulled herself away from her admiring circle and followed, shutting the door behind her.

"Tish, what's the matter with Ben?" I stared at her and she hurried on. "Sidney says Ben said something to Junius about maybe not being in the wedding. I didn't want to upset Mama by asking her. What's going on?"

"Maybe," I said carefully, "you'd better ask Ben."

"I will if I can ever lay my hands on him," Bron said.

"I've been trying for three days. Oh, why does he have to choose now to pull a stunt like this!" Her eyes filled with tears.

I took a deep breath. "I'll get him to the wedding," I said. "Don't ask me how, I don't know yet. But I will. Only in return you've got to do me a favor, too. Get Mama to let me go to the school concert tonight without having Ben along as chaperone."

Bron grinned mischievously. "You two can come along with Sidney and me. We can chaperone each other."

"*You're* going to the high school concert?"

"Junius is in the Glee Club," Bronwyn said. "We have to hear him sing." She sounded like a stepmother already.

It was very interesting attending the concert with Bron and Mr. Albright. For one thing, we got to ride in his stylish cutter instead of walk. For another, I discovered that an engaged couple make ideal chaperones. They didn't pay any attention to us at all, and they let us sit where we wanted, up in the balcony with the rest of the crowd. A lot of the college kids home on vacation were there, too, including Herbie Willis escorting Viney Hodge, and I didn't look in his direction any more than I could help. Mary Lou, conspicuous in red with mistletoe in her hair, was making a fool of herself as usual, climbing all over Doug.

"It may interest you to know," Ken whispered, "that Doug bawled Ben out for the way he's been acting about the pageant. Even offered to punch him in the nose if he didn't go through with it. A fascinating switch on their usual roles."

I tried to blot the problem from my mind and surrender myself to the nearness of Ken and the glory of the Christmas music, for the Glee Club really sounded pretty good. But it didn't work.

"It came upon the midnight clear, that glorious song of old. . . ." *I can't believe those fairy tales any more about angels in wings and haloes.* O holy night! The stars are brightly shining. . . ." *Nobody really knows when Jesus was born, if he ever was.* "O come, all ye faithful. . . ." *What is Truth?*

This is too big for me to deal with, I thought; I should have gone to Pa. But I knew perfectly well why I hadn't. Partly because Pa had enough to contend with already. Partly because it would have been a betrayal of Ben's confidence. And also because, in prying into Ben's problem, I had made it in a special way my own, had taken upon myself the responsibility for helping find a solution. I knew too much; I could no longer wash my hands and run back to the childish Eden of ignorance.

Ken and I rode home in the back seat of the sleigh together, but we hardly spoke. We didn't even hold hands. When we reached the house and Kenneth helped me down, he stood for a minute just looking at me. "I'll hope whatever's bothering you works out."

"It will," I said, and meant it.

I went up to my brothers' bedroom, where a light was still burning and knocked firmly on the door. "Get lost awhile, will you, Peter?" I said when he opened it. "I have to talk to Ben alone."

"Suppose I don't want to talk to you?" Ben said noncommitally from the depths of a book.

"You will. Or at least you'll listen. Because otherwise I'm going to have Pa in here in two seconds flat." I shut the door behind Peter and locked it and stood against it.

"All right," I said, hoping my voice didn't sound as shaky as I felt. "Here it is. I'm not going to try to make you go through with the pageant if you really feel you can't. But you are going to go to rehearsal tomorrow. You don't have to speak any lines, or do anything that makes you feel like a hypocrite, just be there, so in case you change your mind by Sunday afternoon, you'll know what you have to do."

"Who's going to make me?" Ben said coolly.

"You are. Because if you don't, tomorrow night at the rehearsal dinner I'm going to spill the beans. All of them. About everything you've been reading and thinking and discussing. And that just might get Mr. Grimes in trouble if people get the impression he's been teaching atheism in the public schools, because Mr. Albright's not only a Vestryman, he's on the Board of Education, too." I was taking an awfully big gamble with that, because I didn't want to get Mr. Grimes in any trouble. But I didn't think that Ben would let it happen. "You're right about Pa understanding," I added. "He'd be hurt, but he'd understand. But I don't know about Mama. I don't think you're skunk enough to spoil Christmas and the wedding for Mama, especially not with her in her condition."

"You rat," Ben said slowly. "You unmitigated rat."

"If you don't think I mean it, you just try me!" I went out, slamming the door behind me.

Bron didn't come in till after I was asleep, which was a very good thing, because I spent the next half-hour bawling like a stupid baby.

The antagonism between Ben and me was so thick the next morning you could have spread it with a spoon, but fortunately it escaped everybody's attention. This miracle occurred only because there were so many other diversions demanding notice. Whatsitsname had been playing football in Mama's middle all night, which did not leave her in the best of dispositions. Gramps had telegraphed that he was arriving some time that day, but had not bothered telling us what train. Aunt Annie and her family were also due in, but they, thank goodness, were going to be staying with Aunt Kate. While we were still at the breakfast table, the caterer called to inform

Mama of some wedding-reception crisis, and the janitor from the office building where Pa was opening the school telephoned with news that a shipment of desks had been dumped upon the sidewalk.

"S'pose you've got to go tend to that now," Mama groaned. "Might have known! Impossible to have anything go like clockwork around this house!" She couldn't rightly blame Pa, but she was spoiling for a fight, and her eyes lit on perfect fuel for the fire. "Marianna Sterling! You haven't washed those lamp chimneys yet! Told you three times yesterday to do it! Want to disgrace us for the wedding?"

Since the chimneys would have to be washed again before the wedding, anyway, Marnie was annoyed. "I said I'd do it, and I will. Golly Moses, Mama. . . ."

"Don't you cuss at me, young lady!" Mama snapped. "Might have known I couldn't depend on you. *I'll* do it."

Since Mama was determined to be a martyr, Marnie sat back and let her. Mama bent down with difficulty, opened the cupboard door beneath the sink, and let out a screech that shook the rafters.

Cornelius, Peter's blacksnake that had been missing since October, had chosen this moment to let himself be found. He was wound around the top of the bluing bottle, eager-tongued and curious and full of beans, and he was considerably larger than when we had seen him last.

At Mama's scream everybody went running to her except Missy. She, having decided to be helpful, had climbed unnoticed to the dresser where the lamp chimneys reposed and begun trying to polish them with her petticoat. When Mama yelled, she dropped two of them, cut her hand slightly, and set up a competing shriek, followed by a storm of tears and hiccups. Marnie, feeling guilty and therefore angry, took care of Missy, and Bron coped with Mama. Peter was lost in the throes of a joyful reunion with Cornelius. I left to clean up the broken glass, and Pa and Ben, trying not to look relieved at the excuse, took off like shots to tend to the schoolroom desks.

Already, at nine a.m., the day had all the earmarks of developing into a perfectly charming mess. As I swept up the glass fragments, trying to keep Cicero from eating them, I could feel my temples starting to pound. There was fat chance now that Ben would show up at that rehearsal; helping Pa was giving him all too good an excuse. When Stella called, an hour later, to see if I was free for last-minute Christmas shopping, I felt like an absolute saint when I declined; and by the time Kenneth arrived to walk me to Pageant rehearsal, I was feeling very unchristmaslike and very, very glad to leave the house.

As soon as we were out in the street, Ken demanded, "Now what the dickens is the matter?"

"Nothing's the matter."

"Are you mad at me or the world in general?"

"I'm not mad at anybody," I said with dignity.

Ken looked at me deliberately. "For that whopper, I ought to wash your face with snow. In fact, I think I will."

"Ken Latham, don't you dare! I've got my hair curled for the rehearsal dinner tonight!" I was too late; a snowball hit the side of my neck. I threw one back, and in a few seconds we were down in a snowbank and my face was getting thoroughly washed. Naturally, I did as much in retaliation as I could, and if Aunt Kate was watching with her spyglass, she must have gotten quite an eyeful. By the time we got out of the snowdrift, and brushed each other off, and Ken had dried my face with his handkerchief, both my headache and my spirits had improved enormously, and we got to the rehearsal very late.

We walked into the nostalgic winter scent of wet woollens drying over registers, and of the pine needles and hemlock boughs that adorned the altar and pew ends and all the window ledges. Bron had pointed out to Mama that one of the advantages of a Christmas wedding was that the church was already decorated, so we wouldn't have to spend a lot of money on fancy flowers. Candles glowed everywhere, and kids were playing tag in the pews, chased by a couple of harried members of the Ladies' Aid who were trying to drape them into bedsheet and drapery costumes.

"Gee, I like the smell of Christmas," Ken said, and then, in astonishment, "Well, for gosh sakes! Miracles still do happen!"

I followed his eyes, and there, in a back pew next to Doug, sat Ben. He was madder than a hornet, and fairly bristling with animosity, but he was there. I looked away quickly and breathed a silent *alleluia*.

Celinda joined us. "He's been here for twenty minutes," she whispered, "and everybody's been scared to say a word. Except Mr. Derbyshire, who's been too busy! Tish, what did you do to him?"

"I couldn't tell you," I said grimly. "Just for the love of Pete don't say anything!" I didn't have the heart to tell her there was still no guarantee Ben would show up on Sunday.

Thanks to the general chaos, Mr. Derbyshire's preoccupation, and my strong sense of self-preservation, we got through the rehearsal without bloodshed. As soon as rehearsal was over, Ben took off to his own devices, and Ken and I and the other kids in the crowd walked home by way of the Soda Shoppe, where we encountered Anne and Stella having a hot chocolate on their way home from Christmas shopping. By the time I finally got home, I was wetter by several snowballs, my hair was straight as a poker, and it was just about time to be leaving for the rehearsal dinner.

A cloud of vile tobacco smoke and a good deal of laughter indicated that Gramps had arrived, and he took the edge off Mama's annoyance at my lateness. I skinned upstairs, changed into my coral merino, did what I could about my hair, and the next thing I knew Pa had Nellie out front, bells jingling on her harness, and was yelling. "Tarnation, thunder, woman, can't we ever get anywhere on time?"

Mr. Albright, thank goodness, had taken on himself the responsibility of the rehearsal dinner. "It's the prerogative of the groom's family," he said firmly. To our great joy, instead of subjecting us to Miss Albright's cooking, he had engaged a private room at a restaurant. There were quite a lot of us, too, what with the eight of us, and Gramps, and Aunt Annie and Uncle Will and Alice and Leslie—Mr. Albright had insisted all the children be included—and Aunt Kate, and Sourpuss Sadie, and Junius, and Bron's friend Selma who was a bridesmaid, and two grown-up friends of Mr. Albright who were going to be ushers, and their wives. And the dinner party was very posh indeed, with turtle soup, and filet of beef, and Charlotte Russe for dessert. There was even a quartet playing music for dinner dancing, and I wished with all my heart that Kenneth could have been there.

It was all very festive and very exciting, until we got back to the church. I walked into the sanctuary, quiet now in contrast to the afternoon, with candlelight shining on the communion goblet and the altar cross, and my spirits plummeted like a pricked balloon. It was Saturday night, and the pageant was less than twenty-four hours away, and I still hadn't found out how to give Ben back his faith. It was almost enough to make me lose my own.

Amid the subdued merriment and high spirits of the

wedding rehearsal, I moved like a solitary little tugboat, lost in a fog and looking for an anchor. I felt like a lost soul. Correction: two lost souls. Wherever I went, as I moved like an automaton through the ritual of the rehearsal, I felt Ben's eyes, dark and accusing, upon me.

I knew exactly what was in Ben's mind, and it was not only the agony of spirit that came from loss of faith. In sharing his inner thoughts and doubts, Ben had opened himself to me in a way he never had before. And my issuing that ultimatum, my aligning myself with family and church, had been a kind of a betrayal.

The rehearsal was brief and routine, and neither it, nor the words of the wedding service, offered any solace for my soul. We were told how to march in, where to stand and what to do. Junius was going to be his father's best man, since Pa, who was Mr. Albright's closest friend, had to give the bride away. This meant that Junius and I had to march out together, which did not thrill me, but at least it was better than having to march out with Ben, considering the state of things between us. I wished I could stay in the church alone awhile after the rehearsal, but there was no way to manage that without making the whole thing very conspicuous, which I was not about to do. Mama had to go and invite everybody back to the house for coffee and cake, and she was not happy when I pleaded a headache and escaped upstairs.

I went to bed and put the lamp out, but I could not sleep. And it was more than wedding excitement, more than not knowing whether Ben would let Mr. Derbyshire down by not going through with the pageant. I had made myself a part of my brother's problem, and I had not found a solution for him. *What is Truth? And what can I believe?* It wasn't enough that I still believed in Christmas, and in God. If Ben couldn't believe, then for him they might just as well not be real. And I knew exactly what he was feeling, because I was feeling it myself, a loneliness and a terrible emptiness in the bottom of my stomach.

I awoke very early the next morning to snowflakes swirling outside in the pale light and the rustle of my sister getting dressed.

"Go back to sleep," Bron said. "I didn't mean to wake you. I'm going down to church for early morning Communion."

I sat up. "If you don't mind, I think I'd like to come with you."

It felt good to be slipping out together into the pale grey morning. There were few people at the early service, and the scent of pine was everywhere, bringing back sharply all the lonely emotions of the night before. I suppose I'd been hoping I'd receive an answer along with the Communion bread and wine, but it didn't happen, and when we were back in our pew I buried my face in my arms and felt emptier than I had before.

When we reached home, the family was at the breakfast table, including Gramps and Aunt Annie's contingent over from Aunt Kate's. Excitement was percolating with the coffee, which Gramps was making according to his own lethal formula, and Mama was fuming about Ben who'd skinned out of the house before she'd gotten up.

"Stop stewing, Evie," Gramps said mildly, plunking a cup of coffee down before her. "Won't be the end of the world if the boy misses church once or twice."

That's what you think, I thought. I wanted to spill the beans right then and there—it would have felt good to pass the burden on to Pa and Gramps—but I couldn't do it. Instead I impressed my family with my attendance at early Communion, used that to excuse myself from the customary eleven a.m. service, and waited till everybody was safely out of the house. Then I took my Bible and my Journal and went up to the attic, locking the door firmly behind me. What is reality, Ben had asked. Somehow, before the pageant and the wedding, before I could have it out with Ben, I had to battle it out with myself and God.

I read through my Journal from cover to cover, but I found no help there, although I was shocked to discover how much of it was full of me-me-me. Maybe Mama had been right about me being self-centered, after all. I discovered something else, too—how close we all were, how much we cared about each other, deep down, despite our constant surface friction. It was funny how, in the dailyness of life, we never noticed how much we loved each other. That was the glue that held us all together. Even Aunt Kate, I thought, turning the pages of our bleak October. And it went beyond the family circle to embrace others also. Celinda. Stella. Kenneth.

In a way, you couldn't prove there was a thing called love any more than you could prove there was existence of God. You couldn't see it, or reach out and touch it. Even if you believed in its existence, you couldn't quite understand it by reading about it, or by being told—not until you experienced it, and then you *knew*. Any more than I had quite understood until I'd gone through some of the family crises of the past year—until, I added involuntarily, flushing, I had grown so close to Ken.

All this wasn't getting me any closer to the immediate problem at hand.

I opened the Bible and read doggedly through all the different accounts of the Christmas story, and a lot more besides, including whole columns of "begats" in the Old Testament. I ran into a lot of things that disturbed me, things I'd conveniently managed to overlook before, like people being "cast into outer darkness" after the Parable of the Talents, and "to him who hath much shall more be given, but from him who hath not, even that shall be taken away," and "I come not to bring peace but a sword," and some stuff about scourging and crucifixion that made Easter a lot more bloody than I'd realized. I discovered a characterization of God that had no relation to a Santa Clausy figure in a long white beard with a bag of goodies. I found a lot about the relationship of man to God, which I knew would lead me to some heavy thinking later, but I discovered you couldn't use the Bible to prove God unless you first started with a basic belief in the Bible itself, a thing which Ben apparently didn't have.

And time was running out.

I turned for my own comfort to the familiar beautiful words of the Thirteenth chapter of First Corinthians, and a queer thing happened. Coming to it from the illumination of my Journal reading, I began to recognize people I knew in the descriptions of how love acts, began to match up verses with happenings of the past year. The eleventh verse struck at me with new meaning.

"When I was a child, I spake as a child, I understood as a child, I thought as a child: but when I became a man, I put away childish things." That was what had been happening to me, I thought humbly, during the past crowded months. It seemed an eon since I had graduated from grammar school, thinking I knew it all.

"For now we see through a glass, darkly; but then face to face: now I know in part, but then shall I know even as also I am known."

It must be nice to be so sure, to be able to say you absolutely *know*. I certainly could use that right now, I thought.

I sat gazing blankly at the passage, noting idly that I hadn't realized window glass existed way back in ancient Greece, let alone the dark kind. Then out of nowhere, two disconnected pieces of information floated to the surface of my mind. One was a recollection, from my

Shakespeare reading, that people in King James's day had referred to mirrors as "looking glasses." The other was something Mr. Grimes had said, that the mirrors of the ancient Greeks had been made of polished bronze, "in which," he had said, "people saw their reflections like dim dark shadows."

*For now we see a dim reflection in polished bronze, rather than face to face. . . .*

Why, I thought, Paul was talking about Plato's theory of reality—shadows in a mirror, shadows on the wall of a cave. Both of them were talking about the same thing: What is reality? What is truth? How can we *know?*

Only Paul had gone on to give the answer.

*Love.*

In the beginning was the Word, and the word was Love. Prophecy shall fail, and knowledge shall vanish away, but faith, hope, and charity abide. And the greatest was charity, which led to the other two.

He who loveth not knoweth not God, for God is love.

I thought of love, of all the loves that I had known. The love that was silent, that showed itself in acts you had to be sensitive enough to understand—love that didn't push in, but waited to be invited, just as God did.

"God is a gentleman," Gramps had said once; "He never pushes in unless He's wanted."

The love that was stern, that could punish, but only because it cared. The love that forgave, again and yet again. Love that could overcome dislike and prejudice. Love that made age or personality differences unimportant. Love that gave you the strength to reach out, regardless of fear, regardless of personal cost.

And I knew I didn't have to worry any more about trying to prove God; I *knew,* because I had known Him —because I had known love.

All of a sudden I felt awfully sorry for anyone who

hadn't grown up in a family like mine. Without a Pa, it would be terribly hard to understand the idea of God as father.

In the beginning was the Word, and the word was Love. In far-off Judea, a child had been born, and it didn't really matter whether it was on December 6 or 25 or in mid-summer, whether it was winter solstice or Saturnalia. The important thing was that He *had* been born, and that in celebrating His birth we somehow stumbled into a season of loving one another, of caring more about giving than receiving, of opening our shut-up hearts more freely. And that with the death of the old year and birth of the new, we went through a kind of death of our old selfish selves and were born again into a second chance of grace.

Who knows? Maybe even God had recognized the symbolism of Saturnalia and had decided to use it!

I closed the Bible, knowing I had my own head back on straight. Now if I could only sell the idea to Ben.

The family came home from church, including the Stamford contingent, and we had one of Mama's huge Sunday dinners. During the afternoon, folks kept dropping in, leaving wedding or Christmas packages. There was music, and laughter, and candlelight and pine, and the Grandfather's clock kept chiming off the hours, and my heart kept turning to lead within me. I didn't get a chance to talk to Ben, because Ben wasn't there.

Snow began falling, and Kenneth arrived to walk me down to church for the pageant. "Do a good job," Gramps said. "We'll be down to see it, even me, goldurn it." He and Aunt Annie were bringing the younger kids down later. We went out into cool darkness and snow-flakes that tapped like kitten's paws against our faces, and I did a good job of laughing and fooling as we walked along, but inside I felt like crying. Then we went into the steaming warmth of the church basement, and there was Ben.

I could have cried for pure joy.

One look at Ben's eyes told me that nothing had changed inside, except he didn't seem to be mad at me any more. "Don't kid yourself," he whispered when we found ourselves together. "I'm not here because I've changed my mind, or because of anything you said. I'm here because Mr. Derbyshire's a nice old guy, and it dawned on me it was more important not to let him down than for me not to be a hypocrite."

"Ben, I want to tell you. . . ."

"No," Ben said firmly. "Tish, I appreciate it, I really do, but just let me be. It's the best thing you can do for me right now."

The pageant went smoothly, all things considered. Missy's eyes were like stars when she presented her White Gift before the manager, and Celinda looked almost beautiful, and I felt at the same time both happy and close to tears.

Thus ended the Sunday of the Weekend of the Christmas Wedding.

Monday dawned grey and lowering, with more snow threatened, but even that couldn't dim Bron's radiance. Mama kept us busy most of the morning running errands to the grocer's. "Christmas dinner to cook tomorrow, and don't you forget it!" Usually she spent the day before Christmas making advanced culinary preparations, but this year she had to keep the kitchen clear for the caterer's men, which kind of cramped her style.

The dining room table was pushed against a wall and spread with Mama's cutwork cloth. Flowers, red roses and fern and pine, came from the florist. Finally it came time for us to go upstairs and put on our wedding finery. And I still hadn't gotten to talk to Ben, because he had

barricaded himself in the attic, and because instinct
stronger than reason held me back. I did a lot of
praying, though, up to and including when Bron was
hooking me into the green velvet dress and putting up
my hair.

"Just think, this is the last time I'll be doing it for you
in our bedroom," Bron said.

"You'll still have to do it for me on special occasions,
even if you are Mrs. Albright," I said, and started feeling a lump in my throat.

"I will. You can come down to the house any time
you want," Bron said fervently. And then we both
started to cry, and Mama came in, and said, "Stuff and
nonsense! Bron, time you were dressed." Mama was
carrying the wedding dress in her arms and all of us,
including Marnie and Missy, helped get Bron into it.
And at last she was ready, wearing Grandma Stryker's
lace veil, revolving for the last time slowly before the
mirror. The lump in my throat got bigger, and I knew
that Mama had one, too, for her chin was up and her
eyes were very bright.

Bron looked like a dream. The striped silk muslin
clung to her hips and flared out to where seven rows of
satin ribbon zig-zagged up and down around the hem.
The space between zigs and zags was filled with row
upon row of small self ruffles, and more ribbon, criss-
crossed Elizabethan fashion, formed the high collar and
shoulder yoke and bound the sleeves into a multiplicity
of puffs. There was even a fashionable bolero-front of
chiffon lace, and a slight train. I will not even try to
describe the look on my sister's face.

After that things happened in a haze. The ride to the
church through faintly swirling snow . . . a shimmer of
candles, and the scent of pine, and the organ playing
. . . someone thrusting my poinsettia-trimmed muff into
my hands. Ben escorted Mama down the aisle, looking

proud as a queen in the conveniently camouflaging new grey coat. Bron took Pa's arm. The organ music modulated into a joyous peal of chords, and the congregation rose. I saw Missy, hanging onto Gramps' hand, practically falling out of the pew in her attempt to get a first look at the wedding party. Selma led off, assured and steady . . . then Marnie . . . then someone was whispering, "Ready, Tish, *now!*" And I stepped out.

The next thing that I knew with any absolute clarity was handing Bronwyn back her bouquet and taking Junius' arm for our return trip down the aisle, more quickly now. Then the receiving line, then back to the house where lights and music streamed from the windows, then everyone pouring in, relations and dear friends old and new. Presently Bronwyn threw her bouquet from the stairway. She aimed it at Selma, only Missy caught it and wouldn't be parted from it even when she was sent to bed. And Bron and Mr. Albright changed to traveling clothes upstairs and sneaked out the back way to where Gramps was waiting to drive them to the station, thus avoiding the departure planned for them by Jimmy Breidenbach, the Lathams, Junius and Ben, which featured a lot of rice and old shoes and clanking cans. Ben's mood had changed completely, and he was back to his old character of Terror of the Neighborhood. Something certainly had happened, and I was afraid to speculate on what, but despite my stern self-discipline, hope kindled within me.

After awhile the crowd dwindled down to relatives and members of our crowd. We kids took possession of the kitchen, and the boys devoted themselves to disposing of what remained of the feast as the caterers' men cleaned up. And it dawned on Mama that here it was Christmas Eve, Missy was in bed, and for once she had a lot of extra muscle power at hand. So before anybody knew what was happening, she had the boys helping to bring in the tree and had set the girls to sorting out candles and tree decorations.

"This is a lot more fun than doing it in our own houses," Celinda said gaily. The glow she had acquired during the pageant still hung around her like a halo. When we finally had the tree trimmed and had sung a few carols, it was eleven p.m.

"Let's all go down to Grace Church for the candlelight service," Ken proposed.

My heart lurched, and suddenly an angel or demon prompted a wild idea. I took a deep breath. "Great. Let's *all* go," I said loudly, looking straight at Ben.

Miracle of miracles, he neither shot daggers nor looked away. He just turned to Ken in perfectly ordinary fashion and said, just as he might have weeks ago, "Okay, I'll go tell Ma while you kids phone home."

When we went outside into the night-black streets, I could have sworn I heard the angels singing.

The church was crowded when we squeezed in, even Jimmy Breidenbach and the Molloys, who had decided that whether their parents liked it or not, they were going to be Protestants for once. Candles burned everywhere—on the altar, on the window ledges, in tall standards anchored to each end of the pews. I knelt between Kenneth and Celinda and for once I didn't notice how hard the wooden prayer-benches were and how they dug into my knees. I was absolutely overflowing with joy to the world.

The service started with an old Advent hymn sung softly by the choir from the back of the church:

*O come, O come, Emmanuel,*
*And Ransom captive Israel,*
*That mourns in lonely exile here. . . .*

\* \* \*

And then suddenly loud, with a triumphal burst of chords from the organ:

*Rejoice! Rejoice!*

In some strange way, the hymn seemed to be the sum and total, not just of the past week, but of my life and all that I had learned in the past year. I didn't quite understand it; I kind of felt as if I'd stumbled onto something too big to comprehend. But I knew that it was being filed away in some corner of my mind and heart, where it would be when needed. And I knew something else, too, reflecting back on the pages of my Journal that I'd read on Sunday morning. I still felt "different," but it didn't bother me now. I was still, by the world's standards, too sensitive, but I was beginning to learn that sensitivity could be a blessing in disguise if you could use it as a tool for understanding others. And I didn't feel lonely any more, not even when I was alone. I didn't think I ever would again.

In the small, crowded, sense-memory-laden church, I was very conscious of our closeness, and I didn't mean just the tangible one of people's presences. I was very conscious of Kenneth next to me, and Celinda on my other side, and of my brother Ben beyond Celinda. I knew they felt it, too, for Celinda turned to me and smiled and there were tears in her eyes. The closeness built through the Scripture readings and the old familiar carols to that heart-stopping moment of silence before the tower chimes rang in the midnight hour and the ceremony of lighting our individual candles began. How appropriate, I thought, that Kenneth lit my candle and I in turn lit Celinda's. Then there was one last carol, and the candles were extinguished, and we streamed out into the fresh cold night.

We all had felt the magic. We stood around outside, not quite wanting to leave, half not wanting to talk and half searching for some laughter to break the spell. Then Ben did an astonishing thing, which he'd never done before and which rocked me on my feet both figuratively and literally. He looked at me, and before he could chicken out, he wrapped me in a big bearhug that almost broke my ribs. When he let me go, we looked at each other and started to laugh like little kids.

"Ben," I said, "I've been trying to get to tell you for two days. What you talked about . . . I think I've found the answer."

"I don't need it any more," Ben said. He was grinning, and his eyes were clear.

"I know. But I think I needed it myself." And in a whisper, so the others couldn't hear, I rattled out as fast as I could the secret I had stumbled onto in the attic room.

"I went at it kind of the other way round," Ben said. "It dawned on me that if all those other people and other cultures had versions of the same myths as us, there had to be something behind it. It seemed like Somebody had to be trying to tell us something." He grinned ruefully. "It also occurred to me that if you stopped trying to take everything literally, those Bible descriptions of man in hell were a pretty accurate reflection of the state of mind I'd been in."

And the description of heaven, too, I thought silently, falling in beside Kenneth as he reached out to take my hand. Somehow our laughter seemed to have broken the spell of solemnity but not the magic. We still had our little candles, and Ben dug around in his pockets for cigarette matches and relit them, and we walked home through the deserted streets caroling joyously to the night sky, shielding our candle flames with our hands from the chill wind. Only my candle flame just had to take its chances, because Kenneth was still holding my other hand.

Love, I thought profoundly, remembering the mystery I'd felt on the brink of discovering in church. It was the key to knowing God, the magic of the Keeping Days, the secret I had learned like a gift of grace. Not— and this was what I hadn't known before—not the feeling of being loved, but of giving love to others. Even if it hurt. Even if it frightened you with its seeming inappropriateness and its strength.

As we walked along, our various bosom companions turned off at their own corners. When we reached Lathams', Doug departed, but Kenneth didn't let go of my hand. We reached our house, and as usual Jimmie Breidenbach and Marnie raced on ahead, and only Ken and Ben and Stella and I were left. Ben looked from Ken and me to Stella and said magnanimously, "I'll see you on home," which I suspected it wasn't all that much a sacrifice.

Ken and I were left alone together, feeling suddenly shy, and I stared at the frail flickering candle flame, thinking how easily a careless breath could put it out. In the darkness I heard Ken laugh softly. "Merry Christmas, Tish," he said.

"Kenneth," I said, "I'm so happy."

"I know," he said. "It shows." We looked at each other, and looked away. Ken cleared his throat. "There are. times," he said awkwardly, "that a brother has a darn unfair advantage." And before I knew what was happening, he had wrapped me tight in his arms as Ben had done. Only this was different. Decidedly, this was different.

Deep within me, something that had been brought to birth by Herbie Willis in the pantry closet flared to life again, and stiffened in panic, and then surrendered in a tide of joy. Because this was different from that, too.

This was right, and anybody who said we were too young to understand just plain didn't know what they were talking about.

And in our hands, amid the rise and ebb and the cold air and the night sky around us, our candles flamed flickered and burned on like tiny beacons. I could see Kenneth's even after he had released me and gone in silence on his solitary walk toward home.

A Keeping Day was over; a Keeping Day had begun.

Excerpts from the second book
of the *Keeping Days* series
**GLORY IN THE FLOWER**
by Norma Johnston
Coming from ACE TEMPO in October


I begin this new Journal, otherwise known as The
Tears and Trials of Letitia Chambers Sterling, with an
account of New Year's Day, 1901, just in time to record
my family and friends, in regrettably characteristic
form, at the Lathams' open house, the opening of Pa's
secretarial school, and the metamorphosis of the Browning Society. Around our neighborhood, crises usually do
seem to occur in threes.

The first crisis got off with a bang, or maybe I should
say a screech, at the lunch table on New Year's Day.
Mama hasn't made much holiday fuss this year, since
we're still recuperating from my sister Bronwyn's wedding on Christmas Eve. Gramps only departed for his
Pennsylvania farm a day ago, and Mama is looking forward to getting the kids back to school and putting up
her feet in a quiet house, which means that lunch on
New Year's was long on leftovers and short on style. It
was supposed to feature leftover roast beef, but Mama,
who isn't used yet to Bron's not being around to help,
made the mistake of leaving the roast beef unguarded on
the table. When she returned, half the roast was already
inside Cicero, our almost-sheepdog, who was looking

idiotically pleased with himself, and the other half was leaking juice on the Oriental rug.

"Hell and damn!" Mama yelled, an expression she has picked up lately from my thirteen-year-old sister Marnie. "Tarnation children can't take responsibility for anything without I tell you three times! All the thanks I get! Pa not home again when I need him! Me in this condition!"

★ ★ ★

It feels strange and lonely having the bedroom to myself, although it is going to be undeniably convenient when it comes to burning the after-midnight oil with nobody knowing. Snug beneath three quilts while the winds howl outside and the apple tree taps ghostly fingers against the bow window, I can write in my Journal, write extra-credit compositions, write stories. Entering high school opened a new world for me—for the first time I'm not considered weird because I love Shakespeare, history, poetry; because I have a habit of feeling everything too deeply. Both Mr. Grimes, our Greek-god history teacher, and Mrs. Owens encourage me to pretty much follow my own fancy, although they come down hard on such sordid details as organization, quality, and style. I have finally stopped writing about Balkan princesses, haunted mansions, and other things beyond my own experience, and lately my compositions have leaned heavily on anecdotes pumped from Gramps and on other incidents, which happened closer to home. Mama got pretty mad when she found out I'd done one on the time Ben and Marnie got Pa drunk by serving him year-old cider, even though I got A+ and the classroom rocked with laughter.

★ ★ ★

I seemed to be batting a thousand today. I hunted up Mama and broached the subject of the Browning Society.

"Back home by ten." Mama said firmly. "Ben take you. *And* bring you home. School night no time for lallygagging."

That latter was a direct reference to Ken, but I did not rise to the bait, for I had no intention of discussing our relationship with Mama. What with Bron's sudden marriage and her own equally unexpected infantication, I suspected Mama had sex on her mind these days. Or, rather, that she feared it was on mine. She knows perfectly well how moonstruck I am where Kenneth is concerned.

Actually, Mama doesn't have to worry about the perils of me and Kenneth being alone together, worse luck. Although Ken can and does hold lengthy, profound, and unembarrassed discussions of the passions of the ancient Greeks, he shows little inclination to put their exploits into personal practice. Maybe that's because of overexposure to the exploits of his brother and Mary Lou, who don't know beans about Greek but seem to know a lot about lust. As for me—even now, remembering, I find myself flushing. When Herbie Willis, Bron's old boyfriend, mistaking me for Bron, had trapped me in the blackness of the pantry closet, he'd taught me a lot more about the vulnerability of my own body than I'd been ready yet to learn from someone I despised.

But Mama doesn't know that, and I have no intention that she ever shall, so I kept my mouth shut and submitted to Mama's insistence that Ben escort me to the Browning Society that evening.

★ ★ ★

My heart was pounding, and my insides were doing flipflops, but I'd have died on a cross before I'd have admitted it to Mama, who'd chosen me, who was whispering, "Just keep you head—do exactly what I say—" She grabbed the bedposts and dug her heels into the mattress hard. "If you've got time—say a few fast prayers . . . ." Thank goodness Mama, after six kids, was an old pro. She muttered instructions through gritted teeth, and I didn't have a chance to feel scared or squeamish. And in another few minutes I was staring down into the decidedly angry face of my new sister. Only I didn't know she was a sister yet.

I cannot write it. I try, and something stops me, and it's not embarrassment. It was too private, and kind of sacred; private to Mama, and to me because she'd chosen me to share it with her. It was a blooming miracle, happening right there within my shaking hands.

First nothing, then a tiny tear, then something unbelievably large and damp, half-propelled, half-pulling itself through that tiny hole. We watched, scarcely breathing. The thing finally lay there, wet and grotesque and somehow obscene. Then slowly, something stirred . . . the dampness dried, before our eyes wings grew and unfurled. My heart almost stopped with real pain at the wonder and the beauty of that moment. It was like that now. One more pulsing spasm and there she was in my hands, tiny and wet and red in her glistening transparent covering like angel's wings—unmistakably alive and human and fighting mad.

# NOW YOU CAN ORDER
# TEMPO BOOKS BY MAIL!

No library is complete
without the classic novels that have
delighted readers of all ages for years.
Take your pick from these all-time favorites
from Tempo Books:

☐ 17063-9  BLACK BEAUTY by Anne Sewell  $1.50
_____

☐ 17339-5  HEIDI by Johanna Spyri  $1.95
_____

☐ 17108-2  THE ADVENTURES OF HUCKLEBERRY FINN
by Samuel Clemens  $1.50
_____

☐ 17150-3  THE JUNGLE BOOK by Rudyard Kipling  $1.50
_____

☐ 17136-8  THE ADVENTURES OF TOM SAWYER
by Samuel Clemens  $1.50
_____

☐ 16890-1  THE SWISS FAMILY ROBINSON
by Johann Wyss  $1.75
_____

☐ 17121-X  TREASURE ISLAND
by Robert Louis Stevenson  $1.50
_____

☐ 17134-1  THE WIZARD OF OZ by L. Frank Baum  $1.50
_____

Available wherever paperbacks are sold or use this
coupon.
_____

◆ **ACE TEMPO BOOKS**
   P.O. Box 400, Kirkwood, N.Y. 13795

Please send me the titles checked above. I enclose _____ —.
Include 75¢ for postage and handling if one book is ordered; 50¢ per
book for two to five. If six or more are ordered, postage is free. Califor-
nia, Illinois, New York and Tennessee residents please add sales tax.

NAME_____

ADDRESS_____

CITY_____STATE_____ZIP_____

T-20

# HÄGAR
## the Horrible
### By Dik Browne

**Get carried away by America's favorite Viking!**

☐ 12641-9   **HAGAR THE HORRIBLE #1**   $1.25

☐ 12642-7   **HAGAR THE HORRIBLE #2**   $1.50

☐ 12643-5   **HAGAR THE HORRIBLE #3:**
ON THE LOOSE   $1.50

☐ 12644-3   **HAGAR THE HORRIBLE #4:**
THE BRUTISH ARE COMING   $1.50

☐ 12649-4   **HAGAR THE HORRIBLE #5:**
ON THE RACK   $1.50

☐ 17114-7   **HAGAR THE HORRIBLE #7:**
HAGAR'S KNIGHT OUT   $1.25

---

**ACE TEMPO BOOKS**      J-07
P.O. Box 400, Kirkwood, N.Y. 13795

Please send me the titles checked above. I enclose _____.
Include 75¢ for postage and handling if one book is ordered; 50¢ per
book for two to five. If six or more are ordered, postage is free. Califor-
nia, Illinois, New York and Tennessee residents please add sales tax.

NAME_____

ADDRESS_____

CITY_____STATE_____ ZIP_____

# ENJOY THE COMIC ANTICS OF
# CASPER THE FRIENDLY GHOST,
# RICHIE RICH, AND
## ALL THEIR FRIENDS WITH THESE FINE BOOKS

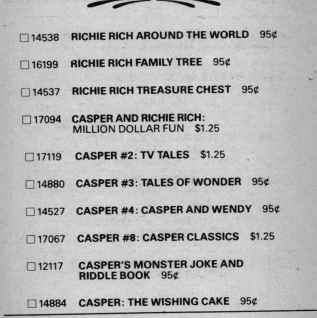

- ☐ 14538 **RICHIE RICH AROUND THE WORLD** 95¢
- ☐ 16199 **RICHIE RICH FAMILY TREE** 95¢
- ☐ 14537 **RICHIE RICH TREASURE CHEST** 95¢
- ☐ 17094 **CASPER AND RICHIE RICH: MILLION DOLLAR FUN** $1.25
- ☐ 17119 **CASPER #2: TV TALES** $1.25
- ☐ 14880 **CASPER #3: TALES OF WONDER** 95¢
- ☐ 14527 **CASPER #4: CASPER AND WENDY** 95¢
- ☐ 17067 **CASPER #8: CASPER CLASSICS** $1.25
- ☐ 12117 **CASPER'S MONSTER JOKE AND RIDDLE BOOK** 95¢
- ☐ 14884 **CASPER: THE WISHING CAKE** 95¢

**ACE TEMPO BOOKS**                                   J-04
P.O. Box 400, Kirkwood, N.Y. 13795

Please send me the titles checked above. I enclose _____.
Include 75¢ for postage and handling if one book is ordered; 50¢ per
book for two to five. If six or more are ordered, postage is free. Califor-
nia, Illinois, New York and Tennessee residents please add sales tax.

NAME_____

ADDRESS_____

CITY_____ STATE_____ ZIP_____

# beetle bailey

## CARTOON BOOKS
### By Mort Walker

Enjoy more madcap adventures with Beetle, Sarge, Zero, Plato and all the gang at Camp Swampy!

☐ 12140-9 **BEETLE BAILEY #1** $1.50

☐ 12254-5 **BEETLE BAILEY #2:** Fall Out Laughing $1.50

☐ 12255-3 **BEETLE BAILEY #3:** At Ease $1.50

☐ 12257-X **BEETLE BAILEY #5:** What Is It Now $1.50

☐ 12258-8 **BEETLE BAILEY #6:** On Parade $1.50

☐ 12259-6 **BEETLE BAILEY #7:** We're All In The Same Boat $1.50

☐ 17266 **BEETLE BAILEY #19:** Give Us A Smile $1.50

☐ 17203-8 **BEETLE BAILEY:** Up, Up and Away $1.95